MRS
HUDSON
AND THE
SPIRITS' CURSE

MRS
HUDSON
AND THE
SPIRITS' CURSE

MARTIN DAVIES

San Diego, California

Canelo US
An imprint of Printers Row Publishing Group
9717 Pacific Heights Blvd, San Diego, CA 92121
www.canelobooksus.com

Printers Row Publishing Group is a division of Readerlink Distribution Services, LLC. Canelo US is a registered trademark of Readerlink Distribution Services, LLC.

First published in the United States in 2004 by Berkley Publishing Group.
This edition originally published in the United Kingdom in 2018 by Canelo.

Published in partnership with Canelo.

Correspondence regarding the content of this book should be sent to Canelo US, Editorial Department, at the above address. Author inquiries should be sent to Canelo, Unit 9, 5th Floor, Cargo Works, 1–2 Hatfields, London SE1 9PG, United Kingdom, www.canelo.co.

Publisher: Peter Norton • Associate Publisher: Ana Parker
Art Director: Charles McStravick
Senior Developmental Editor: April Graham
Production Team: Beno Chan, Julie Greene, Rusty von Dyl

Library of Congress Control Number: 2021953007

ISBN: 978-1-6672-0131-3

Printed in the United States of America

26 25 24 23 22   1 2 3 4 5

No book can give exact laws and regulations which will be found sensible to every house; but common-sense rules apply to every household in all stations of life

Every-Day Cookery and Housekeeping Book

Prologue

✝

It was Scraggs the grocer's boy, taking pity on my impoverished circumstances and the collapse of my spirits, who made the introduction that was to change my life. It was to lead me into so many adventures that my life came to be as thick with excitement as the street that night was thick with fog.

Looking back to that fateful evening, it is hard to believe I could ever have run so fast. Nowadays my frame creaks a little as I shuffle between the piles of papers in my study, and if I venture out to lecture at the Institute I must allow one of my students to escort me home, in case, on the way across the park, I should require an arm to lean upon.

But that night I ran like the wind – or, at any rate, like the stinking breath that passed for wind in those foul, dark, harsh backstreets. Clad in rags, with no long skirts to hamper me, I ran until the blood that pounded in my ears began to fill my mouth, until my hollow chest could breathe no more and my legs gave way beneath me. And when I could run no further, I crawled to the darkest doorway I could find and collapsed there, holding my breath and listening for my pursuers.

I expected footsteps. Young Smale's boots, Mr Fogarty's heels, the laughing clatter of the footmen, confident of dragging home their prey. But nothing came. Somewhere beyond the alleyway there was a busy thoroughfare; carriages and hawkers and the reassuring bustle of a London street. Nothing sinister. Yet I felt no elation. For that minute, for that moment, I was free, but for how long? They say the caged bird forgets the sky; I knew only that I was freezing, penniless and alone.

At the orphan school I had been warned to be a good girl or suffer the consequences. But the months that followed had quickly taught me that virtue came at a price, a price paid in misery and hunger. Which is why, when Scraggs first saw me, I had ventured out of my doorway refuge and was in the process of stealing a cabbage from his ramshackle barrow. In the rags I wore I had nowhere to conceal an object the size of a cabbage, even a cabbage as small and blackened as the sorry item I had set my sights on. My only hope of success lay in flight and in the prayer that I might lose my pursuer in the crowds and the darkness of London's tangled streets.

But exhaustion had slowed my reactions. The cabbage was fumbled, my attempt at escape short-lived and the impact of Scraggs's diving leap dramatic and final. It took my breath away, thumping me into the gutter so hard that only the street's daily delivery of filth and rotten vegetables came between my ribs and instant fracture. And if the physical impact was dramatic, the impact on my spirits was greater. I lay with my face pressed into the rotten-smelling mud, the pain echoing through me, and found myself utterly crushed. Crushed not just by Scraggs's frame, but by the relentless harshness of the world around me and by the absence of any hope that anything would ever be any different from how it had become. Instead of struggling in Scraggs's grip, I laid down my head and began to cry. Every bruise and knock, all the cold and hunger, seemed suddenly to dissolve into tears. I cried so hard that even after Scraggs had returned his cabbage to the barrow, I still made no attempt to escape from the place he'd pitched me. Gingerly, as if reluctant to touch anything so filth-encrusted, Scraggs rolled me over with the toe of his boot and took a suspicious look at what there was to see.

'Crikey,' he exclaimed. 'It's no surprise you ain't up to thievin'. You're in a worse state than a Chinaman's chihuahua, an' no mistake.'

There followed a brief pause while he continued to look me up and down as if embarrassed as to what to do next. Ignoring him, I lay with my cheek on the rotten end of a rotten turnip and wept for all my life wasn't worth.

'Crikey,' said Scraggs again.

I can't recall how long we continued in this manner but I remember Scraggs levering me upright and resting me, now curled into a ball of defensive misery, against the black brickwork of the alley where my attempted larceny had taken place.

'Now, less of that,' he urged. 'What's to be so scared of? I ain't goin' to eat yer. Too skinny, you see.' He laughed, but I was beyond comfort.

'There's a man,' I told him between sobs. 'Looking for me. I can't run anymore.'

'A man?' Scraggs looked around. We were alone in the darkness.

'From one of the big houses. A servant. He locked me up. He's going to... He wants to...'

4

I broke off for want of words to tell my woe. Scraggs just looked bewildered.

'Tell you what,' he suggested suddenly. 'I think you should meet Mrs Hudson.'

He said it with such certainty I felt sure I should know what he was talking about. But who or what Mrs Hudson might be I had no idea. It says something of the state to which I was reduced that when Scraggs commanded 'Wait here', all thought of further flight was gone. He would return and something would happen to me and I didn't care what. All that mattered was that other people would decide it and I wouldn't any longer have to try to lift myself out of the cold, reeking mud.

Scraggs reappeared some few minutes later and by a wave of his thumb signalled for me to follow. He led me down a sequence of alleys and snickleways until we emerged into a broad street where gas lamps inflated the fog with their yellow breath and hansom cabs cut slippery pathways through the mud. Even at that late hour the streets were noisy with hawkers' cries, and the newsboys were calling the latest developments of a mysterious Brixton murder. But such mysteries meant nothing to me then, and Baker Street was simply a street like any other. Around me the house fronts were higher than the fog, and it was to one of these that I was led.

Still following Scraggs, I descended obediently into a dark area below the level of the street where the gaslight falling obliquely onto a white apron suggested a bulky figure awaiting me.

This was Mrs Hudson and never had I met a more striking woman. She was large in dimensions, broad across her shoulders and straight down her sides in a way that spoke of immense strength. Yet there seemed to be no spare flesh on her, and her arms, sticking bare out of her apron and folded across a formidable bosom, were large and roundly muscled. Her face was also round, with a chin just resisting the temptation to double, yet her eyes and nose, set beneath a constantly furrowed brow, were rather more hawkish than otherwise, combining to produce an effect of shrewd interrogation. It was just such a look that she turned on me when I had been ushered unprotesting into the cavernous interior of a darkly warm kitchen.

'Well, child,' she boomed as she prodded me towards the glowing stove and began to wipe at my face with a damp cloth. 'Scraggs here, who is a good lad and generally truthful, tells me you are in a poor state. Out with your story and we'll see what's to be done.'

It may have been the note of authority, or perhaps a vein of kindness in her voice that I detected under the surface granite, but I found myself doing exactly what she asked, telling her the full story of my years in the orphanage, of my positions since that time and of all the misfortunes that had befallen me. She said little, save for the occasional question darted at me from under her dark frown.

'So this fellow knew you were an orphan, did he?'

'Yes, ma'am. I told him, ma'am. He was so kind, you see. I thought him the kindest person I'd ever met. I caught his eye when I was doing the steps at my first house, ma'am.'

'And where was that, girl?'

'At the Fitzgeralds' house in Berkeley Street, ma'am.'

'The Fitzgeralds', eh? That young wife knows nothing of what goes on below stairs. They should never have sent you there. Go on!'

So I continued, stumbling often, especially when I came to my last days in service, and to the brutalities I had suffered there.

'You see, when I went with him as he suggested, ma'am, he was suddenly different. There was no more kindness once I got to the new house. When the cook and the boot-boy beat me, when the footmen were always grabbing at me, pulling at my skirts, he laughed and let them have their way. I was kept indoors, ma'am, and the area door was kept locked.'

'And let me guess…' Mrs Hudson had risen and had begun to fold a pile of laundry, but her attention to my story never wavered. 'It was after a few weeks of this treatment that he put to you his proposition? Suggested a way of escaping your tormentors?'

'Yes, ma'am. But I wouldn't say yes, ma'am. I hated him by then. I hated them all, and I told him so. Told him he was loathsome and disgusting, and called him a slug. Said I'd rather die first. That was when he locked me up.'

The very faintest trace of a smile seemed to play across Mrs Hudson's lips.

'Good for you, girl. And your escape…?'

I hesitated. It was still almost impossible to believe.

'He came to me when I was sleeping, ma'am. Unlocked the cellar door and ordered me out of bed. Told me we were alone. They'd taken away my uniform, ma'am. These rags were all I had, and I was so cold. It would have been easy to go with him. But I wasn't having that. And so I kicked him, ma'am.'

Mrs Hudson's eyebrow rose slightly.

'Kicked him, girl?'

'Yes, ma'am. Well, it was my knee mostly, so not really a kick. I got him in the… in that part where a gentleman is most easily hurt, ma'am.'

Another smile, rather broader this time.

'I'm extremely pleased to hear it, girl. And you were able to make your escape?'

'Yes, ma'am.'

I told her then of my flight through the pantry, of the area door miraculously unlocked, then of my panicked plunge into the darkest, most confusing alleyways. When at last my tale came to an end, Mrs Hudson said nothing for a short while, continuing to fold laundry with her face set in thought.

'And how old are you now, girl?'

'Twelve, ma'am.'

'And what's your name?'

'Flotsam, ma'am.'

'Flotsam, child?'

'That's the name they gave me at the orphanage, ma'am. Mostly they call me Flottie.'

'Well, Flottie, there's no denying it's a sorry tale. A very sorry tale indeed. The man Fogarty you've talked about, the butler whose particular ways caused you to flee, is already known to me.' She exchanged a meaningful glance with Scraggs. 'Let us just say that our paths have crossed. That happens in service. Not everyone you meet below stairs is always as honest as they should be. Indeed sometimes it seems there is no cruelty, no corruption, no exploitation of the innocent in this whole teeming city in which Mr Fogarty would not be prepared to lend a hand. He does it for the pleasure of it, you see, not out of want, for he is a rich man nowadays and has no need to play the butler.'

She paused again and her eyes moved to the glow of the fire.

'Mr Fogarty is everything I despise, Flotsam, so your tale pleases me greatly. I like to hear of someone standing up to him. But Fogarty is not one to tolerate defiance, nor to forgive anyone for such a well-aimed kick. So if our paths are to cross his again, young lady, we had better be ready for him.'

'*We*, ma'am?' I was struggling to keep up.

'Of course, Flotsam. Where else would you go? You've no references, no skills, not even any proper clothes. And there will not be many employers who consider kneeing a butler below the belt buckle an acceptable proof of character. So all in all I think you'd be much better staying here. I have need of a scullery maid and a helper. You have need of a good position and a warm bath. I think we shall get on very well, young Flottie. As soon as Scraggs gets back about his business we shall get you out of what you're wearing and into something that bears a closer resemblance to clothing.'

And that is how I found myself as scullery maid to Mrs Hudson, a housekeeper whose fierceness and fairness were legendary in every servants' hall I ever entered. Under her watchful demeanour I learnt to scrub and polish and wax and shine. I learned to sweep, and curtsy like a real maid, and to answer 'yes, sir' and 'no, ma'am' when spoken to upstairs, instead of blushing and stammering and trembling at the edges.

My education didn't stop there. When I could show that I had mastered my basic duties, Mrs Hudson immediately demanded that I learned the duties of others. Much to my terror, I was apprenticed to Mrs Siskin, the cook, a silent woman and a Methodist, with the instruction to observe the rudiments of her skills. For Mrs Hudson made it very plain that she thought a girl such as myself, with no family and no education, should at the very least be able to tell a blancmange from a jelly.

With similar force of character, Mrs Hudson decided that I must learn to read. A series of tearful encounters in the butler's pantry ensued wherein Swordsmith, the kindly, ineffectual butler, endeavoured to demonstrate the difference between vowels and verbs. After three or four weeks it was debatable whether Swordsmith or myself was the more disheartened, but Mrs Hudson insisted and her will carried all before it.

'Reading and writing, young Flottie, means you'll never end up in the gutter. It's all right for Scraggs and his type to go without. They're boys and this world favours boys. There will always be something out there for Scraggs. But for girls, livings aren't so easy to come by. Anything in the way of learning that comes our way is something that needs to be grabbed with both hands. And with our teeth too if we can reach it.'

So Swordsmith and I were required to persevere and, to the equal surprise of us both, after some months of desperation I suddenly found the strange marks on the page forming themselves into decipherable groups. Soon I had outgrown the exhausted Swordsmith and by the time I was fourteen there wasn't a book in the street I wouldn't have been confident of reading aloud. *The Odyssey* was almost learned by heart and even Mrs Beaton held no mysteries.

It was at about this time, when I had just begun to believe that I was truly safe from the predatory streets outside, that everything changed. The master of the house died by his own hand when confronted with news of a decisive typhoon off Formosa. That meant the break-up of our whole establishment, amidst many tears and bravely gulped farewells. Mrs Siskin moved to a household in Brighton, a town she had been told had a great need of Methodists. Swordsmith, after some vacillation, entered the service of the young Lord Tregavin who shortly afterwards set off on foot for Mongolia. And Mrs Hudson continued to supervise the closing up of the house as though no fear for the future had ever entered her mind.

It was a night in November, and I was sewing by the kitchen fire for almost the last time, when Mr Rumbelow, the family solicitor, appeared at the kitchen door and asked if he might speak a word with Mrs Hudson.

'Yes, sir, of course, sir,' I spluttered, leaping to my feet. 'Mrs Hudson has just stepped out, but will be back any moment now. Shall I ask her to come up, sir?'

But Mr Rumbelow, it appeared, although hesitant in his manner, had no intention of retreating from the kitchen. His eye was resting on a decanter of dark liquid that Mrs Hudson had placed on the shelf of the dresser only a few hours before.

'Perhaps, child, if I may…' He indicated an empty chair by the fire. 'Never one to stand on ceremony, you see… Perhaps wait here… Wouldn't want to miss out… The Mulgrave old tawny! Remarkable! So, yes, perhaps a seat by the fire…'

'I'm sure, sir, that if you would care for a glass…?'

I moved to bring him the decanter, but he seemed suddenly overcome by great shyness.

'No, of course, I mustn't… Most certainly not. Not without… Well, perhaps just a small glass…'

And with that he settled himself beside the fire and watched with something almost like rapture as I placed the port on a salver, along with one of the glasses that Mrs Hudson had laid out in advance. And yet, for all his eagerness, he did not rush to drink. Indeed he cradled his glass in his palm for so long that I began to think his interest lay purely in its colour and aroma. And when he finally raised his arm, his sip was so small that it seemed barely to moisten his lip. Nevertheless he let out a sigh of such pleasure – a sort of blissful, peaceful joy – that I could be in no doubt as to his satisfaction.

'Yes, indeed. A remarkable wine,' he concluded, addressing this verdict more to the fire than to me. 'A very fine wine indeed. Did you know, Flotsam,' he went on, raising his voice and turning towards me, 'that there are barely a dozen bottles of this in London? It is impossible to obtain at any price.'

'Is that so, sir?' I was not, perhaps, experienced enough in these matters to understand the awe in his voice. 'Then how does there come to be a bottle here?'

Mr Rumbelow looked surprised. 'Why, Sir Reginald Birdlip has a virtual monopoly on the remaining supply, and he sends Mrs Hudson a bottle every year. Has she never told you?'

'No, sir.' Mrs Hudson had told me many things, but very few of them related to her previous employment. Of her views on wax polish and grease stains and shoddy fishmongers I knew a great deal. Of her past, nothing. 'Sir Reginald Who, sir?'

'Sir Reginald Birdlip, of the Gloucestershire Birdlips. Mrs Hudson was in service with his uncle at the time of the Italian loans affair. Saved Sir Reginald from certain ruin, she did. Of course she was still only a parlour maid then, and I was a very callow young fellow myself. But when she came to me with her observations there was no doubting her sharpness. Had she not understood the significance of the dust accumulating beneath the stair-rods, the fraud might never have come to light. Sir Reginald pretty much owes her everything.'

'I see, sir,' I replied, although in truth I saw very little. 'I don't think Mrs Hudson has ever mentioned it.'

'Of course after that she couldn't remain with the Birdlips,' the good solicitor continued. 'Too awkward. She simply knew too much. I was lucky enough to be able to point her towards a rather better position, where she rapidly rose through the ranks. And then of course young Bertie Codlington disappeared from Codlington Hall, and only Mrs Hudson was able to offer any explanation. Had she not realised the importance of the half-eaten omelette and the train ticket for Bodmin, we would never have discovered the bungalow near Scarborough, and Bertie would most certainly have committed bigamy with the under-cook.'

Mr Rumbelow shook his head admiringly as he recalled it.

'And so things went on, Flotsam. Of course you'll have heard most of the stories already. And it's been my great privilege, down the years, to have assisted her from time to time. Indeed it was I who found this post for her, when she told me she wanted a little peace and quiet. That was just after the affair at Baltham Hall, you see. Lord Bilborough never knew who rescued the pearls, but Rothebury knew, and so did Rochester and Lord Arlington, and they all wanted her to come to them. But she's never one for the limelight, you know. She likes to keep to the shadows.'

'Indeed I do, sir, indeed I do.' The voice startled us both, coming as it did from the actual shadows by the back door. Mrs Hudson had let herself in so quietly that neither of us had been aware of her presence. 'And if you please, sir, you won't go filling Flotsam's head with all those stories. Flotsam is a bright girl but she has a lot of learning ahead of her, and she'll learn all the quicker if she's not distracted by nonsense of that sort.'

'Er, quite so, Mrs Hudson.' Mr Rumbelow coughed apologetically. 'Yet you cannot deny that over the years your position in some of our great houses has made you privy to some remarkable goings-on. She is too modest, Flotsam,' he concluded. 'Always a good deal too modest.'

'I see you have made a start on the Mulgrave, sir.' Mrs Hudson's voice was stern but I knew her well enough by then to detect the warmth in it. 'Is it to your satisfaction?'

'Why, madam…' Mr Rumbelow seemed genuinely lost for words. 'It is… it is everything you told me and more. When you told me you planned to open a bottle… Why, such felicity, Mrs Hudson, such perfect felicity!'

'Yes, sir, I thought you would enjoy it. And of course as my time here comes to an end, it is I who should be thanking you. I asked you to find me a quiet place free from scandal and skulduggery, and this position has been exactly that. Working here has been a pleasure, hasn't it, Flotsam?'

I bobbed my agreement, and Mr Rumbelow allowed himself another sip of the port. Thus fortified, he took a deep breath.

'Which brings me, of course, to my reason for seeking this interview. For it was not, you understand, solely with the intention of relieving you of your old tawny. Mrs

Hudson, it has come to my attention that you have yet to find yourself a new position and your tenure here will end all too soon. Now, I am aware that a woman of your talents, for there is never a household run in quite the way that yours is run… As I say, a woman of your talents cannot be short of offers of, er, employment, from any number of quarters. But if I could offer any assistance…'

'Go on, sir,' encouraged Mrs Hudson, 'your advice is always welcome, although I have a small sum put away and a mind to wait for the post that suits me.'

'Quite. Just as you say, Mrs Hudson. Quite so. But in the last few days I have received a most earnest missive from Lord Arlington renewing his previous offers. I need hardly tell you…'

'His Lordship's good opinion is most gratifying, sir, but that house of his at Egremont… A most unappealing edifice, and inconvenient in every way. No wonder the soup there is never properly warm.'

'Yes, of course.' Mr Rumbelow allowed his forehead to pucker a little. 'I did indicate to his lordship that I thought your agreement unlikely… But if Egremont does not appeal, how about Woolstanton? Or Rothebury Manor? I know you would be welcomed with great enthusiasm at either establishment. Or failing those, I believe a discreet approach to Lady Carmichael…'

But Mrs Hudson's face remained impassive as a series of great names were listed to her and, when Mr Rumbelow tailed off, the housekeeper reached into her apron and produced a neat square of paper.

'The truth is, sir, that while the positions you mention are all very well, there is a particular post that I have in mind. I believe this address is familiar to you?'

She handed the paper to Mr Rumbelow with great dignity, but it was very clear from the solicitor's reaction that the address she had given him was not one he had anticipated. His eyebrow twitched, then twitched again, and when he raised his eyes there was something approaching alarm in them.

'Why, yes, Mrs Hudson. I handled this lease myself only a few days ago. The new tenants are two gentlemen, medical men of a sort, who have just taken these rooms in Baker Street. And it is true that they do indeed wish to engage a housekeeper. But I must tell you at once, Mrs Hudson, and in the most emphatic terms, that the position would be very different from those you are used to. It is but a pair of gentlemen in rooms who require someone to keep their little establishment in order. The gentlemen will mostly dine out, but there would be no cook to prepare what they may require in terms of breakfast or luncheon. I fear that side of things would all devolve to the housekeeper and whatever help she may have.'

He shook his head again and almost shuddered, as if appalled at the idea being put to him.

'Now, I need hardly tell you, Mrs Hudson, that such a post would be very far beneath those to which you are accustomed. Oh dear, yes, very far indeed. And to be honest with you, the gentlemen concerned are very far from being your usual gentlemen. They have certain requirements of their domestic surroundings that are very far from orthodox. Yes indeed. Very, very far. One of the gentlemen mentioned that the housekeeper he was seeking must have no aversion to blood.'

I detected one of Mrs Hudson's eyebrows rise very slightly above the horizontal, but she said nothing.

'That is not to say,' the lawyer continued hastily, 'that there is anything in the least bit ghoulish about the gentlemen in question. They come with the most impeccable references. One indeed has recently covered himself in glory in Afghanistan. But given their unique requirements, I feel certain they will struggle to fill the position, even though they are willing to agree the most attractive terms with the individual they consider suitable. Quite enormously attractive, in fact. But, Mrs Hudson,' he continued, lowering his voice, 'you must see that such a position could not be for you.'

'Blood, you say, sir?'

'Er, blood, Mrs Hudson. But in vials. Always in vials, I am absolutely assured.'

'And what else, sir?'

'There was, I believe, some mention of bones. And indeed various organs, but always, I am told, safely stored in jars. And of certain artefacts from foreign parts that may be considered a little morbid by our modern society. One of the gentlemen mentioned that there would also be visitors of all descriptions arriving at irregular hours; not to mention various experiments of a chemical nature. Some playing of the violin may also take place, I believe. And the gentlemen stressed that they wished to appoint someone with a rational mind and a keen understanding. A self-defeating aspiration, I fear,' concluded the lawyer, shaking his head, 'for anyone possessed of either would surely see that this was a position to avoid at any cost.'

Mrs Hudson's eyebrow trembled for the briefest of moments. Then she rose to her feet and began to refold the laundry in a way suggestive of deep thought.

'You interest me strangely, sir,' she said at last. 'It is not, as you say, the sort of position I would usually contemplate. But I am sure the gentlemen would also be requiring a maid like young Flotsam here?'

Mr Rumbelow looked momentarily disconcerted but then nodded slowly.

'Well, indeed, Mrs Hudson. I am sure they must. And if you are really serious… Well, I'm sure Flottie here would be admirably suited to the gentlemen's needs.'

'And no doubt on similarly generous terms?'

'Well, Mrs Hudson, if you really are determined to pursue this strange fancy… As I say, if you are so determined, then, yes, I'm sure the gentleman would wish to recognise Flotsam's unique worth.'

Mrs Hudson folded the last piece of linen with a flourish.

'Very well, Mr Rumbelow. You may inform Mr Sherlock Holmes that he has my permission to call.'

–

What took place when the gentleman did call, and just what passed between them, was something to which I was never a party. But on returning home on the evening of the following day, I was passed on the steps by a gentleman ascending. He paused for a moment to look at me and I was greatly struck by his restless, inquisitive demeanour. His features were not unusually defined, though many since have described them so. But the movement of his eyes as they passed over me in exacting scrutiny gave a great impression of restlessness, as if exposed to the winds of many different moods.

'You must be Florence,' he concluded, his examination complete.

'Flotsam, if you please, sir.'

'Precisely!' he exclaimed, beginning once again to ascend the steps with an animal swiftness. 'We shall all do very nicely!' were the last words I heard before he vanished into the fog.

And in that way began a whole new existence. The next morning we said goodbye to our familiar basement and were instead marvelling at the piles of strange boxes and mysterious cases that had been sent on to Baker Street. I confess that as I wandered among them like an Israelite among the Pyramids I was subject to a growing curiosity about the strange gentlemen who possessed such exotic personal effects. Next to a large upright packing case the size of a wardrobe lay a small red chest marked *Poisons*. Beside it was an even smaller box marked *Hair: Northern* and another, *Hair: Asiatic*. Next to the fireplace was an old trunk, inscribed *Various: Strangulation, Asphyxiation, Mesmerism*, which, when moved, revealed the most thrilling of all – a flat case no thicker than a Bible bearing the legend *Blood: Human*.

Mrs Hudson did little to put an end to my ferocious curiosity as she unpacked the various domestic implements that had been sent on by Mr Rumbelow's office according to a lengthy list she had composed the night before.

'Bless you, Flottie, I have scarcely met Mr Holmes and I know very little of the man. Our conversation was confined to my telling him a little bit about myself and what he could expect from me. He strikes me as the kind of man who may benefit from a mite of frankness. Dr Watson, of course, I have yet to meet.'

'And Mr Holmes is a medical man too, is he not?'

'I can't say that he is, Flottie. In fact I understand his interests lie in quite a different direction.'

'Yes, ma'am, it's just that Mr Rumbelow said they were *both* medical men. And from what I can tell, many of Mr Holmes's books are medical books. And he has cases of instruments like I've seen through the windows of the hospital. And many of his cases have markings saying *From the College of Surgeons*, and such like. And the boy from Mr Rumbelow's office who came to check on the deliveries told me that he had heard for certain that Dr Watson and Mr Holmes had met in a hospital.'

Mrs Hudson paused in her unpacking and lowered herself gently onto a box marked *Garments: Old Crones and Naval Officers*.

'Flotsam,' she said, drawing me towards her, 'you're a bright girl and I'm delighted to say so. There are too many people who will tell you that it is not your place to speculate on things that don't concern you, but I'll have none of that. Where would we be if no-one had ever had the sense to speculate a little? And how are we to know what concerns us if we don't do a little investigation first? The older I get, the more I realise that there's very little that passes in this whole heaving city and beyond that doesn't concern us all in one way or another. For if good, decent people don't keep their wits about them, then it is the likes of Fogarty who will benefit.

'So let me give you some advice, young Flottie. At your age I was like you, seeing everything, hearing everything, always looking for the facts beneath things so I could put them together in a way that made sense. Well, Flottie, I've come to understand that in this world facts are very largely used to keep the likes of us in our places. Now I've got nothing against that. I like my place plenty well enough and I'm not looking to move into anyone else's. But I've grown to know that if you start letting facts cloud your judgement you'll spend most of your life being wrong for all the right reasons. No, Flottie, take my advice and learn to heed that little voice inside you that tells you what's right even when all the facts get in the way.'

She stirred from the packing case.

'Now that's enough lecturing, and don't you get the idea that I think it's honest behaviour to go peeking into packing cases that belong to others. If I just went by facts, I'd have clipped your ear and turned you out by now. But right now I need you to unpack the linen. The gentlemen will be here tomorrow night and they'll be expecting the place to be straighter than a sergeant major's trousers.'

But the gentlemen arrived much sooner than we expected. I was making up the beds and looking forward to the bit of bread and cheese that we had brought for supper when I heard Mrs Hudson exclaim, 'My goodness, Mr Holmes, what a shock you gave me! We weren't expecting you till this hour tomorrow.'

A voice I recognised from the previous evening replied, 'Apologies, Mrs Hudson. I fear that Watson and I make a science out of the unexpected. So anxious are we to get down to some serious study in the peace of our own rooms that nothing would deter us from altering our plans and proceeding here at once. Let me introduce the excellent Dr Watson. And where is the inestimable, er, Flottie?'

At that I was called in to perform a curtsy that did Mrs Hudson proud. Despite the proliferation of boxes, Mrs Hudson had created a semblance of order in the principle room, soon known to us all as the study, where the two gentleman were now standing; where, over the years, they were to interview so many visitors and pass so many distinguished hours. It was not a large room but had a good window, curtained now with soft dark drapes, and below it a solid dining table. In the centre of the room, the armchairs faced a welcoming fireplace; behind them a door opened onto a narrow corridor, at the end of which lay the stairs down to the street door and our kitchen; while the gentlemen's bedrooms were gained through a door in the fourth wall. The decoration of the main room was so contrived that by day it was airy and practical but by night the walls seemed closer, the ceiling lower and the space between them dark and comfortable like a cave on a stormy night. In the lamplight, Mr Holmes seemed slightly softer, less lean and angular than before. Dr Watson was a kindly looking man, though not perhaps in the best of health. He mumbled some warm words and then expressed his intention to lie down for a few moments before supper.

'Supper, sir?' Mrs Hudson's eyebrow turned upwards and twitched dangerously. 'Surely you gentlemen will be dining out tonight? There's not a mouthful of food in the house, I'm afraid, sir.'

'Fear not, Mrs Hudson,' Mr Holmes chuckled jovially, 'anticipating just such an eventuality, I took the precaution on the very day we secured the rooms of ordering some foodstuffs to be delivered immediately. And that, if I am not very much mistaken, is the very box, there in the corner beneath Watson's collection of surprising Oriental art works. It will be the labour of an instant for me to transport it to the kitchen and I'm sure we can then prevail upon you to see us towards a little supper.'

It wasn't until we were alone in the kitchen that I dared look at Mrs Hudson's face. To my surprise, instead of indignation there was a certain resigned amusement.

'Well, Flottie,' she sighed with the suspicion of a smile, 'we took this position because it interested us to do so. And I can see that the gentlemen aren't going to disappoint.'

She was halted by a swift knock at the kitchen door, followed in an instant by the entry of Mr Holmes. Our previous employers had never been tolerated in Mrs Hudson's domestic demesne but at Baker Street things were different from the start. The kitchen there was, for me, the best room in the house, warm and safe whether full of angled morning sunshine or lit only by a flicker from the range. And indeed through the years to come, when Dr Watson was out or resting or keeping his room after one of their disagreements, Mr Holmes was often to be found beside our fire with a bottle or two of brown ale, listening avidly to Mrs Hudson's explanations of various domestic mysteries. It was, I think, a side of him that Dr Watson never really saw; perhaps it was a side for which the public wasn't ready.

But this time he was here on more important matters.

'Well, Mrs Hudson, I trust that the few things I sent along will prove adequate for a simple repast?'

'Mr Holmes, just when was it that you agreed to take these rooms?'

'At ten minutes after eleven on the morning of the 22nd,' he replied.

'That would be two weeks ago, Mr Holmes.'

'Fifteen days, to be precise.'

'And are you aware what effect fifteen days may have on a box of meat and vegetables? Even one which appears to have been thrown together by someone under the influence of strong drink?'

'Indeed I am, Mrs Hudson. I have had cause to conduct a detailed study into rates of decay of various foodstuffs under a variety of conditions. The results have proved invaluable on several occasions.'

'Well on this occasion the results have proved something of a mess, Mr Holmes.' Mrs Hudson began to produce an array of vegetables from the box, all of them showing very clear signs of decomposition. An uncomfortable smell began to circulate around the room.

Mr Holmes picked up the remains of a parsnip, now mostly pulp and squashed almost flat.

'Fascinating!' he declared, looking at it closely. 'From the shape to which this has been reduced one could make accurate assumptions about the shapes of the foodstuffs stored close to it, as well as accurate estimates of their sizes and relative densities. Although I would have to concede, Mrs Hudson, that these items are uniformly unenticing. I may perhaps have failed to apply my knowledge in these matters to the practicalities of the domestic arts. Is there anything to be done?'

'Look at it like this, sir.' Mrs Hudson was now engaged in rooting out and discarding an extravagant selection of unrelated comestibles. 'When we have discarded the inedible, what remains, however unlikely, will have to be dinner.'

Mr Holmes paused as though struck by an important thought.

'Do you know, Mrs Hudson, I believe you may have something there.'

No-one ever said Mrs Hudson wasn't the woman to rise to an occasion and by eight o'clock there was a distinctly homely feel to our new quarters. Dr Watson and Mr Holmes, the latter suddenly wrapped in thought, were settled among their packing cases making a healthy supper of bread, cheese, a braised bird we had sent out for and a bottle of burgundy. A much greater air of order prevailed in the kitchen where, the day's undertakings completed, Mrs Hudson and I were sitting quietly by the fire, watching the restful excitement of the small blue flames licking through a shovelful of fresh coal. Mrs Hudson was drinking a glass of the old Madeira that Mr Rumbelow had thought to send.

'You know, Flottie, those two gentlemen are innocents. They need a pair like us who are versed in the ways of the world to see that they come to no harm. And we'll see some excitement in the process, make no mistake. As I always used to say to Hudson...'

But she was interrupted by a flurry of sharp raps on the street door, an urgent, imperious knock that burst through our contented calm like a locomotive through fog. At a signal from Mrs Hudson, I hurried to answer. Fumbling with the bolts I became aware of the insidious cold outside, stealing under the door with a frosty menace. And as I swung the door open, I was confronted by a sight more heart-stoppingly chilling than any freezing night. In front of me towered a figure dressed in black, swathed in a cape so dark its edges seemed of the same substance as the night. He wore on his head not a hat, but a soft dark hood that set most of his face in shadow. But not enough to hide from me the cold silver scar that ran from beneath one ear to just beneath his eye. And where his eye should have been, no eye at all, just a deep, monstrous shadow.

Before I could compose myself enough to scream, something was thrust into my hand and the spectre had stepped backwards into the waiting night.

By the thin light from the windows, I could make out what I held in my hand: an envelope addressed in scarlet and a slim silver dagger.

The Curse of the Spirits

†

It is my firm belief that Mrs Hudson more than any woman of her generation possessed a special talent for reconciling good domestic practice with outlandish and bizarre events. If any example of this were needed, I could cite none better than her response that evening on my return, silent and half frozen with fear, to the fire-lit kitchen. Moving me deftly to the hearth, she asked no questions but busied herself locating a suitable salver on which to convey to Mr Holmes the strange items still held in my grasp.

'Come now, Flotsam, child,' she warned. 'That's the first caller at our new lodgings so we should be making sure that note is properly presented. Which isn't to say,' she continued, pausing to lay a second tray with whisky and soda water, 'that judging by the look of you he may not have been quite the usual sort of caller. But that's the sort of visitor we have to expect now, Flottie, and very accustomed to it we shall become. Now I imagine Mr Holmes will want to ask you a question or two about these here objects, so there's no point us going in until you've had a chance to rearrange your wits. And I imagine Dr Watson will be glad of a drink or two, so there's no point us going in until you've fetched down a pair of them heavy tumblers. And then, if you're to be in the gentlemen's company for any length of time, I think we could lay our hands on an apron that presents them with rather fewer clues as to what you had for your supper.

'As for this,' she pondered, unfolding my fingers from the narrow-bladed knife and holding it up to the light, 'we'd better handle this with a bit of care. In my experience, the sorts of people who send you uninvited knives are generally up to no good and could do with a bit of watching.'

Such was the calming effect of Mrs Hudson's manner that in just a very few minutes, when she once more ushered me before Mr Holmes and Dr Watson, her presence at my side allowed me to repeat my tale with a semblance of calm that belied my inner trembling.

Mr Holmes listened to what I had to say with the utmost concentration, his restless eyes suddenly fixed on a single point, behind them an impassioned light flaring from time to time like a kindling flame. He remained silent until I finished and then Dr Watson spoke first.

'What a remarkable business! Chap sounds like a lunatic to me. Shouldn't be on the streets at all, I daresay.'

'On the contrary, Watson, from Flottie's admirable account it is clear that the actions of tonight's messenger are very far from insane. Think what he has accomplished tonight. He has timed his arrival at that hour of the evening when a housekeeper is most likely to be about her post-prandial chores and the chance is highest that an impressionable young girl will respond to his knock. He has succeeded in using his singular appearance to such effect that he has been able to disappear unmarked into the night. And he has succeeded, I perceive, in delivering his employer's letter to its intended recipient on the very evening of that person taking up a new address. The last of these, although at first glance the greater achievement, is perhaps the least remarkable, for I think I can say without vanity that there are not a few in this great city of ours who could tell you at any time the correct residence of Sherlock Holmes.'

That said, Mr Holmes took a paper-knife from a nearby crate inscribed *Crimes of Passion* and focused his attention on the carefully sealed missive that had been thrust so dramatically into our midst. Before turning to the letter itself, he examined in minute detail its wax seal with the assistance of a magnifying glass that he plucked from the folds of his smoking jacket.

'As I suspected,' he remarked. 'Cheap wax of the sort used by countless people a thousand times a day. But the seal-stamp itself is a different matter. Crude work – of native execution, I'll warrant – showing what appears to be some kind of exotic marsupial.'

He held the letter out towards Dr Watson. As Mrs Hudson passed it to where the doctor was seated, I saw her pass an intent eye across the seal in question.

'Bless my soul,' declared Watson, passing the letter back. 'A strange beast indeed, eh, Mrs Hudson?'

'Yes, sir.' She paused, her eyebrow twitching almost imperceptibly. 'Though not unlike a large rat, perhaps, sir?'

'Precisely!' declared Mr Holmes, after peering swiftly at the letter for a second time. 'I can see you will have to be on your mettle, Watson. Mrs Hudson clearly has a sharp eye in these matters!'

Rather hurriedly he slipped the letter open and tilted it towards the lamp. For a short moment, every occupant of the room seemed suspended in a state of breathless concentration and time hung motionless at the edge of the lamplight. Then Mr Holmes gave a short exclamation and thrust the document at Dr Watson.

'If you would be so good, Watson. I'm sure it will benefit from your admirably uncomplicated delivery.'

The letter comprised one piece of paper, folded twice, unevenly, as if in a great hurry. It carried no address but that day's date, scratched in the same scarlet ink across the top of the sheet. Below, scrawled in an unsteady hand at an angle acute to the horizontal, was a message speaking as much of panic as simple fear.

> *Sir I find myself in mortal peril and daily fear for my life I beg to be allowed to wait on you tomorrow at the hour of eight o'clock in the evening, I shall presume to call at that hour in the hope that you receive favourably this most urgent request of -*
> Nathaniel Moran

The room seemed even quieter as his words were absorbed by the cushioning silence of our concentration. Some-where inside me a tiny thrill of excitement passed through my spine to my feet, making my toes tingle.

'Mystifying,' murmured Watson.

'Transparent!' declared Holmes. 'You have some small notion of my methods, Watson. I beg you to apply my principles and tell me what we can glean from this most irregular epistle.'

'Why, Holmes, I can glean nothing from it except that the writer is clearly afraid for his life. How else can one explain the frantic style, the lack of care for presentation or punctuation, the oversight of including no address to which you might direct a reply?'

'My good Watson!' retorted Holmes with a chuckle. 'Your openness is such that you find it difficult to penetrate beyond the first face the world presents to you. While Mrs Hudson helps you to a well-deserved drink, let me suggest a few conclusions that I feel can be safely drawn from this missive.

'When our correspondent calls in person, I strongly suspect that we shall find him still some years short of what is described as middle age. In the last ten days he has returned to London from a prolonged period in the tropics and is still affected by an illness he contracted there. He has recently fallen on hard times but hopes that this state shall be a temporary one. And, if I am not very much mistaken, he is also something of an amateur naturalist and has made a careful collection of native fauna while he has been overseas.'

'Really, Holmes!' Watson expostulated. 'You cannot seriously expect us to believe that even a mind such as yours can deduce all that from just a few lines of prose. Why, it's an impossibility!' And in his perturbation he pushed his newly empty glass towards the drinks tray with a gesture more instinctive than conscious. Even Mrs Hudson's eyebrow twitched slightly as she replenished his glass in silence.

'On the contrary, Watson. Nothing I've said requires anything more than the most basic observation. Firstly as to his age: his handwriting shows signs of haste and powerful emotion. It is not impossible that you are correct in surmising it is fear that has made his hand unsteady.

Yet beneath the surface emotion it remains a strong hand. See the vigour of the downstrokes and deep impression his signature has left on the paper. There is none of the uncertainty here that so often betrays the septuagenarian, none of the small weaknesses that suggest a man past his prime. So a man of middle years, perhaps? And yet surely the composition of the letter, the scant regard for the niceties of correspondence, suggest a failure in the writer to master his immediate emotions. One would not expect to find such surrender to his prevailing mood in a man of mature years. So a young man then? Yet a sojourn in the tropics of some years' duration, of which more presently, dictates that he can no longer be termed a youth. And so, Watson, I am forced to conclude that our correspondent's age is somewhere in between. In short, I fully expect him to be a man of thirty.'

'But, Holmes,' rejoined Watson, throwing an inclusive smile at Mrs Hudson as if certain that his friend had over-reached himself, 'how can you deduce that he has so recently returned from the tropics, and after a stay there of some years?'

'Surely, my dear Watson, the reasons begin to suggest themselves? His seal with its grotesque foreign rodent is a clear indication of a time spent in warmer climes. Its rough finish and poor delineation speak of the native workman. You may also have observed the small palm tree under which the creature rests. The man who has chosen to adopt this as his seal clearly feels an attachment to the motif that argues a period of accustomed usage, almost certainly during a foreign sojourn of some years' duration.

'And yet we know him still to be a relatively young man, so his return must have been comparatively recent, particularly if, as I suspect, his health still bears the imprint of his travels. For where you see only fear, Watson, I also detect a hand undermined by fever. A vigorous hand rendered strangely unsteady, an unexplained brevity as if the effort of writing was a great one... Given what we know already of our friend, a tropical fever, not quite shaken off, is the most likely explanation. Meanwhile, the absence of any return address, far from being the over-sight you imagine, suggests to me a man uncertain of his whereabouts from day to day. Clearly he has yet to find permanent lodgings. Yet ten days is ample for a man of average resource to establish himself in the metropolis, so I deduce our correspondent's arrival fell within that period.'

'But what of the rest, Holmes? The depleted funds and the interest in native species?'

Mr Holmes leaned back in his armchair and began to light the pipe he had been most carefully filling, his face affecting a look of the most pained surprise.

'Really, Watson, surely the rest is most readily apparent? The cheap wax and cheaper writing paper both argue that he is not currently able to afford the luxury of a reputable hotel. He should hardly be using these materials if the writing room at Claridge's was at his disposal. I suspect he is staying in one of those nameless, semi-respectable East-End boarding houses while seeking daily for lodgings that will suit his reduced circumstances. The services of a servant – for I feel your apparition must be characterised as such, young Flottie – indicates that his fortunes have not always been at their current ebb. And I have yet to meet a man reduced to unaccustomed poverty who does not yet harbour hopes that another minute will see all his fortunes restored.'

'And a naturalist, Holmes?'

'The ink, Watson! The ink! No-one outside those publications commonly known as the Penny Dreadfuls ever uses scarlet ink. The only exception of which I am aware is the habit of collectors in some remote parts of the Empire to use red ink for the labelling of exhibits in their cabinets. They generally find that it holds its colour much better than black ink of local manufacture, which fades disastrously when exposed for long periods to the fierce sunlight. And our writer's choice of seal, revealing as it does the preoccupations of the naturalist rather than the anthropologist, would appear to place the matter beyond doubt.'

'Why, I believe that is the finest thing I have ever heard!' exclaimed Dr Watson, draining his glass with a gulp. 'What do you say, Mrs H? I'll wager you've never heard the like of that in all your born days!'

However true that was of Mrs Hudson, I confess that I for one was spellbound by the image Mr Holmes had revealed with such elegant strokes. As he basked in a satisfied atmosphere of admiration and tobacco smoke, I simply didn't have words to express the wonderment that filled me, wiping away the memory of my earlier fear. Everything seemed to make sense. Perhaps there was nothing that couldn't be explained.

And that, I found, was something with which Mrs Hudson could concur, though for reasons that were very far from my own. It wasn't until we had regained the warm fastness of our kitchen that I understood Mrs Hudson did not necessarily share the views expounded so brilliantly by the great detective. As I readied myself for bed I noticed that she could not settle, preferring to refold the laundry rather than take a second glass of Mr Rumbelow's excellent port.

'Tell me, Flottie,' she asked at last, laying the final bedsheet down so folded that it would have served as a study for budding geometricians, 'what are your feelings about Mr Holmes's explanation of that letter of ours?'

'Oh, Mrs Hudson, ma'am! It was the most surprising thing I've ever heard! I thought that stranger appearing at the door was a shock but it was nothing to the way Mr Holmes showed us how all the facts fitted together. Before he began, there were no imaginings I wasn't imagining. But now I know it was just an ordinary gentleman that sent that letter, I know it was silly to be frightened. I feel I almost know the gentleman myself!'

Mrs Hudson looked even sterner than usual.

'And do you not think, Flotsam, that there could be other explanations for all those things Mr Holmes pointed out?'

'Ma'am?'

'You see, there was nothing Mr Holmes said that I could actually say was *wrong*, but it just didn't feel *right* either. In *here*,' gesturing somewhere in the region of her bosom. 'It's not to say that Mr Holmes isn't very clever and scientific, but I couldn't help seeing it another way.

'I mean, Flottie, what sort of gentleman sends his man around at that hour, at just the time when his startling appearance will appear most sinister? Why couldn't he have used the penny post like anyone else? His letter would have arrived in a nice orderly way tomorrow morning, in plenty of time for Mr Holmes to have prepared himself for a visit that evening. And then there's that dramatic scribbling in an ink that no decent soul would dream of employing. I don't know what they write in out in the Indies, but it's hard to credit that in this country he couldn't have found a more honest colour for his purpose. However poor his accommodation, I don't believe there was no pot of black ink to be had if he needed it. Don't you think, Flottie,' she continued softly, 'that his reason for writing could have been quite different from the one he claims? If he had deliberately set out to disconcert us all as much as possible and create around himself an aura of mystery, he could have found no surer way to go about it. It occurs to me, young Flottie, that Mr Moran may prove a slightly trickier character than he would have us believe.'

–

And yet the appearance of the gentleman himself at precisely eight o'clock the following evening seemed to bear out everything that Mr Holmes had predicted. It was a day made busy by the duties associated with new lodgings. Mrs Hudson was up well before dawn and by the time I awoke had already been attended by Scraggs and a small army of similar boys who had been dispatched all over London with different orders relating to our comfort and provisioning. I spent an exciting morning assisting Dr Watson in the unpacking of his many packing cases until Mrs Hudson, deciding Dr Watson was better able to begin the sorting of his artworks without my aid, sent me off to communicate to Scraggs some additional requirements.

It was one of those rare November days when the sun pierced the fog and suffused the streets of London with a golden haze that softened for a few hours the harsh lines of brickwork and stone. Scraggs proved in high spirits and endeavoured to convince me that it was my duty to accompany him to Smithfields where, he promised, he would be able to point out to me an associate of his in the butcher's trade who could provide Mrs Hudson with the finest Tamworth sausages in the kingdom. However, conscious of events awaiting me in Baker Street, I determined that on this occasion I would return promptly, the better to prepare myself for a glimpse of our mysterious correspondent. For all that, it was growing dark by the time I began to make my way back to Baker Street and the warmth of the day had evaporated into the chill of incipient fog. I shivered as I sensed in the fading light the menace of the night returning, and my footsteps quickened as the shadows grew deeper, while the gradual lighting of the lamps accelerated the gathering darkness.

Imagine then the feelings of relief and happiness on my return to find the shutters closed for the night, fires already blazing in the grates and the warm, rich smell of a deep stew wrapping itself round Mrs Hudson as she surveyed with imperturbable satisfaction the domestic scene.

'Oh, Mrs Hudson, ma'am,' I gulped, half aghast at the evidence of so much labour in my absence.

'Your timing, Flottie, is perfect. I thought you would wish to keep a good eye on that rascal Scraggs to make sure that everything about our delivery was in order, so I took it upon myself to get the fires going and the lamps lit. But now I'll be putting my feet up for a moment or two with a glass of the sherry that Mr Rumbelow's office saw fit to send round this morning. I shall leave it to you to finish off the knives and forks and when you're done we'll go up to the linen room and have a go at the rest of the silver. And I daresay you'll be interested to answer the door tonight should the gentleman with the unusual ink care to call in person.'

So while Mrs Hudson sat by the fire, turning the pages of a large tome that had been delivered to her by special messenger that morning, I polished cutlery with all my heart and soul, until it shone in the lamplight like the steel of a guardsman's sword. Up in the study, Mr Holmes nestled in thought as deep as his armchair, the drawing of his pipe and the lazy clouds of tobacco smoke the only evidence that the great mind was at work under the inert exterior. Opposite him, Dr Watson leafed idly through one of the illustrated periodicals that were sent to him by subscription. Eight o'clock seemed a long time coming and through both rooms an unacknowledged current of expectation crept like a low draught.

When the knock at the door finally came, I jumped like a startled sparrow for all that I had spent the previous hour anticipating it. It was a very different knock from the previous evening, low but repeated very rapidly three or four times as if the visitor were in a state of barely suppressed agitation. My eyes turned to Mrs Hudson who remained unmoved beside the fire, her concentration apparently unbroken.

'If you'd be so kind, Flottie,' she asked without looking up, but I noticed that her glass had been rested on the hearth and she no longer seemed to scan the printed page in the way she had before.

When my excitement had been mastered sufficiently to allow me to open the door, Mr Nathaniel Moran proved to be a sallow gentleman of around thirty years of age. Indeed so closely did his appearance conform to the image I had created from Mr Holmes's description that any doubts I had harboured about the great detective's perspicacity were instantly and completely set aside. Beneath ginger whiskers his face was unnaturally pale, as if recently ravaged by illness. He was a strongly built man whose movement and appearance suggested a good deal of natural grace, yet his demeanour and manner betrayed a hesitation or nerviness that did not sit comfortably with his strong features or a pair of cool eyes. When I took his coat I noticed that the clothes beneath were old-fashioned in cut and designed for warmer climes. Inwardly marvelling at Mr Holmes's prescience, I proceeded to announce the visitor to his expectant hosts.

Dr Watson immediately jumped to his feet and made Mr Moran welcome while his colleague made only a desultory effort to rise, then sank back into his armchair, his eyes barely open and his smoking uninterrupted. Before I could withdraw, Dr Watson had already established his guest in a chair by the fire and gallantly followed behind me to hold the door as I passed through it. For a brief moment each of us met the gaze of the other and I fear my wild curiosity must have communicated itself to the good doctor in that exchange of glances for, instead of pushing the door closed, he closed one eye in a half-wink and the door, unseen in the shadows, remained open a good inch or more.

The linen room was little more than a store room opposite the study. Soon after our arrival Mrs Hudson had colonised it for domestic purposes and now the effect of Dr Watson's charity was to enable someone placed in its doorway a narrow line of vision across the slim corridor that separated the two rooms, through the open door, into the heart of the study itself. With a casual nonchalance that only served to reveal my precise motives, I sauntered into the tiny room and edged the pile of waiting silver to the place that best allowed me to follow events in the other room. To my great surprise Mrs Hudson, on climbing the stairs and finding me in this position, raised a questioning eyebrow but made no attempt to prevent my inexcusable breach of manners, so that when Mr Moran began to speak his words were as clearly audible to us in our niche as they were to Mr Holmes by his hearth.

'Gentlemen,' Moran began, 'I hope you will excuse me for disturbing you at this hour and for the brevity of my note to you last night. I am only too aware how irregular my conduct must seem.'

'Nonsense, sir. Dr Watson and I never stand on social niceties. Besides, you have been suffering from a fever, I perceive.'

For a moment Mr Moran seemed genuinely taken aback and he took a moment before he replied.

'I see your reputation is richly deserved, Mr Holmes. Even in Sumatra, where I have passed the last seven years of my life, word had reached us of your talents.'

'Sumatra, you say?' returned Holmes casually, raising an eyebrow in the direction of Dr Watson. 'A place with a rich native fauna, I imagine.'

Again Mr Moran seemed startled.

'Indeed, Mr Holmes, as I am only too well aware. It is partly just that aspect of the country which has brought me here tonight. That and other attendant details which I trust a man of your talents will be able to make something of.'

'Perhaps if you were to start at the beginning, Mr Moran, and confine yourself to the facts of the case...' He settled deeper into his chair and sent another cloud of tobacco smoke drifting out towards the linen room where I had just begun to polish the same candlestick for the third time. Mrs Hudson had taken up the small candelabra and, with her back turned to me, was working away with crisp, powerful strokes.

'Mr Holmes, the story I have to tell is not one that I tell lightly. Like yourself, I am a passionate believer in scientific knowledge. Yet I now find myself beset with the most unscientific and superstitious apprehension.

'My father, sir, was a successful merchant who found in his dealings in Malaya the means to a substantial fortune. If I had wished it, I could have continued his ventures upon his retirement but my father and I quarrelled and, with the impetuosity of youth, I vowed to make a fortune of my own that would surpass his and prove to him how far short his estimate was of my true abilities. I had acquired a good practical knowledge of trade in the tropics and through an acquaintance I was introduced to four others, young men such as myself, whose daring and determination promised to make up for any lack of capital. After much discussion we decided to seek our fortunes in Sumatra. There is a string of islands there off the west coast which have been untouched by the big trading concerns. We formed the Sumatra and Nassau Trading Company operating out of Port Mary and took an oath on our lives that we would labour shoulder to shoulder until our fortunes were made.'

Down the thin line of light, I saw Moran shiver.

'On arrival, sir, Port Mary proved to be little more than a dispirited collection of huts containing a handful of transitory Europeans and a small population of Chinese. Around it, the jungle rose like a mountain, swathed in mist, encroaching on the town at every opportunity, and at night the cries of strange creatures invaded your dreams. It was as if the island itself resented our intrusion and was trying to reclaim our outpost as its own. And the people were no more welcoming. From the Chinese there was blank indifference, and beyond the town we faced the suspicion and hostility of the natives. From the day of our arrival, a dreadful loneliness began to engulf us.

'And yet what we called the town soon became, for all its shortcomings, our refuge. For those islands are a wild place, Mr Holmes. A place of savage beauty and dark, muttering superstitions. The tribes worship the forest and its spirits, each of which appears to Western eyes more cruel and vengeful than the last. Before we had been on the island three days, we received a visit from their chief priest. Our presence there offended the spirits, he told us. If we remained our ventures would fail. If we failed to respect the spirits of the island we would pay with our lives.'

Dr Watson shifted slightly in his seat and I found I had paused in my polishing. Moran coughed nervously. Only Mrs Hudson and Mr Holmes appeared unmoved.

'The jungle which we hoped would provide our fortune is dark and threatening. It contains creatures unknown to European science – spiders the size of birds, venomous snakes no bigger than your thumb, a bestiary of the disgusting and the frightful. And amongst these creatures, taking their animal shapes to work their mischief, are any number of malevolent spirits.

'Three in particular are revered by the savages. First there is the tiger spirit, who represents life and vitality. Then there is *maki*, a spirit who takes the shape of the purple cobra and who represents both death and sleeping. These two are more respected than feared. But between them comes *enoki*, the stealer of souls, and this is the spirit who truly provokes terror. Just as vermin are drawn to carrion, so *enoki* is drawn to the evil in men's hearts. Where

42

there is vileness, *enoki* feasts. He comes at night and nibbles at the evil in you, growing more rapacious with every visit, until your whole soul is devoured. For those destroyed in this way, there is no death, no sleep, just an empty eternity waiting for *enoki* to return to feed on you once more. In native legend, *enoki*, if he is ever seen at all, takes on the form of an enormous carrion rat, and tales are told of sick men visited in the dark by a foul creature which sits upon their chests to await their passing. They feel its weight, smell its evil breath, but see nothing at all.'

The silence that followed was distinctly uneasy, broken finally by a faint tutting from Dr Watson.

'Oh, come now, sir,' he spluttered, 'that's a bit much, isn't it? Rats of giant proportions stalking invalids and what-not. It's enough to make one feel quite uncomfortable. Surely you aren't asking us to believe such stories?'

'On the contrary, Dr Watson, I am very much hoping that you and Mr Holmes will show them to be nonsense. But let me continue my tale.

'Mr Holmes, I will not dwell on the early years of our venture. Suffice it to say that I learned to my cost why the riches of the islands had remained for so many years unexploited. Of the five of us who set out with such high hopes, two were to find nothing but a grave in that unforgiving jungle; the first, Whitfield, was taken by fever within a month of our arrival. That left Postgate, Neale, Carruthers and myself determined to persist in our venture. We stayed afloat by selling a little opium to the Chinese but the natives remained resistant to our overtures and without their assistance the island's wealth was beyond our reach.

'This stubbornness began to provoke us and we began to sneer at their superstitions. In a light-hearted moment I even commissioned a seal depicting the imaginary rat and used it on company correspondence. Yet we were not to be deterred, and a new line of business suggested by Neale seemed set fair to prosper – only to be overtaken by a sequence of events that led to the ruin of our ventures and may yet, I believe, cost us our lives.'

There was another pause as Moran mopped his brow. Watson shifted uneasily again and a little shudder passed softly down my spine as though something of the damp jungle loneliness that Moran described had crept into the room. Mrs Hudson, habitually stern, seemed sterner than ever, but there was something about the faint nodding of her head that, if she were listening at all, expressed a cryptic satisfaction in the gentleman's tale.

After gathering himself, the visitor continued.

'It was a day in October, just over a year ago, that things began to unravel. Postgate had been on a short expedition into the interior looking for minerals. Postgate liked these expeditions. The cold watchfulness that surrounded our days in Port Mary was beginning to get to him and he was drinking too freely. He used these expeditions to escape our disapproval and to discharge a great deal of ammunition at any target the jungle provided. When he returned that day he was literally whooping with elation, a dead creature the size of a spaniel hanging from his saddle. A small crowd gathered as he dismounted and in front of everyone he whirled the thing around his head, shouting my name. 'Moran!' he cried, 'I've shot their precious rat! Come and look at this!' And it was in truth a remarkable specimen, easily the largest creature of its kind I'd ever seen. It's fur was black, its tail furred like a squirrel's. It had mean, powerful jaws and vicious claws. 'Eater of souls indeed!' he cried.

'Let's see what they make of this!' And before I could stop him, he had attached the carcass to the string of our flag pole and was hoisting it high above our compound.

'That night Postgate got drunk. Neale and Carruthers put him to bed, leaving me on the veranda, eyeing the jungle with unease. Postgate's had been a silly, juvenile gesture but it made me afraid. That may seem absurd to you but in the tropics shadows take strange shapes. That night I slept badly, my dreams full of horrible images, and when I awoke it was to find myself staring at something more horrible still, something on my pillow, little more than an inch from my face.'

Mr Moran broke off his tale to pass a hand across his weary features.

'It was the carcase of a rat, a rat of ordinary size, skewered by a narrow blade through my pillow, into the bed frame below. A carcase so fresh that the blood still seeped from it, so fresh I swear to you that its limbs still twitched. And stuffed in its mouth, cut from my head while I slept, was a lock of my own hair.'

Safe in the linen room by the small pile of unpolished silver, I could see both Holmes and Watson lean forward slightly. Mr Holmes's pipe was long since set aside and now his eyes were alert and searching, trained on the speaker with a vital intensity. The fire was dying down and flick-ering shadows played over the faces of the three men. I imagined the dark malevolent night drawing in around Moran's jungle dwelling and I shuddered.

Moran took a deep breath and continued his tale.

'I quickly learned that I was not alone in this horror. My colleagues had all received the same visitation, and I think it's fair to say that all of us were badly spooked. There was

45

an old man in Port Mary, half native and half Chinese, and we sought him out in hope of an explanation. He told us that the meaning of the objects we had received was clear. It was the curse of the high priest, calling down upon us the spirit *eroki*. Now, he told us, coolly as you like, the spirit would visit each of us in turn and would begin to eat away at our souls. When he had taken enough – enough for him to claim possession of us – we would die. We would die by the knife of the high priest, guided by the spirit's hand, but death was only the beginning. After death, our torment would begin in earnest, as *eroki* would return to feast upon us for the rest of eternity.

'The following morning, I found that Postgate had risen early, taken a mule and was gone. Two days later he was back. A rubber prospector called Cartwright emerged from the interior with his dead body strapped across the mule. Cartwright brought the body to our offices and told us how he had been disturbed in the night by the sound of a man's screams. In the islands off Sumatra, a scream in the night is not necessarily something to investigate, but there was something in these screams that Cartwright could not ignore. 'It was as if a man's soul was on fire,' he said – and Cartwright is not a man given to poetry. At dawn he had set off in the direction of the noise and in a small clearing he found Postgate, still bent in agony but cold to the touch. Around him lay the few things he had taken with him – his gun unfired, some food untouched, an empty bottle or two of liquor.

'Beyond, but for the marks of birds and animals, the leaf mould was unmarked by any footprints save those of Postgate and Cartwright himself. And when he turned over the body, Mr Holmes, he found blood on the man's fingers and face. But it was his eyes that caused a hardened man like Cartwright to recoil in horror. For where his eyes should have been there was nothing. Nothing but thick-caked blood. The spirits had taken his sight, Mr Holmes, and he had died in the agony of their vengeance.'

The Tell-tale Stain

✝

To say the room fell silent would be a considerable understatement. For a full five seconds there seemed to reign not a silence but an absence of sound like a vacuum that drew from everyone all power of speech. Then abruptly the vacuum broke and sound came rushing back.

'I say!' exclaimed Watson, knocking over his drink with a strangled flourish.

'Extraordinary!' rasped Holmes, rising from his chair abruptly and sending over a small incidental table.

'Blimey!' I squeaked, back in the linen room, dropping the candlestick and bringing down a pile of assorted silverware with a reverberating crash.

And Mrs Hudson, putting the finishing touches to the small candelabra, murmured, 'Well, well!' very softly with the air of a scientist whose experiment has produced a result both satisfactory and slightly unexpected.

The uproar allowed Mr Moran to sink back in his chair while Dr Watson refilled his glass with brandy and shrub and retrieved the table. Mr Holmes remained standing, tapping his pipe hard against the mantelpiece as if in agitation. Outside, Mrs Hudson was helping me to retrieve the scattered silver.

Dr Watson, aided by a healthy swig, was the first regain a degree of coherence.

'Really, sir! I don't know what you're about, trying to scare us out of our wits! I've never heard such ridiculous nonsense!'

'Dr Watson, my intention is the opposite. Confronted at every turn with facts that seem to permit no natural explanation, I turn to you in the hope that you may find reason and logic where increasingly I can only detect a supernatural hand.'

'Let us, as you say, concentrate on the facts of the case,' rejoined Mr Holmes, frowning at his pipe. I was aware of Mrs Hudson tutting very softly by my side.

'Was there a surgeon resident in Port Mary who could examine the body?'

'Alas not, Mr Holmes. I was forced to conduct the examination myself and it was clear, although I'm not a medical man, that the poor fellow had been blinded in the most horrible manner. But by what means, I cannot guess.'

'This man Cartwright, was he well known to you? Is it safe to believe his tale?'

'I knew him slightly, more by repute than otherwise. But he had been a familiar figure in those parts for some years. He was liked by the other Europeans in those islands and seemed a regular fellow.'

'And where is he now?'

'I couldn't tell you, Mr Holmes. It was the nature of his work to spend most of his life in the jungle. He could be anywhere in the Orient.'

'And was he quite clear there were no tracks other than his own leading to the body?'

'Perfectly clear. I'd heard of Cartwright off and on for a few years at that point and knew him to be a tough type. Yet I swear he was badly spooked by what he'd found. I never saw him look so rattled. I questioned him carefully about tracks near the body but he is adamant there were none.'

'What about disease? Might there have been some natural cause of this sudden affliction?'

'I have since consulted experts in the field and they can suggest no such cause.'

'Very well. That is helpful for now. What happened next?'

'My colleagues took it hard. Where before we had felt isolated now we felt afraid. But it was an insidious, nagging fear, a terror of the unknown, made worse when a persistent, clammy mist descended upon us from the jungle. With it came the nightmares. The night after Postgate's death I awoke with the sense of a terrible weight pressing upon my chest, and when I opened my eyes I swear for an instant I saw a pair of yellow eyes — animal eyes — staring back at me. This dream was repeated many times in the nights that followed. And then the killings began.

'The first was a native hunter, one who sometimes traded with us and so had been made an outcast by his tribe. The circumstances of his death were identical to those of Postgate's, his wounds the same in every respect. And we had plenty of opportunities to make comparisons, for the very next day another hunter who had traded with us was found dead with the same appalling scars. The fourth victim was a white man, an eccentric settler who had gone native years before and lived alone in the jungle. He would occasionally appear in Port Mary with the skins of creatures he had trapped which he exchanged for as much gin as he could carry. Judging by the state of him, he had been dead at least two weeks when he was found.

'By now my colleagues and I were seriously unnerved. No-one would trade with us after that, and our business ground quickly to a halt. The next victim was an old man who lived alone in a ramshackle hut near Port Mary. He was an outcast from the tribe, surviving on scraps and hand-outs. Postgate sometimes gave him liquor. On the night he died, there was no part of Port Mary where you did not hear his screams.'

Outside, the cold was beginning to press against the shuttered windows. Inside, in the warm half-light, Mrs Hudson paused in her polishing and placed a hand quietly on my shoulder, where it stayed when Mr Moran continued his tale.

'The final straw came one evening, just before sunset, when the high priest called a gathering of the elders to ratify the curse he had pronounced. They gathered in the small area of open ground in front of our offices. By now we were living as if besieged and my companions were nearing nervous collapse. I believe the situation could still have been saved by a show of courage and determination, but that night, in front of us all, illuminated by the blaze of the setting sun, the priest performed the calling down of the spirits' curse. It is a ceremony that the European might mock, but I was there, Mr Holmes, and as I listened to its low chant grow louder under our windows I could feel within it the gravity and weight of a death sentence. At its climax, a dagger is soaked in the blood of animals and the spirits are called down to inhabit that knife. The knife is then delivered to the person or persons accursed, and from that point forward the spirit *enoki* will not rest until he has claimed that man's soul as his own. That night, still reeking with warm blood, the knife was delivered to our door.'

Mr Holmes continued to stand rigid against the mantelpiece, his thin angular body catching shadows from the fire. Dr Watson fidgeted uncomfortably as if he, like me, had suddenly remembered the silver dagger of the previous evening, now glinting red in the firelight on a table next to his brandy glass. Mrs Hudson's hand on my shoulder gave an extra squeeze.

'It was too much for my companions,' Moran continued. 'The following morning they planned their departure. I tried desperately to change their minds. What remained of our investment would be irrevocably lost if we quit the island and I begged them not to invite ruin in this way. But their nerve had gone and their fear was too great. I confess we quarrelled, Mr Holmes. In fact my efforts to dissuade them took such a toll on my health that when the day set for our departure arrived I was too ill to travel, laid low by a crippling fever. Fearing for their own lives if they lingered, my companions left me in the hands of Penge, my loyal attendant, and set sail for London. So virulent was my fever, it seemed unlikely I would survive it, but survive I did, and as soon as I regained some semblance of consciousness, Penge made arrangements for me to be moved to a small sailing boat. Before I was properly aware of my surroundings we had been smuggled out of that fateful island and were bound for Singapore.

'As I recuperated, I realised that events in Sumatra had left me a ruined man. The small amount of stock the Company held outside the island was just sufficient to cover our debts, but none of our initial capital remained.

Relations with my father had been too deeply affected by my perceived defiance for me to hope for help from that quarter. I resolved to return to London where Neale and Carruthers, my erstwhile partners, had retreated to attempt the salvage of their fortunes. However, on the very eve of my departure, I was disturbed by a visit from a Chinaman newly arrived in Singapore. He was a so-called medicine man who travelled the islands gathering herbs to sell to his countrymen. He had been in Port Mary when I was there and knew of the shaman's curse. He informed me that we were not forgotten by the priest and his acolytes. Indeed, guessing our destination, a second dagger had been cursed and was to be put aboard the Matilda Briggs, the regular London packet ship that served the islands. An acolyte of the priest's was charged with delivering the dagger. And once delivered, nothing could stop the spirits achieving their purpose.'

The speaker's eyes sought out those of the great detective.

'Mr Holmes, when I wrote to you last night, I sent you a knife. Last Tuesday I passed the night in a boarding house on the docks. When I awoke the following morning, that same knife lay by my bedside. Two days earlier, five days after my own arrival, the Matilda Briggs had docked at Gravesend.'

There followed over the course of the evening a great number of questions from both Mr Holmes and Dr Watson. They rapidly established that the second dagger was, as far as Moran could say, identical to the first, that no-one in the boarding house, least of all Moran or the watchful Penge, had been able to account for its mysterious delivery. That very day Moran had consulted with his former partners and the three had resolved to seek the assistance of Sherlock Holmes. His companions, Carruthers and Neale, had taken the precaution of changing their lodgings but were both happy to wait on Mr Holmes at any time should he feel it necessary. Dr Watson took a note of their addresses.

To my great surprise, Mrs Hudson showed very little interest in any of these questions, choosing instead to return to the kitchen to prepare the breakfast things for the next day while sending me about my round of bedtime tasks. It was late in the evening when I heard Mr Holmes bring the interview to a close with a promise to make enquiries on Mr Moran's behalf.

'I need hardly say that the solution of a mystery with its roots so many miles away is not to be attempted with any guarantee of success. But what steps Dr Watson and I can take shall most certainly be taken.'

I heard Mr Moran reply that he would be collecting messages from the offices of the Rangoon & Occident Shipping Line should Mr Holmes wish to communicate with him, and then the bell was rung and I was summoned to show Mr Moran to the door. It was not until he had reached the street that something surprising occurred. Mrs Hudson, moving down the corridor with surprising alacrity, called Mr Moran back.

'Begging your pardon, sir, Mr Holmes has asked me to put to you a question he forgot to ask earlier. He wishes to know...' and here Mrs Hudson paused, apparently out of breath but just possibly so she could position herself better to see his face in the lamplight. 'He wishes to know if you shall continue to keep your rooms in New Buildings for many more days?'

The effect of the question on Mr Moran was extraordinary. He began to reply, hesitated, began once more and again came to a halt. Even in the pale light from the street I could see a flush rise to his cheeks. Finally he mastered himself.

'I can see Mr Holmes is an even more remarkable man than I had been led to believe. Yes, you may tell him that I shall remain in New Buildings until further notice if he should wish to contact me there. He is clearly already aware of the address.'

And with that he turned on his heel and made his way into the night, the ring of his boots on the cobbles marking his progress long after the night had enveloped him.

Mrs Hudson chuckled to herself.

'Come on, Flottie. It's bed for you and me.'

And I went quietly, deciding to keep my questions for another day. But my hearing is sharp and I could have sworn on the Bible that the bell had not been rung a second time; that Mrs Hudson had not been called to the study; that in following us to the door she had most certainly come directly from her own kitchen.

–

The rain that had set in during the night continued off and on for a further three days. Even the broadest streets turned slowly to mud and, by the Thursday, pedestrians, horses, carriages, even the pigeons, had begun to take on in their lower parts the same drab grey covering that is the true colour and texture of London. Or as Dr Watson put it, after three days of rain you might begin to believe that the mud and filth of every inhabited part of the Empire had emptied itself into our crowded streets.

The morning after Mr Moran's visit was another of great activity. Mr Holmes had been called to an incident in Paddington and Dr Watson accompanied him, so for a few hours at least the contemplation of Mr Moran's plight was laid aside. Mrs Hudson, however, was displaying the energy of a desert dervish, commissioning errands, summoning representatives of tradesmen from all over London, dispatching messages and turning the rooms in Baker Street into an oasis of warm welcome amid those splattered streets. At one point, returning from the post office where Mrs Hudson had sent me with a bag full of letters, I discovered her in the kitchen surrounded by a dozen scruffy boys between the ages of eight and fourteen among whom I instantly recognised Scraggs and seven or eight others who were regular suppliers of provisions to Mrs Hudson's previous establishment. One had just finished speaking and Mrs Hudson was nodding thoughtfully in his direction.

'Thank you, Mills. Remember, say nothing to Wiggins. He seems to be going to the bad.'

She looked up when she heard me at the door. 'Now here's Flottie,' she continued warmly, 'so you'd better all go about your business sharpish and not get under her feet. Some of you seem to imagine that the presence of a pretty girl is an excuse for malingering up here when there's work to be done.'

The boys filed out, nudging each other and grinning, while I looked as reproachfully at Mrs Hudson as I dared. She watched the last one depart with a look that was only superficially stern.

'They are good boys, each of them, Flottie, and it's a proper scandal that in this whole city of do-gooders there's nothing done to set them on their way to a decent calling that would get the best out of them. Still, they see and hear everything that goes on in this city, for there's no house however grand that doesn't open its doors to the butcher's boy and the grocer's lad and the young man from the chandler's. They're like a web of knowledge, they are. Keep in with them and you never need pay a penny more than you need for anything from lettuces to lamp oil. Now, Flottie, let's get to work and never mind my teasing.'

And with that the whirlwind of activity continued, keeping me far too busy to ask questions about the gathering I'd interrupted or about the series of messages delivered directly to Mrs Hudson in the course of the afternoon.

The evening post brought more letters, one for Mr Holmes and two for Mrs Hudson, and what with reading them, planning supper, folding the laundry and setting me on another round of dusting and polishing, there was no rest for her or for me until five o'clock, when we'd lighted the fires and closed out the blustering night. This was my favourite time of day and we pulled our chairs to the hearth with a rich sense of self-indulgence. As a reward for the work completed, which I honestly believe would have taken two days in another household, Mrs Hudson treated me to a piece of candied peel from a box sent by Mr Rumbelow with the previous day's sherry. Mrs Hudson was clearly in an excellent humour under her stern exterior and she held her glass up to the light with the air of a satisfied woman.

'Once the work's done we can move on to the important things, eh? Look at that, Flottie. This is one of the finest sherries. Not at the height of fashion just at the moment but magnificent nonetheless. Remember that light straw colour. One day, when you're mixing in far better company than mine, it will help to know these things.' And I nibbled my peel meekly and felt flushed at being included in such remote, adult knowledge.

After a short, contented silence, Mrs Hudson turned to the subject that had been on my mind all day, regardless of the tempest of activity that had engulfed me.

'So, Flottie, what's your feeling about Mr Moran's strange tale?'

'Ma'am, I don't know what to make of it. This morning, with rain dripping down my neck, it seemed hard to believe in men being tracked down in London by a strange foreign curse. But last night, when he was talking, I could almost feel that dagger was watching us all, waiting for its moment. Do you think it could be poisoned?'

'I have a feeling there was something dangerous present here last night, Flottie, but I don't think it was that knife. However, Dr Watson will be able to show you how to test for poison on something like that. You should learn from those two gentlemen, Flottie. If we're to stay in this house it's no good being scared of all those chemicals and equipment. Besides, the doctor needs an occupation. It's a year since he came back from Afghanistan and trotting around after Mr Holmes all day is no sort of a way for a man to pass his life.'

However, Mrs Hudson's schemes to further my education were of far less interest to me than the matter in hand.

'Wasn't it amazing how Mr Holmes was able to know so much about him from his letter, ma'am?'

'It is and it isn't, Flottie. It certainly seems as if Mr Holmes got a good deal right but somehow I just wonder...

For instance, Mr Moran went to a lot of trouble to show how afraid he was of this strange threat that hangs over him. Afraid for his life, he said. Both of our gentlemen agreed his note was dashed off hurriedly in a mixture of fear and fever. He was supposedly in too great a haste to write in a straight line across the page or find a decent pot of ink.'

'Yes, ma'am.' I could only concur with Mr Holmes and Dr Watson. Everything from his handwriting to his nervous manner seemed to suggest a fear approaching desperation on the part of Mr Moran.

'Let's have another look at that letter, Flottie. I took the liberty of tidying it away when it became clear Mr Holmes had no further use for it. You'll find it in the drawer in the dresser, next to the mousetraps.'

I scurried to retrieve it and Mrs Hudson spread it open under the lamp so it was visible to us both.

'Now is there anything on that page that you didn't notice before, perhaps because it was too dark to make out?'

I looked at the letter and its now familiar scarlet ink. It seemed exactly as I had remembered it.

'What about there at the bottom of the page, Flottie?'

Peering more closely I made out a small circular discolouration near the edge of the writing paper.

'It looks like a grease stain, ma'am.'

'Just what I thought, Flottie. But what kind of grease? There are thousands of possibilities and I'm sure Mr Holmes could list a host of ones I've never thought of. But you don't spend over 50 years working in kitchens without learning a thing or two about grease. Come, Flottie, let's try a little experiment. Fetch me one of those cheap tallow candles that we found under the stove, a drop of the frying oil and half a pound of best butter from the pantry.'

Despite her frown, there was a confidence in her manner that gave me a little thrill of anticipation and I hurried to fetch the objects she requested with a little hop of excitement. When they were assembled in front of her, Mrs Hudson leaned intently over the sheet of paper that lay like bright in the arc of lamplight. First of all she lit the candle, a very cheap yellow object made from a dubious combination of unattributable carcasses, all boiled down together. It's pungent smell made me wrinkle my nose as it infiltrated the shadows of the polished kitchen.

'Now look,' she whispered and tilted the candle gently until a small drop splashed on to the piece of paper an inch away from the original mark.

'Now while that dries in, let's try this,' and with a steady hand Mrs Hudson lowered the lip of the oil jug, allowing a second drop to fall onto the paper beneath.

'Now, Flottie, take a look at them and let's see what we've got.'

I lowered my head very close to the paper. The candle fat had left a dark mark of a yellow-grey colour. The oil had soaked in deeper, leaving a stain in a slightly darker shade of grey.

'I don't think it's either of those,' I said at last. 'The original mark is much lighter than these two, almost colourless really. These look a lot *dirtier*. I'm sure if the mark had been made by either of these we would have noticed it straight away, even by lamplight.'

'All right. Let's try one more then.' And Mrs Hudson, still frowning slightly, took a sliver of butter on the end of a knife and held it over the candle flame. When the edges of the butter began to liquefy she moved the knife to the notepaper and tilted it until a small drip of butter had landed next to the other three stains.

I waited till it had dried into the paper before I spoke, but when I did there was already awe in my voice.

'It's the same! See how it's left the same mark! They're both slightly darker at the centre and almost invisible at the edge. It was a butter stain on Mr Moran's note!'

I paused for a moment, then continued, my voice suddenly less excited.

'But what does that tell us?'

'Look at the two butter stains again, Flottie. There is a slight difference, isn't there?'

It was true. I had been concentrating only on the colour of the original stain so I had noticed without comment the small brown mark left at its centre. Now I studied that mark even more closely until Mrs Hudson, to my enormous surprise, produced a magnifying glass from the front of her apron.

'Well, Mr Holmes leaves them all over the place, child. I'm sure he won't begrudge us the use of one for a few hours. Now use this to look and tell me what you think.'

Now my view was transformed and I could see the brown spot I had been peering at was not a stain but a tiny rough-edged object pressed into the paper's surface. It looked very familiar.

'It's a crumb,' I ventured, slightly disappointed that my first attempt at scientific observation had ended on such an unremarkable note.

'A very small toast crumb was what I thought,' confirmed Mrs Hudson, nodding approvingly. 'Now, Flottie, how could such a stain have come there?'

'I suppose it just dropped on, ma'am. If a small piece of toast fell onto the paper and was shaken off very quickly it may have left just such a trace behind. If the writer was working by lamplight or candlelight he wouldn't particularly notice it. And if a crumb stuck to the grease, it was probably pressed down into the paper when he folded the sheet and sealed it.'

'Flottie, you will go every bit as far as I ever imagined.' Mrs Hudson put her arm around my shoulders and rewarded me with a squeeze of approval. 'Now let us imagine the scene as conjured up by Mr Holmes, the scene Mr Moran would have us see.

'It's night. Mr Moran has returned to his humble lodging. He's out of breath because he has gone through the streets quickly, afraid of what he'll find there. The dagger is burning a hole in the coat pocket where he thrust it after showing it to his friends, two gentlemen so perturbed by what he tells them that they leave their dwellings that very night and go into hiding with what belongings they can carry. Moran has been tasked with finding help and on his return he grabs a sheet of cheap note paper and the first pot of ink he can find. He scribbles a rough note, running sentences together in his fear and haste, oblivious of his sprawling hand. The note is dispatched that very moment in the hands of his faithful servant, who is ordered not to rest until he has tracked down the famous Sherlock Holmes…

'Well, Flottie, how does that look to us now? Can we imagine the panic-stricken Mr Moran scribbling feverishly at his desk with one hand while with the other he helps himself to a cheerful afternoon tea? Flottie, *does a man fearing for his life eat generously-buttered toast?* I have to say I find the idea highly unlikely.'

I stared at her with my mouth rudely open, for every word she said seemed to resound with good sense. I had so believed in the desperation that lay behind Mr Moran's note that it was impossible to reconcile the image I had formed in my mind – an image that Mrs Hudson had described in uncanny detail – with the image of Moran settled comfortably in a leather chair, feeding himself toast as he penned his letter.

'But, Mrs Hudson, if Mr Moran was only pretending to be afraid when he wrote his note…'

'Exactly, child. We will do well to treat everything he tells us with a large pinch of Cheshire salt.'

And with half a wink and a joyous nudge from the point of her elbow she ambled back to the pantry for another glass of sherry.

–

However, if Mrs Hudson's revelations had convinced me that Moran's tale was not entirely to be trusted, events the following morning left me floundering in renewed uncertainty. Shortly after breakfast the bell rang and both Mrs Hudson and I were called to the study where we found Mr Holmes and Dr Watson examining an item that had arrived in that morning's post.

'Ah, Mrs Hudson!' exclaimed Mr Holmes in great good humour. 'We have received a communication that has some relevance to events here the other night. Since you and young Flottie were both involved from the outset, I thought you may be interested in seeing how the case develops. The workings of great minds will always inspire, even if they cannot always be understood – a piece of wisdom that I'm sure Dr Watson will readily endorse. Eh, Watson?'

'What was that, Holmes?' asked Watson, peering up from the letter he had been examining with the most desperate determination.

'Nothing at all, dear fellow,' said Holmes, smiling affectionately before turning again to Mrs Hudson and me.

'Watson tells me that you are already aware of the salient points of Moran's tale and you will not be surprised to learn that my task for today is to verify as many details as possible of that queer narrative. Mrs Hudson, as a woman of excellent good sense you will understand that I can have no truck with the suggestion that these individuals met their deaths by supernatural means. A perfectly natural explanation will exist, and when we have discovered it we will be in a far better position to take measures guaranteeing the safety of Moran and his associates. I do not doubt that great villainy is at work here, but villainy in a human form, perpetrated by someone who will prove as eager to avoid contact with Dr Watson's heavy stick as any other villain.

'The task of interviewing Neale and Carruthers I have assigned to Dr Watson here, while I myself shall concentrate on some of the other details in Moran's account. But before we set out, let us share with you another development,' and at that Mr Holmes took the new letter from Watson's grasp and offered it to Mrs Hudson with a flourish.

It was short and succinct.

46 Old Jewry
Nov 19th
Re: Evil Spirits

Sir,

Our client Mr James Winterton of Winterton Shipping, London, owner of the Matilda Briggs and other vessels, has made some inquiry from us concerning evil spirits. The aforementioned vessel being recently returned from Borneo and Sumatra, Mr Winterton has received a visit from one Mr Norman, passenger on said vessel's latest voyage. Mr Norman has alleged said vessel is possessed with an unnatural presence that, he claims, repeatedly harassed him, on one occasion pitching a small leather Bible into the sea. He exhorted our client to take measures before the vessel makes its next voyage. Mr Winterton, having interviewed the captain, a Spaniard, and the crew, mainly Lascars, has discovered that they support this tale. As our firm specialises almost entirely upon the assessment of nautical equipment the matter hardly comes within our purview, and we have therefore decided to enquire of you if there is any specialist in this field that might be recommended to our client.

We are, Sir, Faithfully yours,
LAUNCESTON, PHELPS AND FINCH

When she had finished reading, Mrs Hudson looked up thoughtfully.

'I should say, sir, that this is an extremely interesting document.'

'And so Dr Watson found it too, Mrs H. I admit it has a certain sensational interest, though I personally do not place a great deal of store by it. I'm sure we shall find that this is the result of suggestible individuals and a superstitious crew, made aware before their departure of fanciful rumours circulating about their cargo, then cooped together for long periods at sea. It is, I feel, of more interest to the psychologist than the criminologist. We can dismiss it as no more than an intriguing diversion from our primary business.'

If I had expected Mrs Hudson to bridle against such casual dismissal of her opinion, I had again miscalculated. When on the gentlemen's departure we returned to the kitchen her expression was almost jocular as she began to change into her outdoor clothes.

'Bless us, that Mr Holmes is quite a one. How he got this far without us, Flottie, is something I'll never know.'

'But, Mrs Hudson, ma'am, doesn't that letter suggest that there is something in Mr Moran's tale after all?'

'Of course, Flottie. I'm convinced there *is* something in his tale. Our investigations last night were decidedly useful but we mustn't confuse ourselves. If you feel you're losing touch with what's what, there's another telegram you'd better have a look at. It's in the dresser drawer, at the back, under the tongue-press.'

By now Mrs Hudson was ready to go out but she waited until I had found the telegram.

'It's from Lord Ponsonby at the Colonial Office. I was once able to help his lordship solve a little problem concerning his daughter's second coachman. I sent him a note yesterday morning and he was good enough to investigate and reply the same afternoon.'

The telegram seemed to leave no room for doubt.

CAN CONFIRM TWENTY THREE
UNEXPLAINED DEATHS PORT MARY OFF
SUMATRA MARCH APRIL STOP TWO

EUROPEAN ONE CHINESE OTHERS
NATIVE STOP ALL MALE STOP
INVESTIGATION BY DUTCH AGENT JUNE
STOP DEATHS MOST HORRIBLE STOP
CAUSE UNKNOWN STOP AGENT BAFFLED
STOP COMPLETE MYSTERY STOP FOND
REGARDS
PONSONBY

'You see, Flottie, we do have a mystery on our hands after all,' commented Mrs Hudson, raising an eyebrow in a parting wave before slipping out for her afternoon off.

It was later that afternoon that I discovered the problem posed by Mr Moran was not the only one for me to consider. I passed the afternoon working on the gentlemen's rooms, reflecting happily that in doing so I was in a small way assisting one of the eminent men of our times. Time passed quickly and though it was no later than four o'clock it was already growing dark when I made my way back to the kitchen. As soon as I entered I knew there was something wrong. There was something foreign there, something chill that did not belong. The lamp had not been lit and there was a presence in the air that made my whole being cold.

'Who's there?' My voice trembled.

'Hello, Flotsam,' came a voice I remembered from the days I was trying to forget. 'I was passing so I thought I should drop in.'

'Mr Fogarty,' I whispered, almost to myself.

'Indeed,' he replied, moving out of the shadows so I could see his face and its fixed, mocking smile. 'I can't stay,

Flotsam, but I'd like to ask you to come round and visit me soon. You see,' and he passed the tip of his finger very slowly down the line of his jaw, 'I believe I have found your brother.'

The Lost Child

✝

Although at that time I had neither a name nor a family to call my own, I knew it had not always been so. I have a memory, misty like the moon through fog, of a time before the orphanage. I remember a woman holding me close to her, so tight that at night I can still dream of that tightness. There was warmth and softness and my nose pressed into sweet-smelling hair. And a memory of a different woman, faceless and formless like a figure in a dream, who lowered her forgotten face close to mine and whispered 'take care of your brother.' And my third memory, much sharper in focus, like a dream interrupted by waking, of the doors of the orphanage closing behind me and a tiny parcel of white blankets being forced out of my arms, and corridors ringing with loud, loud sobs that were my own.

I lost my brother when I was too young to remember him. All I recall is an arrangement of blankets and, as he left my arms, a desolation inside me so cold that I thought it would never melt. To survive, I learned to keep the secret of his existence safely inside me. It could not be mentioned at the orphanage. To do so was willfulness and ingratitude. It could not be mentioned when I was sent to work in the kitchens of the hospital where to speak at all was expressly forbidden. It was not to be told to the series of brief, disapproving employers who found temporary use for the labour of a girl too small to reach the bolts to run away. The first person I told was the first to ask, the butler who ruled the big house where I had hoped for salvation and found only bondage worse than any that had gone before.

Mr Fogarty was a butler in name but he ruled that house with a grip colder than iron. I had never met anyone whose power seemed less questioned or more absolute. His empire was founded on fear yet he was able to win a small girl's trust with the same casual carelessness he used to light an Egyptian cigarette. He had first seen me scrubbing doorsteps, and at once recognised an easy prey. Softly he drew from me my fears and hopes and discovered in my tears the story of my lost brother. He made me understand with reassuring half-sentences that he would make enquiries on my behalf if I proved to be a good girl; that, if I deserved it, it should be possible for a man such as himself to identify my brother's whereabouts.

'They said he was dead, sir,' I told him.

'They say that to keep you quiet, Flotsam. I have no doubt I can find him.'

There were many cruelties inflicted upon me in that house but there was none to rival that.

The months I stayed there seemed to last as long as the rest of my life in total. I found myself at the very bottom of a hierarchy based on misery. From the carefully planned punishments of Mrs Flegg the cook to the gloating pain inflicted by Smale the boot boy, it seemed there was nothing that could not validly be inflicted upon me. I was only sustained by the thought that when Mr Fogarty heard of the cruelty I should be spared. But when Mr Fogarty called me to him again, the escape he offered was not the one of which I'd dreamed. The proposal he put to me was starkly clear even to my innocent understanding, and it seemed as though the harshness towards me from every quarter intensified in the days leading up to it, until the present seemed every bit as wretched and degrading as the future he proposed. And above it all, impossible for me to ignore, was the thought that by working for Mr Fogarty as he suggested I could earn a way back to the brother I had given away.

In the end it was the cook who saved me, the individual in the house who had perhaps done most to make my life unbearable. By then I was being kept by Fogarty in a cellar room and it was there, when Mrs Flegg brought me a bowl of her thinnest gruel, that her drunken spite blew away all my clouds of indecision.

'Eat this,' she screeched, twisting my ear until my head was forced to the ground next to the bowl she had brought me. 'Eat this and be grateful for it. And don't give me any of your meek manners and proper ways, young lady! *They* won't last long with what Fogarty has in store for you. He'll throw you to his wolves an' no mistake. And all for a brat that died in the gutter long ago! You think he's alive? Ha! You think Fogarty would do that for you? You think he has helped any of us? Look around at what's he's done for us – and then think how much worse it's going to be for you!'

That night, thanks to my sharp knee and to a strength of spirit I scarcely knew I possessed, I made my escape. The few objects I called possessions were left behind. I had no coat and no proper clothes but none of that mattered. My brother was dead.

Yet that was not the end of everything after all. I was saved by my pursuit of a rotten cabbage and, in the two years that followed, Mrs Hudson and Scraggs and Swordsmith and even Mrs Siskin the Methodist had managed between them to warm the parts of me that seemed to have frozen in the chill of Fogarty's cellars. Suddenly among friends, even the pain of that missing white bundle lost its pre-eminence in my thoughts. So many children died, it seemed, that surely the cook had spoken the truth. In my own way I mourned him and tried to pass on. But now Fogarty's words, in a kitchen rendered suddenly grey and lifeless, touched me in places I thought had ceased to feel. Could it be true? Even while fear and disgust flooded my thoughts, a small candle of hope was lighting up lost corners within me.

'Of course, you would visit as a respected guest, Flotsam. I can see that you have come a long way since we last met and I must apologise that I so greatly under-estimated your potential. But it would be wise of you to call. I came upon your brother quite by accident but he is in a poor state and needs someone to help him.'

Fogarty smiled in the grey, grainy light.

'Don't think I haven't made quite sure. His path from the orphanage was a straightforward one and easy to verify. You will be quite safe, and one day you may thank me. Tonight, Flotsam. Later will be too late. I shall be waiting for you.'

And then he was gone. I watched him ascend the area steps then stride boldly into the swirling dusk. A passer-by might have taken him for a superior servant, but his bearing was of someone accustomed to command. And among those he was accustomed to commanding was me.

I was quiet when Mrs Hudson returned and she busied herself about me in the most heartening possible way.

'Flottie, I have had an excellent day, and have taken a most rewarding walk along Oxford Street with a gentleman who owns ships. His observations have been most enlightening in every respect. What do you say to that, eh?'

For once, however, my mind was not on her words. I had decided. If I was to evict the shadow of Fogarty's presence from this place he had invaded, I had no choice. I must visit him as he ordered and find out where the truth lay.

My decision made, I could not settle. I passed a listless evening unable to concentrate on any of the books Mrs Hudson had brought me. Since our arrival in Baker Street she had decided that I was ready to move my education in the direction of the physical sciences, having already mastered reading, writing, arithmetic and baking, and having achieved some knowledge of Latin from the Irish knife-grinder who Mrs Hudson paid in pastries while he sat and talked of Ovid in a soft Cork burr. Much to my surprise, I found the sciences interested me greatly. The gentlemen's microscopes and their rows of slides had filled me with an itching curiosity. It seemed to me that Mr Moran's butter stain was only one of the things out there to be seen more clearly if you looked closely enough. The racks of test-tubes and the neatly labelled bottles of chemicals appealed to my sense of order, too. It felt as though there was another alphabet out there that I had yet to learn, one which could prove the key to a whole new world of understanding.

But on this occasion my wandering attention would not be reined in by the written page. My eyes stole to the movement of the fire and my thoughts strayed across a perilous landscape. Tonight, he had said. It must be tonight. I would be able to slip out when Mrs Hudson slept. The front door would have to be left unbolted behind me. And out there beyond the door lay Fogarty and the night. My eyes flicked to Mrs Hudson's comforting form but it seemed my restlessness had communicated itself to her, for tonight there was no port by the fire, no open book. She stood at the table behind me, folding sheets with military precision, a deep furrow on her brow and the line of her eyebrows thin. I longed to confide in her then, longed for her to place an arm around me and tell me what to do. But I knew her opinion of Fogarty and knew what her advice would be and dared not ask. Instead I sat in silence and tried not to think at all.

My bedroom was a box bed adjoining the kitchen, so close to where Mrs Hudson slept that sometimes when I woke at night I could hear her breathing. Sleeping was rarely a problem for me in those days but that night it was easy to stay awake. I listened for the chimes of the clock on Chiltern Street until I counted the midnight and then slid quietly from under my covers. In those days I could move so lightly I barely touched the ground and it was a simple thing to gain the kitchen without disturbing the steady rhythm of Mrs Hudson's breathing. From there I moved quickly, pulling on clothes and my heavy coat, making no sound until the door had closed behind me and I was free to slip away from the only home I had, out into the anonymous dark.

The rain had left the streets treacherous and the fog was thicker than ever. Light from the gas lamps gathered the fog into yellow circles, leaving the roads below in darkness. The streets were not yet completely deserted but the remaining hansoms seemed dark and hunched, and looming pedestrians were more sinister for being alone. For a moment I wavered, but if I went back Fogarty would be with me there forever, hovering on the edge of every evening. If I went on, I could meet him and know the truth, even if his truth was simply a further web of lies.

By night the streets took on the menace of a veiled threat. Unseen creatures scuttled down alleyways, feeding on rubbish and fattening in the fertile shadows of my imagination. And there was no warm fire waiting at the end of this journey, only the great, blank-faced house where Fogarty was employed. It's front door opened onto the grandest of squares; the back entrance was hidden in a brick-black alley littered with rubbish and unlit but for a blue lantern suspended above the steps. The fog in the alley was full of silence.

I pulled my coat tightly around me and stepped towards the blue light.

The arm that seized me roughly out of the darkness was so swift there was no time to scream. A strong hand was over my face in a moment and another round my waist, pinning my arms to my sides. I was wrenched backwards, dragged into shadow, then pulled tight against a man's body, my spine rasped by the buckle of his belt. The hand in my face pressed my head back with a jolt, the pain turning my mind white with panic until a man's voice spat my own name in my ear with hissing contempt.

'Flotsam! You came back to us, did yer? Knows where yer future lies after all, do yer?'

It was Smale. I knew him by the poison in his voice and the smell of his breath on my face. Smale the boot boy, my torturer-in-chief at Fogarty's; a Smale grown in size and strength and capacity to damage.

'You made a mistake walking this street.' He gave my head another jolt backwards and sneered at my gasp of pain. 'We've got no mercy on runaway whores round here. You see, I'm not the boot boy anymore. Now Mr Fogarty pays me to keep his girls in order. So that's what I do. Keep 'em in order.'

And with a derisive snort he pressed me suddenly even closer, the arm around my waist lifting me against him, the other abruptly leaving my face and reaching into my coat for the front of my dress. I gave a sharp exclamation, then kicked backwards as hard as I could with my heel. At the same moment there was a movement in the darkness and a loud crack by my ear and Smale went limp. His weight dragging me sideways into the gutter as he crumpled. A dark figure in silhouette stood over us, gently massaging his knuckles.

'Flotsam is my guest, Smale. She is here tonight at my invitation. If you had paused long enough in the pursuit of your grimy and tiresome lust you would have noticed that Flotsam has risen quite beyond any circle you are ever likely to inhabit. You will confine your animal desires to the sort of women I allow you. If you were slightly less unclean I would require you to assist Flotsam to her feet, but I fear that would only expose her further to the contamination of your touch. Allow me...'

Fogarty raised me to my feet with immaculate apologies and escorted me to the narrow steps that led to the house. There I paused and looked back to where Smale lay. The darkness hid him completely but I could feel his eyes like prickly heat on my skin. Then Fogarty's hand touched the small of my back to guide me down the stairs and I remembered that danger comes in more forms than one.

But it seemed that for a moment Fogarty's claws were sheathed. He showed me into a room furnished like a small study. A solitary light burned on a writing desk, which lay open revealing papers piled in disorderly heaps. Fogarty moved the chair that stood before it to the edge of the light and seated himself. I remained standing before him as I always had.

'It was put in my power recently to do you a good turn, Flotsam. A man who owed me money happened to mention something that reminded me of the sorry tale you once told me. I promised to help you then but in this world promises don't come for free. I felt it only fair to look out some means by which you could repay my services. But to my surprise and disappointment you chose to decline my offer. You have clearly done well as a result of that decision. I'm afraid the same cannot be said of your brother.'

I stood in front of him cold and bruised, but not defeated. I had prepared myself for this.

'The man who owed me money gave me the name of another man, a man who had once worked at your orphanage. His job was to provide newly-born infants to families that would pay for them. He assured me that each transaction was carefully recorded. I investigated and found this to be true. The full documentation is there on the desk for you to examine should you wish to. Finding your brother was easy with that. Saving him will prove more difficult.'

'Saving him?'

'Your brother did not fare well with his new family. He was supplanted by first one and then two natural children.

His temporary parents turned him onto the streets where, after some misadventures, he has developed habits that are likely to destroy him. Follow me.'

He led me along a corridor and down steps to a dank cellar room. I could see by the sickly yellow candlelight that the room contained only a bed where a small fragile boy of nine or ten was being tended by a cold-faced woman. I had never witnessed such pain. He was barely conscious and his writhing seemed driven by an inner agony of unimaginable dimensions. He seemed unaware of anything except the pain within. And every movement he made as he struggled etched itself into my soul.

'Now watch,' whispered Fogarty, nodding to the woman. From somewhere out of sight she produced a bottle of laudanum and poured a small draught. Then she raised the boy's head and brought the liquid to his lips. The effect was immediate and a look of blissful release transformed his face in the way I've seen dawn change the Thames – fleetingly lighting its corrupt surface with an impossible beauty.

Fogarty was watching me as I watched.

'Like magic, Flotsam. But magic doesn't come cheap. While I pay for his addiction he will probably survive for a while. A good doctor might yet save him. But if I were to stop paying, were I to take away the laudanum and leave him locked in here, unattended, for nature to take its course…' His eyes waited for me to look at him. 'Well, it would be a pitiful, painful death, Flotsam. Thankfully he would never know that it was a fate his sister had chosen for him.'

I looked at the small broken figure who had now subsided into sleep. My brain was racing to keep up with Fogarty's intentions.

'What do you want from me?'

'Oh, I can assure you that the method of repayment is infinitely less demanding than before. It would give me no pleasure at all to see someone of your refinement in the hands of a disgusting creature like Smale. No, Flotsam, I recognise that you have moved on. In fact I would be tempted to make a present to you of the pathetic creature over there if it were not for the fact that you are in a position to do me a simple favour.'

Shivering slightly in the dim candlelight, I still could not see where we were heading. And now, more than anything, that was what I wanted to know.

'A favour, sir?'

'You work in the household of Mr Sherlock Holmes. Two nights ago he was visited by a gentleman recently returned from the East. I'm very interested in that visit, Flotsam. Very interested. And very interested in what Mr Holmes makes of his case. You might well find a way to overhear what goes on. If so, there is a doctor in Shadwell who for five pounds would undertake to free your brother of his unfortunate addiction. When I am aware of Mr Holmes's conclusions, your brother will be delivered to that doctor with just that sum in his pocket.'

For a moment surprise at his request threatened my composure. I grasped at the first words that offered themselves.

'How do I know you'll…?'

'Oh, quite. You may well feel I'm not to be trusted. But think of it from my point of view. Five pounds is nothing to me. It isn't much to pay to avoid the inconvenience of a messy death on the premises. And what do I gain from cheating you? Very little. Who knows, when you are happily reunited with a recovering sibling we may be able to do business again at some point in the future. Goodwill always has a value, Flotsam.'

There didn't seem much to say. For a fearful moment I thought he would offer me a hand which I knew I couldn't bring myself to take, not for all his deadly reasonableness. But the moment passed with a dismissive nod before he ushered me to the door. For now our business was complete.

Outside, the fog seemed to hang undisturbed. I heard the bolts slide across the door behind me and shivered as I turned to face the cold. I was thinking hard as I climbed the steps to street level and it was not until I reached the top that I realised something which made my footsteps freeze. *Someone had extinguished the lantern.*

I knew from my own time in the household that a blue lantern was set outside to burn all night. Without it, complete darkness filled the narrow alleyway. I stood very still and listened. A horse's hooves, smothered by the fog, could have been two streets or twenty yards away. Much nearer, a gutter dripped hesitantly on to the cobbles. My eyes searched for anything to give shape to the fog-filled darkness. A very faint smudge of light to my right came from the gas-lit street where my path lay. From there, a right turn and thirty hurried paces would take me to wider streets where ambush was less likely. To turn away from the light, up the narrowing alley, would plunge me into a bewilderment of unnamed passageways.

I took a tentative step towards the light and paused. The dripping gutter paused too, waited a moment, then dripped again, softly, like a final heartbeat. I took a second step. Nothing. Then a third – and in a blur of sound and shapes three things happened at once. A clear, decisive footfall rang out at one end of the alley, near the light; a sudden movement in the corner of my eye sent me ducking to the cobbles; and somewhere above my head I heard Smale's curse as he tripped over me in the dark and the fog, knocking us both to the cobbles.

He fell harder than I and in a moment I was gone, quickly to my feet and flying in the other direction, away from the light, up the alley, into the blackness. 'Two of them,' my brain registered briefly just before my knuckles banged the brickwork of an unseen wall. Using it as my guide, I pushed on into the gloom, stumbling over invisible obstacles but not slowing down. Behind me I was dimly aware of another crash like someone hitting the cobbles hard and headlong and from then there was only one set of footsteps on my trail.

I was moving faster than the fog allowed. I could see almost nothing and I stumbled more than I ran. I kept my right hand to the wall, turning into every unseen alley revealed by my fingertips, once splashing through water up to my hips and scrambling out up a bank of mud and slime. The footsteps behind me seemed relentless, unerringly choosing the path I had taken. Sometimes I heard a voice, muffled by the fog, calling my name, and I thought of Smale's hand over my face, the dreadful helplessness as he forced his body against mine. He would be ruthless this time. I knew what had driven him to wait for me in the fog. There was no Fogarty to rescue me this time and Smale had never been slow to settle his scores. So I struggled on, hoping to gain enough distance to find myself somewhere to hide. Then, turning a corner, I slammed into a post that sent me crashing to the ground, one knee numb and the other bleeding. My eyes blurred with tears as I stumbled forward again. Desperation was beginning to weaken me. A stitch seemed to be burning my side. The footsteps behind were regular and less panicked than my own. They were closing now, slowly hunting me down.

I turned another corner and ran into a dead end. A thin light from a solitary warehouse showed me walls on three sides, their tops lost in the fog. I tried to double back, but I could hear the footsteps approaching, and again that voice, barely audible over my panting breath and beating heart, still calling my name. Gasping now, I ran to the darkest corner and sank to the ground, groping frantically for something to hide me. My fingers closed on a piece of sacking, no longer a sack, its contents once something thick and foul, now rotting. Without hesitation I pulled it tightly over me.

My gasping breath wasn't enough to stop me hearing the footsteps of my pursuer at the entrance of the alleyway. They paused there, perhaps puzzled at their quarry's sudden silence. Then they began to inch up the alley, stepping carefully, risking no mistakes. I could hear breathing as heavy as my own and then three final steps that ended right beside me. Even under the sacking, I could sense the height of the figure looking down on me. Suddenly calm, I realised my eyes were full of silent tears. Somewhere in the darkness a small boy was sleeping. A tiny figure in a blanket had been taken away from me, letting in the cold. It was cold now, very cold.

The unseen figure above me took a deep breath and a voice filled the darkness.

'Flotsam, my girl,' it pronounced grimly, 'if you are not back in your bed in twenty minutes I shall ask Dr Watson to give you a taste of his heavy stick. Not,' the voice continued grumpily, 'that I can imagine that particular threat striking much fear into anyone.'

The warmth seemed to flood through me and well out in fresh tears.

'Oh, Mrs Hudson!' I cried, throwing aside the sacking and leaping upwards with my arms open. 'Mrs Hudson, *it wasn't my brother!*'

The Sailor's Widow

✝

The fire was burning brightly in the kitchen range and, for all Mrs Hudson's threats, the distant church clock had struck four before I was back in my cupboard bed. Before that, as we picked our way homewards, I had been subjected to a scolding that can rarely have been surpassed for eloquence. Clutching Mrs Hudson's hand as the streets became familiar again, I was far too happy to do anything but hang on tight and take comfort from her masterful invective and the unthinking certainty with which she navigated the fog-filled yards. To my astonishment, only a few minutes walk saw us turning back into Baker Street.

'It's not so difficult,' she growled, seeing my surprise. 'When I was a girl I knew all these streets better than you know your way to the biscuit jar. That's why it wasn't so hard to keep up while you ran around in circles like a pony at the circus. If I thought I was losing you, you did an excellent job at running straight back to me.'

'But how...?'

'How did I come to be there? Well, lucky for you I was, my girl. You had trouble written all over your face this evening, Flottie, and you could have woken Nelson on his column with your clumping around when you tried to sneak out. And since you weren't going to tell me what had happened to you this afternoon, I thought I might find out for myself by giving you a bit of company.'

She broke off with a low chuckle.

'Mind you, there's some of the company you were keeping will wake up tomorrow with a headache as ugly as his face. Chasing girls in the fog is a dangerous business. He should have been more careful,' she concluded, rubbing her elbow with some enthusiasm.

Only when the fire was lit and I had been wrapped in warm blankets, with an unheard of hot brandy in my hands, did I have to account for my desperate escapade. To my surprise, Mrs Hudson took my account of Fogarty's approach with grim-faced calm and even my first encounter with Smale elicited no more than a raised eyebrow and a slight tightening of her knuckles. However I could see curiosity in her frown when I recounted my visit to the sick boy's bedside. As I talked, she began to move around the kitchen, rearranging objects with a fixed concentration.

'He was in pain, ma'am,' I told her. 'And because of what Mr Fogarty had said about him, I felt it so hard, every bit of it. I almost cried with relief when they gave him that draught.'

'But Flottie, child, could he not perhaps be your brother? How can you be so sure he is not what Fogarty claims?'

'If he's alive, ma'am, I'll know him when I see him. I know I will. I remember the feeling when they took him away. I still remember it now, ma'am, just as it was then. If something went that deep, I must feel something when I meet him. I just must.'

Mrs Hudson stopped moving things and looked at me carefully.

'When I knew it wasn't him, I was afraid I wouldn't feel anything at all. But I did. I felt this terrible pain for him because he could have been my brother but wasn't.'

'I don't like leaving him in that house, Flottie, whoever he is. Especially if Fogarty thinks his bait has failed.'

'Oh no, ma'am. I knew I mustn't let him think that. And I wanted to find out what he wanted from me.'

'And what was that?' she enquired cautiously.

I watched her widening surprise as I told her about Fogarty's interest in Mr Moran and his tale. Her eyebrows raised in the middle and she got up and began to tidy again.

'Mr Moran, eh? Well, well. More and more mysterious. I wonder what concern it is of Fogarty's? I know there is nothing criminal in which Fogarty doesn't take an interest but I hardly imagined he would concern himself with this little matter of ours.'

'Mrs Hudson, ma'am, could you tell me about Mr Fogarty? You seem to know so much more about him than I do.'

The housekeeper came forward and knelt next to me by the fireplace. She had arranged a pile of blankets near the hearth and now she wrapped one round each of us so that the wool rubbed my chin.

'Maurice Orlando Fogarty is the Machiavelli of crime. His pleasure is more in the plotting, in the successful deceit, than in the profit itself. His ingenuity and his unscrupulousness have made him rich but his real reward comes from the sense of power he feels over others, knowing he can manipulate them, deceive them, bend them to his will. He seems to derive the same thrill of power whether it's a peer of the realm or one of those poor girls he puts on the streets. His father was Irish, his mother Italian, but it would be hard to say that Fogarty has any nationality at all. He can pass as a gentleman in a dozen different countries.'

'But if he's a butler, ma'am…'

'Oh, don't be fooled by that. Fogarty has chosen to be many things. But he was born into service and sometimes chooses to hide himself below stairs in great houses where society won't notice him.'

Mrs Hudson took the brandy from my hands, fortified herself with a sip and continued.

'When I first heard of him he was a young man making a name for himself in the kitchens of London. I don't know where he learned to cook but he was a genius with food. Soon his name was everywhere, though of course he took good care to make sure the name that went everywhere was not his own. Back then he went under the name of Maturin, and it was a banquet he cooked up for the Marquis of Bute that sealed his reputation. After that he could go anywhere. At the house of Monsieur Bertillon in Paris he presented a series of triumphant dinners to the cream of French society. Monsieur Bertillon had them all there – royalty, generals, ambassadors, statesmen. And every one of them ate bucket-loads of the best food they'd ever tasted. It was three months before the scandal broke. It came out that Monsieur Maturin had been cheating with his ingredients. The more successful he became, the more irresistible he found the temptation of making fools of them all. While Monsieur Bertillon was paying for the best, Fogarty was buying meat from the dirtiest butchers in France. Horse meat, condemned meat, it didn't matter what sort. Such was the man's genius he could make it taste like anything.

And for three months he got away with it, channelling hundreds of thousands of francs into his own pockets.'

I tried to reconcile this image of Fogarty, a humble domestic making a fool out of his employers, with the cold dangerous man I knew. Yes, I could see him relishing the trick, but not with amusement, just with sneering contempt for those he tricked.

'By the time the news was out, Fogarty was gone. Old Monsieur Bertillon shot himself in the Bois de Boulogne and the talented Monsieur Maturin disappeared forever. None of this was any concern of mine of course, but the next time Mr Fogarty surfaced it most definitely was. You have heard of the Plinlimmon diamond affair? At the time there was a great deal of suspicion attached to Lord Plinlimmon's domestic staff and only a handful of them could prove their innocence. I was still a junior housekeeper then and I was one whose whereabouts were vouched for. His lordship's valet was another. Long before I connected this valet with the missing French chef, I had become certain deep inside me that he was the person responsible for the crime. Of course, events proved me right, but not before both diamond and valet had disappeared without trace.

'From that point on, I've made it my business to keep an eye on Fogarty's career. Whenever the newspapers report a family ruined or a gentleman disgraced, I look to see if perhaps a figure resembling Fogarty was instrumental in their downfall. Whenever I read of a famous theft, I look to find the quiet valet at the gentleman's shoulder or the innocent butler who has disappeared.'

'And now he's here, ma'am?'

'For the last five years he has been lying low in London. And in keeping a low profile, he has immersed himself in low crime of the sort that your friend Smale might under-stand. The Fotheringays are so often abroad their butler has few duties and ample opportunities to dirty his hands in London's uniquely sordid underworld of crime. It is as if he wishes to disappear from the larger stage completely.'

'And does he know you?'

'Our paths have crossed more than once. I know he blames me for preventing the suicide of the Lawrence heir, an event that would have earned him 30,000 guineas. And as I always used to say to Hudson...'

But at that moment the clock struck the hour, Mrs Hudson sensed my smothered yawn and I was bustled to bed. In the dark, the night smoothed round me by Mrs Hudson's sleeping breath, I thought of the boy who was not my brother and of how differently we lived. Then the darkness blurred gently and I slept.

–

The following morning, just before the breakfast hour, Sherlock Holmes surprised us in our kitchen. Resplendent in a crimson silk dressing gown, he had a twinkle in his eye and a newly-delivered letter in his hand.

'Ah, Mrs Hudson!' he declared warmly. 'I was about to enquire if you slept well, but that is so clearly the case that the question is unnecessary.'

'And how is that, sir?' replied Mrs Hudson placidly, continuing to arrange crockery on the dresser without turning around.

'It is not a difficult piece of reasoning. I can see from the state of the flame in the stove that it is newly lit, which suggests a later start than is your custom. At this hour it is usually ablaze. Flottie's colossal yawns convey the impression of a young girl recently arisen. In addition, I am aware that Watson was in here very early, foraging for breakfast. Now Watson is not a quiet man, nor a man at ease in a kitchen. If his clattering did not wake you, and he assures me it did not, I feel it is reasonable to conclude that both you and Flottie were enjoying an unusually full night's rest.'

He waggled the letter under his chin with a pleased smile. Mrs Hudson finished with the crockery and pulled out a chair for him with a friendly nod.

'As you say, sir, Flotsam and I were up a little later than usual this morning. Although I did have time to observe that Dr Watson had already set off for a day in the country.'

Mr Holmes looked up sharply and for a moment ceased to wave the letter under his chin.

'Mrs Hudson, that is remarkably perspicacious. May I enquire how…?'

'Oh, you can tell a great deal from a larder, sir, particularly after a gentleman has been in it. Provisioning a kitchen is a precise science, you see. Gentlemen seem to imagine that a larder contains a feast of random edibles where their plundering will go unnoticed. On this occasion, it didn't take a lot of thought to realise that Dr Watson would not have endeavoured to create for himself such very substantial ham sandwiches if he were spending the day in town, or indeed within reach of a country inn. A day in the hills, is it, sir?'

'Quite so, Mrs Hudson. I see my presence inspires you. Your reasoning is still rather unsophisticated but on this occasion you have stumbled upon something very close to the truth. I have sent Watson, in the guise of a walker, to see what information he can surprise from Moran's father. A remote establishment in the Downs.'

Mrs Hudson nodded approvingly.

'And would it be out of place for me to ask what Dr Watson found yesterday when he visited Mr Moran's colleagues?'

'Not at all, Mrs Hudson. I consider you and Flottie worthy helpers in this case; you are the rods of base metal that help to conduct the lightning. However in this matter I am hardly better informed than yourselves. Watson returned late last night and showed rather indecent haste to retire when I informed him of his impending early start. But tonight we shall hear all and I would be honoured if you and Flottie would join us. Watson with an audience will no doubt be less precise than ever but I daresay I shall be able to extract the salient points.'

'And does that letter concern this case, sir?'

Mr Holmes was still waving the note under his chin and at this he looked at it a little blankly. Then his face lit up and he settled back in his chair.

'Indeed it does, Mrs Hudson. Dr Watson being absent I thought I would share it with you. When you have furnished me with some of your excellent brown ale in lieu of breakfast, I beg you to read it and tell me if you grasp its significance.'

The beer supplied, Mrs Hudson and I left Mr Holmes to draw the cork while we turned our attention to the letter. We looked at it with some excitement. Then we looked at it a second time. Then we looked at each other. We were underwhelmed.

Re: The Sumatra and Nassau Trading Company
7 Bishops Yard

Sir,

Subject to your enquiry of the 19th, we can confirm that the above company ceased to trade as per the information you have received. It is not our place to comment on any rumours pertaining to that circumstance. I trust this information is of use.

Your faithful servants,
Marsden and Trocklewood, Stockbrokers

'Well, Mrs Hudson?' asked Mr Holmes, dabbing foam from his upper lip with the end of his dressing gown cord.

'This would seem to confirm the collapse of Mr Moran's company in much the way he stated, sir.'

'Precisely! I daresay it may seem to you a very trivial confirmation of detail, but to me it is a vital part of the whole. By pinning down the details, the disciplined mind frees itself to focus on wider horizons. Unfortunately, by confirming Moran's story, this letter has rendered Dr Watson's journey somewhat redundant. But I am sure the fresh air will do his constitution a power of good.'

This happy thought was accompanied by a further swig.

'The same, however, cannot be said for myself. Instead I foresee a cosy afternoon in front of the fire with a good pipe and some serious consideration of the question in hand.'

The great detective rose to leave but at the door he paused as if suddenly troubled.

'Mrs Hudson, were you truly able to deduce how Watson's day was to be spent merely by a glance in your larder?'

'Of course, sir.'

He nodded to himself, as if uncertain what to make of this.

'Extraordinary!' he concluded.

'Very simple, Mr Holmes,' returned Mrs Hudson steadily. 'One should never overlook the alimentary.' And she turned quickly to the dresser as if a great deal of rapid concentration was required to disguise the joyous convulsions of her eyebrows.

It was only when Mr Holmes had ensconced himself firmly by his own fireside that Mrs Hudson revealed a surprising plan for the day.

'Flottie,' she said, 'I have a mind to go to Limehouse today to visit Mrs Trent and I have a mind to take you with me. What do you say?'

'Today, ma'am? Shouldn't we...?'

'I don't think we need to trouble ourselves too much about domestic affairs today. Dr Watson's gone for the day and Mr Holmes is determined to see no-one. Poor Mrs Trent has had an unfortunate life which she enjoys sharing with visitors but for once I am eager to hear her story. There was something we heard yesterday that makes it urgent I speak to her as soon as I can.'

She mused for a moment.

'I'm not generally a believer in coincidence, Flottie. But sometimes it appears to have a very long arm indeed. So a visit is required. Besides, you and I haven't been out for a jaunt in ages. I can tell you the story of Hudson and the jellied eels. Now, quick. It's a long way and we haven't a moment to lose.'

So enthusiastic was Mrs Hudson that I was hurried out of the house into unexpected sunshine with a piece of bread still uneaten in my hand. I was still trying to make sense of the multitude of scarves and mufflers that Mrs Hudson had draped around me on the area steps when a carriage pulled up purposefully at our door. My attention was now so firmly fixed on the attempt to tie my muffler while holding mittens, hat and breakfast simultaneously that I paid it little heed. I had just hit upon the idea of placing all the remaining bread in my mouth at once when a young man with whiskers leapt from the carriage and hailed Mrs Hudson with good humoured familiarity.

He was a remarkably good looking young man with a bright eye and a smile brighter than his waistcoat. Even to my inexperienced eye, it was clear he was dressed in the height of fashion although the way he splashed cheerfully through the mud as he approached us suggested that he was not overly concerned with matters sartorial. He shook Mrs Hudson warmly by the hand and before I had realised what was about to happen he had turned towards me for an introduction.

'This is Flotsam, sir. Flotsam, Mr Rupert Spencer.'

'How do you do, Miss Flotsam?' and he met my gaze with a pair of brown eyes that smiled at the corners as he held out his hand.

It was not a happy moment. I had seldom felt a greater desire to acquit myself with dignity but was rendered speechless by the fact that I had just filled my mouth with my entire breakfast. Both cheeks bulged alarmingly. Unsure whether to attempt to swallow, I instinctively held out my hand towards his, only to realise that I was still clutching a pair of mittens and one end of my scarf. The other end, I noticed with dismay, dangled limply in a puddle.

'Allow me!' he offered gallantly and bent to retrieve it, giving me time to achieve a feat of swallowing of which a London sparrow might have been proud. When he looked up only my reddened face and some nervous undulations in my throat remained to give me away.

'On the contrary, Mrs Hudson, the privilege was all ours.' He turned to me again. 'Our big gloomy town house was the most miserable place for a small boy like me. Mrs Hudson was the only reason I'd agree to come. Do you know, when I was seven she showed me how to stuff a squirrel?'

This was certainly not the sort of activity I imagined Mrs Hudson undertaking and only the fear that my mouth was still full of crumbs prevented my jaw from dropping.

'Never you mind all that, Flotsam. I've learned how to do a lot of useless things in my time.'

Mr Spencer smiled at us both. He seemed genuinely pleased to be standing in the sunshine with us.

'I *am* glad I caught you, Mrs H. Your message said you intended to travel to Limehouse and I thought I could take you part of the way. I have an appointment at eleven, otherwise I should take you *all* the way. Do you know, I don't think I've ever been to Limehouse.'

'I imagine you haven't,' returned Mrs Hudson, 'but we should be most grateful for a ride, sir. It will give us an opportunity to catch up.'

If I imagined the process of catching up involved a polite exchange of news, I was very far wide of the mark. As I arranged myself shyly in the corner of the carriage, still worrying about how I looked in my muffler, Mrs Hudson nudged me and whispered, 'Mr Spencer is a rather promising young scientist. I thought he might prove useful.'

Then the carriage jolted into motion and by the time Mr Spencer was settled opposite us, we were rolling gently out of Baker Street. He wasted no time on pleasantries.

'I received the report from old Ponsonby last night,' he began. 'It lays out the agent's findings about this Sumatra affair very clearly. Ponsonby's people at the Colonial Office say the agent is very sound. Trouble is, those islands are technically the Dutch East Indies and by the time anyone thought to tell Singapore about it, the trail was already cold. All they could do was ask the Dutch to investigate. However, the report gives what details there are of the deaths. The thing is, I don't know what to make of them.'

'We were wondering about poisons, sir?'

'Very sensibly. The obvious cause would be some sort of violent poison. I flirted with the idea of blowpipes and poisoned darts but rather disappointingly the report seems to rule them out. No puncture marks, you see. So I looked for something administered through food or drink that has, first effect, pain in the eyes so acute that the victim might be driven to self-mutilation, and, second effect, death. Trouble is, I can't come up with anything like that either. I've been through the poison lists – up all night I was – and it's remarkable how many poisons have been catalogued. Some people seem to spend their whole lives doing nothing else. But they haven't come up with anything to fit the bill, I'm afraid. I'm terribly sorry to let you down, Mrs H.'

He paused sadly for a moment then brightened. 'Of course, it doesn't have to be plant-based. It could be some creature they trapped. You never know with animals. I was reading the other day that eating polar bears is terribly bad for you.'

'Thank you, sir.' Mrs Hudson nodded solemnly as if this latter piece of information was of the greatest interest to her. 'On a different note, sir, we have a knife that Flotsam would like to test for poison. Do you think you would be able to assist us?'

He turned to me with his brown-eyed smile.

'Of course, I'd be delighted to assist. Do you know much chemistry, Miss Flotsam?'

'Very little, sir,' I mumbled from under my muffler. His friendly gaze made it difficult to be shy and even harder for me to serve Mrs Hudson with the outraged glare I had been intending.

'It is an area Flottie intends to study, sir.'

'I'm delighted to hear it. It's always a pleasure to meet a fellow scientist, Miss Flotsam. If I am ever able to assist you in your studies…'

And at that point Mrs Hudson turned the conversation to the Spencer family, where it remained until the parting of our ways.

It was not until Mr Spencer was preparing to get back into the carriage after handing us down with a polite farewell that Mrs Hudson paused as if a thought had struck her.

'What is it, Mrs Hudson? Can I help?'

'It's just a thought that has struck me, sir. Only a small thing. But an obvious question, now I come to think about it. Tell me, sir, how often does a doctor generally pronounce his patient dead?'

'Once is usually considered sufficient, Mrs Hudson.'

'My thought exactly, sir. After all, we can only die once, can't we?'

Mr Spencer had time to throw a conspiratorial look of puzzlement in my direction before his carriage rumbled into motion and we were left to continue our journey rather less comfortably amid the jostling of a London omnibus.

Mrs Trent, when we eventually reached her, proved to be a small and shrinking woman whose frame seemed crumpled by the careless pressing of the years. She had worked with Mrs Hudson briefly when both were girls, but when Mrs Trent married a sailor their lives took different courses. It was less than a year previously that they had met again by chance. Mrs Trent was by then a widow who had lost her husband and one of her sons to the sea. Certainly, seeing the two women beside each other, it was hard to believe they had ever been the same age or shared the same station in life. Mrs Trent was weak where Mrs Hudson was strong, was cowed where Mrs Hudson commanded. She lived humbly in a basement room near the docks where the one proper chair was hastily vacated for Mrs Hudson and a stool and a biscuit provided for me.

'So good of you to visit, my dear Mrs Hudson,' she warbled as if simultaneously pleased and disconcerted. 'Such a long way to come on a winter's day.'

'It's good to see you well, Betty,' replied Mrs Hudson with brisk informality, and there followed some minutes of conversation on the subject of Mrs Trent's ailments past and present. As they talked, I looked at the damp-stained walls and wondered at the strangeness of a life that seemed to contain so many opposites. Only hours after Smale had held me helpless in an alleyway I was being handed from a private carriage by a gentleman with white gloves and brown eyes. I looked at Mrs Hudson and found myself smiling deep inside.

'And tell me, Betty, how's that son of yours?'

'Arthur's still away at sea, Mrs Hudson. I pray for him every night and god willing he'll be back in March. Since Jeb was lost, I fear for Arthur most terribly.'

'Oh yes, poor Jeb. How long ago was that, Betty? I forget the circumstances exactly.'

'It will be a year ago in February. As to the circumstances, I wish I could forget them.' She turned to me. 'I've said it many a time, Jeb was a wild lad but he didn't deserve what happened to him. He'd been at sea since he was a boy and he'd picked up some hard ways by all accounts. When he came home he used to shock me with all his drinking and his fighting and the like. I used to think it would be the gin that would be the death of him. In a way I wish it had been.'

She dabbed at her worn-out eyes with a threadbare handkerchief. She was no longer directing her story at me.

'The letter from his captain arrived last spring. There'd been some trouble ashore and Jeb had been locked in the hold for a few hours while things quietened down. The captain wrote that he must have picked up something nasty ashore, because when they let him out he had gone quite mad, raving and screaming, seeing invisible creatures swarming over the deck. Think of it! My poor Jeb! The captain was on a regular run out in the Indies and decided to carry on to Java. But it was of no help to Jeb. They were caught by a sudden squall with Jeb blundering about on deck. The pitch of the ship took him overboard when the crew were busy with the sheets and he was never seen again, God rest him.'

Mrs Hudson was leaning forward eagerly as if she had suddenly remembered something.

'And all this from the captain's letter, Betty?'

'Indeed, Mrs Hudson. He was a good man to write to a poor widow like me. I heard later that he was dead before I got the letter, struck down by a fever in the Straits.'

'And the name of the ship, Betty? I'm sure you mentioned it to me once. Can you still remember it?'

'Of course I can. The ship where my Jeb met his end? I could no sooner forget it than forget Jeb himself.'

'Yes, Betty?' Mrs Hudson was struggling to suppress her eagerness. 'What *was* the name of the ship?'

'Poor Jeb. It was an unlucky name for him. I hate to think of him screaming and raving like that. The name, Mrs Hudson? Oh, yes. The name of the ship was Matilda Briggs.'

The Fell Sergeant

†

The long journey homewards was a silent one. The sunshine had given way to a sky pregnant with winter and the chill seemed to creep out of the ground into the opaque afternoon. It seemed that Mrs Trent's tale had given Mrs Hudson something to ponder and for the first time since our move to Baker Street she seemed a trifle perplexed. She sat and watched through the window as our omnibus shook off the docks and shuffled westwards. Her brow was knitted in the most fixed of frowns and very slowly she stroked one finger backwards and forwards along her lower lip. It was not until we were walking back up Baker Street in the evening gloom that she let out a low, rumbling chuckle.

'Well, Flottie, events can make fools of us all and at least you know now why I was anxious to visit Mrs Trent. What do you feel we've learned from her story?'

That was the question I had been puzzling over myself but I was no nearer an answer as we reached our front door than I had been when we waved goodbye to Mrs Trent in the shadows of the warehouses.

'It seems a strange coincidence, ma'am. It was only yesterday that we heard reports the ship was haunted with evil spirits, and now it pops up again. Perhaps Mr Holmes was wrong to dismiss that letter so out-of-hand.'

'A very sensible answer, Flotsam. I am convinced that Mr Holmes made a very grave error in disregarding the letter about the Matilda Briggs. And you are right that it is a strange coincidence.'

By now we had reached the corridor and she popped her head into the study as we passed.

'Excellent! Dr Watson's not yet returned and Mr Holmes is fast asleep in his armchair. That means we have a little time to get the place sorted for the evening before the doctor arrives.'

'Do you think, then, that Mrs Trent's story is important?'

'Oh, yes. I think we've learned something of great significance. In fact, now that I've had time to pull together a few threads, I think I'm beginning to understand a lot more about what was going on in Sumatra.'

'Golly!' I exclaimed.

'Young ladies do not say "golly", Flotsam.'

'You mean you know how all those people died, ma'am?'

'Yes, I think that is becoming very clear, although there are one or two details which it would be prudent to check. The important thing to understand, Flottie, is that those unhappy deaths are the least of the mysteries that face us. We have much deeper questions to consider. However, I think there are two lessons we have learned today. First of all, we shouldn't rush to dismiss coincidence. And then we should remember that getting the right answer isn't always as important as asking the right question.'

And with that she shrugged off her coat and bent to revive the kitchen fire while I endeavoured to look alert and knowing.

'No, there are much more worrying mysteries that face us, Flottie. Such as why does Mr Moran use cheap writing paper? Why is Fogarty suddenly taking an interest in Mr Holmes's maid? And why,' she added slowly, 'why on earth don't we know more about Penge?'

–

It wasn't until much later in the evening that Dr Watson arrived home after a tramp across the moors that had proved as damp as it was dispiriting.

'I like a good walk as much as the next man,' he declared as Mrs Hudson helped him out of his dripping coat, 'but to walk ten miles through a bog only to be sent about my business like a common tramp... Well, it's enough to make a fellow's blood boil!'

And as if to prove the point the doctor began to steam gently in the warm corridor.

'I take it, Watson, that Mr Moran senior wasn't inclined to talk about his son's doings?' asked Holmes with a smile of amusement.

'He most certainly was not, Holmes! The blighter almost set his dogs on me. He met me in the hills before I had even reached his house. Asked me what I wanted there and when I said I knew his son you'd have thought I'd said I was planning to steal his silver. The fellow wouldn't listen to a word after that. Said his son had made his choices and could rot in hell. Nothing for it but to hike back the way I came and wait for the last train soaked to the skin. Dashed poor form if you ask me!'

'Come, Watson. Let us make amends for your wasted trip. While you change into some dry clothes, Mrs Hudson will serve you some supper and I myself shall mix you a drink. No, no, sir, I know how you like it. Plenty of water. I am quite the connoisseur.'

He beamed proudly and continued before Watson could speak.

'Let us gather in the study in thirty minutes time. I have promised Mrs Hudson and Flottie here that they may hear your tale from the horse's mouth, for they are developing a taste for sensation and if you were ever to do as you vow and commit one of our adventures to paper, they would be your most loyal readers.'

Dr Watson directed a nod in our direction.

'Jolly good! It will be a pleasure, Mrs Hudson. I daresay that in your line of work you observe a great deal of human nature.'

'Come, Watson, no time for idle pleasantries or you shall have to cut short your ablutions. We expect you in thirty minutes.'

And he turned regally into the study bequeathing a lingering scent of tobacco and brown ale to the troublesome process of separating Dr Watson from his watery boots.

An observer would have found an unlikely scene laid before him had he been shown the Baker Street study thirty minutes later. On each side of the fire, in their familiar armchairs, sat Mr Holmes and Dr Watson, but just behind them, owlish in the half-light, loomed Mrs Hudson. Having discreetly examined the port on offer, she had resisted all Dr Watson's offers of refreshment and now waited by the drinks tray blending so perfectly into the background that our observer may not have been immediately aware of her presence. Even less obtrusive and even further away, perched at the insistence of Dr Watson on a velvet footstool, I sat so deep in the shadows that I might have been hidden from observation altogether.

Dr Watson, looking warmer and rosier, was peering dubiously into his glass when Holmes interrupted his meditations.

'So, Watson, we are gathered to learn what your examination of Neale and Carruthers revealed. I have no doubts that you have acquitted yourself admirably. First, for those less familiar with the principles of scientific thought, it may be helpful if you summarise the situation as you saw it when you set out.'

'Certainly, Holmes. I hope you will feel that I have repaid your confidence.' Turning in the direction of Mrs Hudson and myself, he went on. 'The most important task of these last few days has been to test the details of Moran's story. Such an outlandish tale must clearly be subjected to scrutiny, though as Holmes here pointed out, the process of verifying an account of such distant events must necessarily be a lengthy one. I was happy to leave the technical aspects to the expert and confine myself to interviewing the witnesses.'

Here Holmes gave a slight nod of acknowledgement.

'Indeed, Watson. An admirable exposition of our approach.'

Watson glowed a little more rosily and drained his glass with a determined gulp.

'I interviewed Neale first. He has taken rooms at Brown's Hotel in Mayfair in a bid to evade any pursuer who may have obtained his address in Cavendish Street. I have to say, he proved a strange cove. I expected that he would be eager to receive any emissary of yours but throughout he seemed quite disturbed, as though his mind wasn't really on the answers he gave me.

'My first impression of him was one of weakness. The man is of impressive physique but there was something about his carriage that suggested a man accustomed to following the lead of others. He held himself badly, for a start, and never quite met my eye.'

'Really, Watson!' interrupted Holmes. 'We are gathered here to discover the *facts* of the case!' He turned to Mrs Hudson. 'You must forgive Dr Watson. I'm afraid his army training has left him with an innate distrust of anyone who lacks the military bearing.'

'Merely painting a picture, Holmes,' mumbled Watson, mostly to himself. 'Anyway, in response to my questions he confirmed pretty much every detail Moran had told us. The hideous mysterious deaths, his terror of remaining in Sumatra, his precipitate escape. He even confirmed Moran's fever, though he glossed over the business of leaving his friend behind in Sumatra. The fellow must realise he comes out of that looking pretty shabby.'

'And what of his subsequent activities?'

'He says he and Carruthers hope to raise the capital for another venture closer to home.'

'What else, Watson?'

'That was about it, Holmes.'

'That's *all*? Really, Watson, I hadn't expected you to ask every question that I should have posed but I did expect a little more than that! What of the man's history, those little clues that tell us what sort of man he really is?'

'He seemed a dashed plain blighter to me, Holmes.'

At that Mr Holmes's face warmed into an affectionate smile.

'Exotic enough to have attracted a tropical curse, my friend. However, we must be content with that for now. Do you have any observations to make, Mrs Hudson?'

Mrs Hudson considered for a moment, her face still impassive. I waited, hoping desperately that she would demonstrate to Mr Holmes some breathtaking piece of deduction. She considered carefully.

'Brown's Hotel is reputed to be a very fine establishment, sir.'

'Is that so, Mrs Hudson? I shall make a note of your recommendation. Now what of Carruthers, Watson?'

'I found him at the old St James's Hotel in Knightsbridge, Holmes. A mean-looking man, all moustache and eyebrows. I could imagine him leaving a friend in peril to make good his own escape. I daresay he would find someone like Neale easy to influence, too. Anyway, he seemed absolutely solid on the Sumatra story. Said it was the worst time of his life.'

'Any new details, Watson?'

'Sorry, Holmes.' Watson looked gloomily at his empty glass.

'Not to worry, my friend. You have succeeded in confirming Moran's story, which was our primary objective. If we wish to know more, we can visit Mr Carruthers again. And Mrs Hudson and Flottie have learnt that not all the work we do is as sensational as they might expect.' He stirred in his seat. 'Now, after my exertions today I feel I would benefit from an early night. If you and Mrs Hudson will excuse me…?'

'May I ask Dr Watson a question, sir?' Mrs Hudson's face was still motionless but at the very top of her nose her brow was ever so slightly wrinkled.

'Of course, Mrs Hudson.'

'Well, sir, I don't pretend to be very scientific, Dr Watson, but from the human point of view, as it were, I should be very interested in learning how the two gentlemen struck you. I mean, sir, what was the overall impression you formed?'

'I can give a very simple answer to that question, Mrs Hudson, for it was particularly striking in both cases. I have never in my life met two men more terrified. If I were to abandon the language of precise observation, I'd say each was quite simply scared out of his wits.'

–

'So, the mystery deepens, eh, Flottie?' chuckled Mrs Hudson when we were back in front of the kitchen fire.

'Does it, ma'am? I thought Dr Watson's story was going to be a bit more exciting. Doesn't it suggest that Mr Moran was telling the truth after all? Or at least,' I added thoughtfully, 'that they are all telling the same lie?'

'Very good, Flottie. Now there are things Dr Watson said which I need to mull over. Their fear, for instance. I hadn't entirely expected that.'

'But the curse…?'

'Now, Flottie, you can't go believing in that sort of thing. I think it must be a sign that your bed is beckoning. You get yourself ready. I shall just write a quick note.'

But as I watched her write I seemed strangely awake. My arms and legs ached from the unusual exercise of the night before and all the bumps and cuts that were beginning to throb again seemed to amplify the call of a warm bed. But my mind refused to be tired. There seemed to have been so many events happening so quickly that, as I changed into my nightdress in front of the fire, it seemed only a matter of time before a sudden visitor would pound on our door and demand our attention.

Mrs Hudson sealed up her note and handed it to me. It was addressed in her neat handwriting to Mr A J Raffles at the Albany.

'Tomorrow morning, Flottie, you and I need to work like navvies. Even Mr Holmes and Dr Watson expect certain standards. But when you're through your list of chores, you may be good enough to deliver this for me. For myself, I would like another word with young Mr Spencer when the chance arises.'

She eyed me quizzically as I stood before her, still uneasily wakeful.

'Come on, Flottie, if that brain of yours is still turning over we may as well put it to some proper use. Do you remember the word game that Swordsmith used to have you play? I was thinking we could play a round or two. If running around in the gutter all night doesn't wear you out, perhaps some mental exercise will do the trick.'

I ran to fetch paper and pencils with a childish enthusiasm. It was rare for Mrs Hudson to suggest a game, though once she and Swordsmith had wracked their brains to devise ways of entertaining me when I was sleepless.

'I'll choose the first word, Flottie. How about *orchestra*?' and she turned over the one-minute timer with a twist of her wrist.

Before the first dozen grains had fallen my mind was entirely occupied with the game, trying to find smaller words contained in the word Mrs Hudson had chosen. The game was to find most words, but the real honour lay in finding the longest. After a minute of scribbling, we agreed that my *search* matched Mrs Hudson's *starch*. Four or five more games ensued before Mrs Hudson sat back and smiled at my enthusiasm.

'Now off to bed you go, Flottie, and no lying awake. I'll give you one more to think about, just in case you can't sleep. It will be easier than solving mysteries and better than counting pigeons. Just a simple one, I think. Try 'Norman'. That should be about the right size.'

And as I cuddled under my blanket in the velvet dark, my mind tried to play with the word Mrs Hudson had given me.

'Norman,' I considered. 'There's Roman and roam… manor… arm… roan… moan…' But sleep was creeping up from my toes and before the thought was complete it had faded into the night.

–

Elsewhere in that same night not even the driving rain that had come with the darkness could empty the streets of London. Braziers burned in nameless yards. Ships slipped their moorings and edged from the pool of London into thick mist. Somewhere Mr Fogarty was at work, laying his plans, plotting his plots, smiling his thin, menacing smile. Somewhere else again, his collar hunched against the rain, Smale was smiling too, crouched in a doorway and looking up at a window where the last light had just been extinguished. And, nearer and nearer, a small boy was running with gasping urgency ever closer to our door.

When it came, the rapping I had been half expecting broke in on us with the violence of thunder. Mrs Hudson and I were awake at once and stumbling into a state of dress. But, fast as we were, by the time Mrs Hudson reached the corridor wrapped in an old gentleman's over-coat, Mr Holmes was already there, running a hand through unexpectedly tousled hair. Dr Watson and I joined them a moment later, the doctor yawning dazedly in what appeared to be a regimental dressing gown.

Mrs Hudson made her way to the door while the rest of us were still making embarrassed adjustments to our attire. We heard the street door open, a hushed exchange and then Mrs Hudson's footsteps returning. There was a note in her hand that she held out to Mr Holmes with a short nod of her head.

'From Inspector Gregory, sir.'

Holmes took the note and opened it eagerly. After a quick glance at its contents he stepped back and passed the note to Dr Watson.

'It appears we shall not be interviewing Carruthers a second time, after all. He is dead, Watson. Murdered.'

The three of us crowded round the letter but there was little else to be gleaned.

'As you see from his postscript, Gregory found your card in the man's pocket, Watson. So for once he has sent for us with commendable promptness.'

'The boy is waiting, sir.'

'Of course, Mrs Hudson. Tell him I shall accompany him at once. Dr Watson shall follow us with all available speed. Watson, this might be the perfect opportunity to test the Niermeister equipment you have been so interested in. We can test Herr Niermeister's theory of electrostatic irregularities. Would you be so good as to prepare the equipment and follow on?'

'I say, Holmes, that's a bit steep! It's the middle of the night, it's pouring with rain and I've only just dried out from my last soaking. And that German paraphernalia is dashed heavy for lugging around.'

'Of course, dear fellow. How selfish of me. I shall insist that Flottie accompany you with an umbrella.'

For a moment I thought Mrs Hudson was going to object but she caught my eye and seemed to understand the pleading there.

'Well really, sir,' she began, but by now I was essaying the most melting expression I could muster. 'Of course, sir, if Flottie can be of assistance… I'm sure Dr Watson will answer for her well-being and perhaps the young need their sleep less than the rest of us.'

Bending down, apparently to untuck my hair from my nightdress, she added in a low voice, 'Keep your mind open as well as your eyes, Flottie. I know I couldn't have a better deputy.'

And it was with those words of praise still warm inside me that I found myself, ten minutes later, seated next to Dr Watson in a grumbling hansom as it shook its way southwards, its destination Knightsbridge.

The Vanished Witness

✝

The St James's Hotel had a uniformed policeman at the entrance, another at the main desk and a third patrolling the space between with solemn, impressive steps. They stood guard on a place that was by some distance the most opulent I had ever entered. It smelled of leather and polish, and I seemed to sink into the carpet as if stepping onto velvet. The purple drapes and hangings soaked up sound so that even the bustle attendant on a murder was reduced to a meek murmur. An elaborately moustachioed man behind the desk was talking softly in a French accent to the nearest policeman, apparently upbraiding him for the temerity of the detective force in intruding on such carefully crafted luxury.

But murder knows no aesthetics, as I was soon to find out. As we made our way across the foyer, the Frenchman's glance followed me and I was glad Mrs Hudson had taken such care with my appearance. With some deftness my hair had been bundled up, a neat plain hat located and pinned and a slim navy dress produced from nowhere and slipped over my head while Mrs Hudson briefed me in a whisper on various questions of etiquette. To my surprise, in five minutes I had been transformed into the smartest and neatest I had ever been, from my piled-up hair to my never-worn best black shoes. I didn't look at all like the Flotsam I recognised and the knowledge made me somehow taller and straighter so that when the Frenchman's eyes met mine he dropped his head in a respectful bow. Would Smale recognise me now, I wondered with a little flash of pride? Was I the same person who had greeted Rupert Spencer with her mouth full of bread and her scarf in a puddle? The policeman showing us through the hotel had relieved Dr Watson of his cumbersome wooden chest and now the doctor slipped my arm through his and escorted me towards the gilded lifts with an air of protective gallantry.

The scene upstairs brought my mind very firmly back to the grim purpose of our visit. Mr Carruthers had clearly met his end in a most horrible way. His body lay face down near the fireplace, collapsed as if his limbs had given way as he crawled towards the grate. His face was turned so it rested on one check, making his expression plain to all who entered. And what an expression! His features were contorted horribly, his mouth open with his tongue, swollen and distended, hanging out of it. A trickle of blood ran from the side of his mouth to the rug, where it gathered in a dark, congealing stain. And worst of all, both his eyes remained open so it seemed as you entered the room that he watched your entry with a frozen scream of pain. Around him the ornate furniture was overturned, as if the room itself had shuddered in horror.

Mr Holmes looked up when we entered. His manner was remote, like a man absorbed in a landscape of his own, but his movements by contrast were short and jerky as if dictated by a barely suppressed energy. Nevertheless he lightened when he saw Dr Watson and beckoned him over to where a neat young man in tweeds knelt beside the body. Mrs Hudson had told me that I should learn most by being noticed least but even from a position by the door I could hear that Mr Holmes's voice was fired with excitement.

'Gregory here has done an excellent job, Watson. Nothing has been moved, not a single item disturbed. This is exactly how the body lay.'

I looked again around the rooms that had belonged so briefly to Mr Carruthers. Beyond the living room, through an oak-panelled double door, I glimpsed a bedroom where clothes sprawled in confusion across a bed that seemed to reach for ever. Both rooms were high-ceilinged and expensive in purple and gold, brightly lit by electric lights concealed in cut-glass chandeliers. Around the body, murder had wreaked havoc. A plush divan had been toppled over and lay alongside an overturned chair. A velvet foot-stool lay upside-down in one corner. Next to it a wooden box, still partly wrapped in brown paper, had been swept from an adjacent table and lay amongst its disordered wrappings. Near the door someone had sent a whisky decanter crashing to the floor, where it lay in pieces near its crystal stopper. The escaped liquid had crept across the floor until it reached the dead man's feet. The air smelled of whisky.

By the fireplace, Mr Holmes and Dr Watson continued to examine the body in the company of the man referred to as Inspector Gregory. I had no great urge to join them for, although death was not uncommon on the streets of London, I found I had no great curiosity to examine it at close quarters. In addition, Mrs Hudson's advice as she pointed me towards the waiting cab had been quite clear. 'You can leave Mr Holmes to spot the bizarre. What the likes of you and I must do, Flottie, is to keep an eye on the commonplace.' And so, while the convulsed corpse was the focus of attention, I lingered on the edge of the scene and endeavoured to observe what was ordinary. But I found my mind turning like a barrel organ, there was so little here that was commonplace to me. From the silk carpets to the ornately plastered ceiling, everything seemed overwhelming in its richness and luxury. But I did my best. I duly noted the design of the half-wrapped box, the position of the fallen decanter, the colour of the curtains, the maker's name on the clock, even the number of horned cattle in the vast Highland scene above the fireplace.

Finally I felt I had no choice but to turn my attention to where the dead man lay. The sense of motion in the collapsed body was unnerving, as if at any moment he might resume his final desperate crawl to the beckoning bell-pull that hung by the fire. But his face vanquished any doubts. The skin was sickly pale and his lips were drawn back in a snarl or grimace that distorted every feature. My attention was caught by Mr Holmes's voice – low, urgent and excited.

'Certainly poison, gentlemen, and judging by its effect a powerful one. Note the swelling of the tongue. I suggest, Gregory, that since no alternative presents itself we assume the poison was administered in the decanter. The whisky would mask the taste...' Then his voice dropped lower amongst the nodding heads as they clustered closer over the victim.

The dying man had nearly reached the bell-pull, I thought. His head was no more than a foot away from the marble surround of the fire. One more lurch forward on his knees and he would have reached it. Would that have helped? By then the poison was already spreading through him. Even as he crawled he must have known it was too late. In the grate, the fire was almost burnt down but the embers still glowed brightly. I noticed automatically that it needed stoking and then, almost simultaneously, I noticed something strange amongst the ordinary. Next to the grate, so bright and clean that I wondered if it was simply for ornament, stood a smart brass fire set of hearth brush, fire-shovel and poker. Except it didn't. One of the hooks was empty. The brush and the shovel were in place but the poker was missing. I looked around the fireplace but there was no sign of it. In a place such as this it was impossible that the set might have been incomplete. The poker must have been removed.

I made another hushed circuit of the apartment but failed to find it. In the bedroom everything was orderly but for some open drawers and the pile of garments on the bed, as if Carruthers had been contemplating a rapid departure. I knew little about Carruthers but felt sorry for him: it seemed that a great deal of his last few months had been spent in flight – from Sumatra, from his London home and now from here. Making sure I was unobserved, I sorted quickly through the scattered clothes, then checked under the bed. There was no poker. I tried to make sense of it. A missing poker might be anticipated had Carruthers been bludgeoned but why should it be moved if he had met his death by poison? I stepped back into the living room to try again. Could it have rolled somewhere? I peered again under the furniture but the room was brightly lit and even an ornamental poker should have been obvious. Then I came to the overturned footstool that I had noted in my initial inventory. It lay to one side of the room, near the small table under which the open parcel now lay. As I looked at it this time, I realised that it wasn't lying quite flush with the floor. As if there was something underneath. Very gently I tilted it upwards and peeped beneath it.

'Dr Watson, sir,' I called, taking great care to replace it exactly in the position I had found it. Dr Watson was standing now, his attention still on the group crouched over the body. 'Dr Watson, sir, I think perhaps someone should look at this.'

'One moment, Flotsam,' he replied and continued to direct his attention downwards, to where Mr Holmes was addressing Inspector Gregory with unusual animation.

'There was no struggle, Gregory. This disorder represents the frenzied blundering of a dying man, a man who can feel himself stricken and stumbles repeatedly as he seeks in vain to summon help. And, of course, there is something else of importance to note...'

By now I had resorted to tugging Dr Watson by the sleeve and rather grudgingly he left the two gentlemen to their discussion.

'Well, Flottie, what is it?'

I indicated the overturned footstool and Watson advanced towards it slightly impatiently. He lifted it casually to one side then dropped it with a sharp cry, leaping backwards and shielding me from the stool with an outstretched arm.

'Great Scott!' he exclaimed.

'It's quite all right, sir,' I offered from under his arm. 'I made sure it was completely dead before I called you.'

His cry had attracted Mr Holmes and the inspector, and Watson stepped forward gingerly and moved the footstool further to the side. Under it lay the missing poker and, under the poker, its head crushed flat, a slim blue snake the length of my forearm.

Inspector Gregory let out a low whistle of surprise. Holmes stepped forward and peered more closely at the strange tableaux. 'It seems, Watson, that you may have been premature in concluding that the poison was administered through the whisky. However, you have more than redeemed yourself by discovering something that Gregory's men, in their anxiety not to disturb the evidence, rather remarkably appear to have overlooked.'

The two men began to protest together but Holmes silenced them with a raised hand. 'Let us consider how this discovery alters our thinking, gentlemen,' and stepping deftly over the upturned divan he moved to where the body lay. We gathered around as he lifted first one of the victim's arms, then the other. After a close examination of the second, he let out a small cry of satisfaction.

'Ah, just as I imagined!' He produced a magnifying glass with a flourish and held it out to Gregory. 'Note the small puncture marks. I think we have our murder weapon.' While Gregory and Watson took turns to examine the wound, Mr Holmes had returned to where the poker lay but this time his attention was held by the box under the nearby table.

'It all becomes clear. What a fiendish device! We are dealing with a criminal mind at once both ruthless and cunning.'

'The parcel, you think, Holmes?' murmured Watson as he and Gregory joined Holmes in examining the box. 'Dashed unpleasant trick. The chap opens the lid, pushes aside the layers of paper and bang! One bite and before he knows it he's as good as dead.'

'Precisely, Watson. In the first few seconds, before the poison began to take effect, Carruthers had time to stride to the fireplace, seize the poker and make certain his executioner would do no further harm. Then he begins to understand his peril. He may have had an idea to use spirit from the decanter to cauterise the wound but by then the poison was already beginning to tell. He tries to support himself on the furniture but his desperate attempts to reach the bell only lead to the disorder we currently witness. How was the body discovered?'

'The gentleman below, sir. A Belgian gentleman. He was woken by a series of crashes from the room above. He rang for the night porter and made a complaint. When the porter investigated, he found the door locked from the inside and the lights burning. After getting no reply to his knocking, he put his ear to the door and claims he heard a groan. He then spent some time finding the manager, who used his shoulder to burst through the door. They found Carruthers dead and the furniture in disarray. The key was in the lock on the inside.' Despite the hour, Gregory seemed wide awake. 'We shall of course make enquiries at once about the delivery of this box. It is likely that someone in the hotel will remember its arrival.'

Watson was examining the box, a small square object of polished wood inlaid with an intricate pattern. Two small holes had been punched through its lid.

'Some sort of tropical timber, Holmes. It would appear the curse...'

'Nonsense, Watson! Although these events justify Moran's fears, it was a hand made of flesh and blood that punched those holes and a human hand that dispatched it to Carruthers.'

He turned to Gregory, his eyes full of bright energy. 'As you correctly surmised, Inspector, Dr Watson and I know something of this case already. I shall be happy to lay the facts before you. But first there are two men who must be warned of tonight's events at the earliest opportunity. A moment's delay may cost them their lives. Unfortunately I have only a forwarding address for one of them. Would you be so kind as to dispatch a man immediately to the offices of the Rangoon & Occident Shipping Line? They are holding mail for one Nathaniel Moran. It is imperative that his whereabouts are discovered and that he is informed of what has occurred here tonight.'

'Please, sir!' Timid though I was, I felt it important to intervene.

'Not now, Flottie. Watson, can I ask you to take the news at once to Neale at Brown's Hotel? Warn him that he is likely to be the target of a similar attempt. And make haste. The man's life is at stake.'

'Of course, Holmes. I'll go at once.' He indicated the heavy wooden chest he had brought with him. 'Shall I…?'

'I will have one of Gregory's men return it to Baker Street. Your enthusiasm is admirable but I hardly think this it is appropriate to conduct experiments at a moment such as this.'

'Please, sir…!' I tried again.

'Yes, indeed,' Holmes smiled benevolently. 'You must go with Watson, my girl. Now, if you will all excuse me, I always prefer to analyse the data while it is still fresh. I shall return to Baker Street on foot and give these matters my careful consideration.'

The next twenty minutes or so passed in a blur; a last fleeting look at the murder scene before the body was moved, a hasty passage through the soft corridors to the hotel lobby, some last rushed words with Gregory and then a fretting wait while a cab was sought. It was not until Dr Watson and I were in motion, a cabbie rushing us dazedly through the night, that I had another chance to express my concerns.

'Dr Watson, sir, Mrs Hudson says that Mr Moran lives in New Buildings in Portman Street. If it is very urgent to contact him...' Now that we were safely on our way and there was a moment to relax a little I noticed that the doctor's head had begun to nod and his breathing was becoming heavy.

'Dr Watson?'

'Er, what?' He looked slightly alarmed. 'Oh, yes. Mrs Hudson. Of course.' He took my hand and patted it fondly. 'Mrs Hudson is a very fine woman, Flottie. Must have misunderstood. Chap told me himself he didn't have an address.'

And with that he settled his head back and shut his eyes. He still held my hand and now he gave it another pat.

'I knew a girl like you once, Flotsam. Out in India. Long time ago. Eighteen, she was. Used to wear her hair up like you did tonight. Vicar's daughter. Beautiful when she laughed. Died of a fever in Peshawar in '82. Still think of her though. Dashed shame. Such a dashed shame...'

The doctor's head drooped again and somehow, for all the danger to Mr Moran, it seemed wrong to bring him back to the rushing, turbulent present.

–

Our arrival found Brown's in a state of genteel repose. Although lights still burned on the ground floor only the to-and-fro of the doorman, like the breathing of a gentle sleeper, gave any indication of life. His progress was interrupted by our headlong arrival, and he leapt to attention as the cab pulled up, then held open the door with a smart salute while Dr Watson handed me down. Inside, the profusion of red and gold was oddly reminiscent of the hotel we had just left, but here there was none of the unwonted activity we had found in Knightsbridge. However Dr Watson struck the bell with such urgency that in a few minutes the manager himself had been roused and, accompanied by a liberal assortment of staff, was greeting us with a respectful bow.

'I have heard something of your work with Mr Sherlock Holmes, sir. If Brown's can offer any assistance…'

'It is imperative that I speak to Mr Neale at once. Please show me to his room. It is a police matter of great urgency. I would also be obliged if you would ensure that no other callers for Mr Neale are allowed past the lobby until Inspector Gregory of Scotland Yard has interviewed them.'

'Of course, sir. If you will allow me one moment…' and with another small bow he retreated to the desk where the hotel's large leather register rested.

Watson turned to me with a frown. 'Heaven send that we are in time, Flotsam. To think that only yesterday Carruthers was telling me of the threat that hung over him. He was right to be afraid, Flottie. There's devilry at work tonight.'

Over at the desk, the manager was conversing animatedly in undertones with a uniformed young man, his face troubled and his hands gesturing nervously. 'Dr Watson, sir,' he said, advancing with a nervous cough. 'It seems there is some mistake. Mr Neale checked out an hour ago, shortly after receiving Mr Holmes's message.'

'Mr Holmes's message?' For a moment Watson looked puzzled, then his expression changed and the colour began to drain from his face. 'Good God, sir! There was no message from Mr Holmes! I have been with him myself for the last hour or more. Tell me what has happened!'

The uniformed young man shuffled forward meekly, flushing as the eyes of the room fixed upon him. 'If you please, sir, someone came with a message for Mr Neale from Mr Sherlock Holmes. She was most insistent that it was delivered straightaway, despite it being so late. Said it would cost her half a crown if it wasn't and she wasn't going away till he got it. She made a right racket. I mean a great deal of noise, sir.'

'She? It was a woman?'

'Yes, sir. A flower seller, sir. Had a few flowers in her basket and one of them squashy shapeless hats. Said a gent had given her half a crown to deliver an urgent note to Mr Neale and promised her another one, to be collected from Baker Street tomorrow, if he got it before dawn.'

'Great heavens! What did she look like? Would you recognise her again?'

The young man looked concerned. 'I don't rightly know that I would, sir. She was rather ordinary, sir. Not a young woman, sir, a bit untidy, a bit shapeless, you know the sort, sir. You walk past that sort on every street corner. Normally, I'd have sent her on her way, but the note coming from Mr Holmes, sir...'

'She told you that?'

'No, sir. It was written on the note. 'From Mr Sherlock Holmes. Urgent.'

'What did you do?'

'I sent the note up, sir, then tried to move the woman on. But before she'd gone, sir, Mr Neale came running down in a right state. Breathless, he was, and eyes open really wide. "Where is she?" he shouted. He caught her up at the door and the two exchanged a few words. And that was it, sir. He came straight over and settled his bill and he was gone inside half an hour. It was all so sudden I forgot to tell him about the parcel.'

'*The parcel?*' Dr Watson and I exchanged startled looks.

'Yes, sir. A lad arrived with a parcel for Mr Neale at about nine o'clock. A tough looking type he was. Asked for the parcel to go right up, but Mr Neale had left instructions not to be disturbed so I told him it would have to wait till morning. Turned quite nasty, he did. Swore and cursed, but he wouldn't leave the parcel. Said Mr Neale wanted it urgently and that I'd just talked myself out of a job.'

'My God!' Dr Watson was badly shaken. 'Flotsam, we are too late! Their first plan failing, they hit upon another. That note was Neale's death sentence!' And with a groan of honest anguish, he sank, head in hands, into a chair of exquisitely upholstered cinnamon leather.

–

It was a weary journey home through the bitter lees of the night. The city had turned an indeterminate grey and when we reached Baker Street the rain had become a sporadic sooty sleet that would have stained all it touched had its predecessors not already done so. Even the cheerful lights still burning in our windows did little to alleviate our gloom. As we mounted the stairs in solemn silence, my body ached and I longed for sleep. But Sherlock Holmes was waiting for us at the top of the stairs, his eyes alight with restless energy.

'Well?' he demanded sharply when we reached the landing. 'What news? I expected you before this.'

'I have let you down, Holmes,' muttered Watson. 'Neale is gone, tricked from his hotel in your name and vanished into the night.'

Briefly, in terse, weary sentences, Watson told him what we had found, while I stood beside him swaying slightly, too cold to listen and too tired to despair. Holmes had become still, the vitality draining from him as he heard Watson's tale.

'They could tell us little more, Holmes. A common-looking woman and a rough-looking man. We shall find neither. Neale is surely dead.'

Before Holmes could reply, a voice cut through the darkness from the kitchen door.

'What nonsensical creatures you gentlemen are! There's a young girl dead on her feet and you two wringing your hands about things there's no changing. You should be thoroughly ashamed.' Mrs Hudson was advancing on us out of the darkness with bustling energy and the same formidable combination of nightdress and overcoat that she had sported earlier. In her hands she held a small envelope and a large blanket, and it was only after she had nudged Mr Holmes to one side and wrapped the latter tightly around my shoulders that she deigned to offer him the former.

'This arrived tonight, sir, after you had all gone out. I thought it could wait till morning, but since we're all up… Now, Flottie, into the kitchen and out of those things. Whatever these gentlemen may think, there's more folk perish from the cold than die from Oriental curses.'

And with that I was once more whisked into a kitchen where the warm orange firelight defied the encroaching dawn and the smell of cloves curled round the kitchen from a promising pot on the stove.

But my night was not quite over. As Mrs Hudson put me to bed, a part of my mind was trying to fight the rising tide of sleep.

'I found a snake,' I told her dizzily. 'It was under a footstool. The footstool was made of dark wood and pink satin.'

'You can tell me in the morning, Flotsam.'

'But we didn't warn Mr Moran, ma'am. I tried but Dr Watson fell asleep. He was dreaming of a girl with hair like mine.'

'There's nothing to worry about, Flottie.'

'But they tricked Mr Neale. He must be dead by now.'

'Don't be foolish, Flotsam. Mr Neale's alive and well and tucked up in a boarding house in St Pancras. Now you need to sleep. And if you want something to think about, think about this: tomorrow I'm arranging your first chemistry lesson.'

The Guard Watch

✝

It is perhaps an unnatural child that sleeps untroubled within hours of attending a scene of violent death, but it was fully eight o'clock before I awoke on the following morning. Even then it was not a harrowing memory of the previous night that first filled me but a panicking realisation that, in Mrs Hudson's household, to sleep beyond six on consecutive mornings was not so much a sin as an acceptance of inevitable perdition. Nevertheless, Mrs Hudson was unconcernedly washing the gentlemen's breakfast things when I emerged and she greeted me with an almost approving nod.

'For a girl not too fond of the dark, you've taken to spending a lot of time running around at the dead of night, young Flotsam.' She paused for a moment to attack a darkened pot with a sudden flurry of vigour. 'However, today we're going to get back to normal. There is work enough for ten to be done this morning, errands galore for the afternoon and tomorrow you and I are going out into society so an early night wouldn't do either of us any harm. In the meantime, get yourself some breakfast and while you eat it I want to hear every little detail about last night's goings-on.'

And so I told her everything, from the colour of the cows in the painting to the dark blue and pale blue markings on the dead snake. I was glad of my diligence because the examination proved searching.

'And where exactly was the wooden box, child?'

'Under a small table near the upturned footstool, ma'am.'

'Near the door?'

'No, ma'am, on the other side of the room. Near the bedroom.'

'Describe it to me.'

'It was made of dark wood with white inlay in a pattern like the one on the front of the Mecklenberg Hotel, all squirls and squiggles.'

'What did the gentlemen say about it?'

'Dr Watson told me he thought it was from Java, ma'am. They were all quite sure it was from those parts.'

'Hmm… You say it was only half unwrapped. Was the paper around it arranged so that it might have hidden the design of the box from the person who opened it?'

'No, ma'am. The pattern was clear to see.'

'And it was delivered when?'

'At about half past eight, ma'am. That's what Inspector Gregory told us as we were leaving. He says the boy remembers taking it up.'

'Isn't it all a bit strange, Flottie?'

I considered for a moment. 'It's all *very* strange, ma'am. But do you mean it was strange that the box had been unwrapped?'

'Strange that it was opened at all, Flottie. We are to assume that Mr Carruthers lived consumed by fear of a vengeance from overseas. We know from Dr Watson that he really was afraid, so much so that it was obvious to the most casual observer. Yet on receiving a box *that was clearly Oriental in origin*, he showed no hesitation in opening it and he took no precautions against what it might contain. Is that likely, Flottie?'

I imagined the course of events as Mrs Hudson had described them – the box arriving, Carruthers opening the paper and seeing the design, stepping back in horror.

'Perhaps he dared to open it because he wasn't alone, ma'am. Or perhaps there was a note inside the paper that reassured him.'

'But the door, Flottie.'

'Locked from the inside, ma'am. So he must have been alone. And we didn't find a note.' I ran through it all, imagining the scene again and again. 'Could it have been that he was just swept along, ma'am? I mean that he knew there was danger but opened the box just because he couldn't help himself?'

Mrs Hudson nodded slowly. 'You are very astute, Flottie. It could have happened as you say. Or it could be,' she continued after directing another energetic burst of scrubbing at one of the heavy iron pans, 'it could be that he was afraid of something else altogether.'

She finished the pan with a flourish and turned to face me. 'You did very well faced with such a terrible scene, Flottie. Tell me what happened when you left the hotel.'

I described our journey to Mayfair and repeated the story of the young man who had dealt with Mr Neale's callers. It was only as I was talking that I found myself recalling her last words to me the night before.

'But, ma'am, last night you told me where he was…'

I tailed off, suddenly aware of a fractional quiver on the edge of her lips.

'A common-looking woman indeed!' she tutted contentedly, and I found my eyes drifting to a large bunch of carnations that lay on the window sill. Mrs Hudson allowed the quiver to wriggle into the trace of a smile.

'Well, Flottie, it didn't take a master detective to see Mr Neale was in danger, so after I'd got you all out of the house I took the precaution of removing him from Brown's to somewhere a little less conspicuous. I may perhaps have dressed down a little before doing so, but there's nothing to be gained from drawing attention to yourself and, after all, Mr Holmes is hardly likely to think it is my place to interfere.'

'But what about the note?'

'Oh, just something I rushed off on the way. I needed to make sure he would see me, and people seem to find anything with Mr Holmes's name on it surprisingly persuasive. Once I had explained the danger he was in, he was only too happy to go with me. A distant cousin of mine runs a guest house near St Pancras so I left him there. Although he agreed to avoid all mention of me, I'm afraid he would insist on writing to Mr Holmes.'

'Was that wrong, ma'am?'

'He would do better to disappear completely, Flottie. As it is, I fear we'll have our work cut out to look after him.'

'On the contrary, Mrs Hudson, you look after me superbly,' interrupted a voice from the kitchen doorway. The door had been ajar and now Mr Holmes's head appeared there, his sharp features contrasting with the curve of the pipe that he flourished near his chin. 'Indeed, I was commenting to Watson only the other day how fortunate we have been in securing your services. And your actions last night were further proof of your admirable qualities.'

'Sir?' Mrs Hudson was about to start polishing the silver but she stopped what she was doing and looked round sharply, her lips slightly pursed.

'I refer of course to your quickness of thought in keeping the fires burning until our return. There are not many women, Mrs Hudson, who would have borne the disturbances of last night with such equanimity. At my previous lodgings, the landlady succumbed to hysterics whenever a murder was announced.'

He came into the kitchen and perched on the edge of the table.

'In recognition of your splendid fortitude, it is only right that I should share with you the contents of the note you took in last night. You will be relieved to know that it was from Mr Neale, who last night had the prescience to avoid his pursuers. He is currently at a rather common address in St Pancras.'

Mrs Hudson, her sleeves peeled back from her forearms, had been about to begin the daily task of polishing the big silver candelabra. But she continued to hold it unpolished above the sink while a small frown appeared between her eyebrows.

'He has sent you his address, sir?'

'Indeed, Mrs Hudson. A most sensible precaution.'

Mrs Hudson looked him directly in the eyes. 'Sir, I'm sure you will go to great lengths to ensure that information is shared wisely.'

Mr Holmes, intent on lighting his pipe, seemed oblivious to her earnestness.

'Quite so, Mrs H. I'm glad you appreciate the need to guard the information carefully. We must tell no-one. I made the same point earlier this morning when I called on Mr Moran.'

There was a terrible crash from the sink as Mrs Hudson dropped the candelabra. 'You did *what*, sir?'

'I understand your surprise, Mrs Hudson. When you retired to bed last night, I was still unaware of Mr Moran's whereabouts. However, driven to action by my concern for his safety, I left the house at once and spent the night with two uniformed officers outside the offices of the shipping company that holds his mail. Shortly after dawn, when the caretaker arrived, we conducted a search and found a note from Moran. It appears he has now found lodgings and I tracked him down to the New Buildings in Portman Street. But rest assured, Mrs Hudson, apart from Watson, Gregory and yourself, Moran is the only person aware of Neale's address.'

Mrs Hudson had abandoned the candelabra where it lay and from behind the door had taken my muffler, which she was folding and unfolding as she moved to where I was sitting, quietly ignoring my breakfast.

'Mr Neale is in great danger, sir,' she said at last.

Mr Holmes, his pipe now lit, was eyeing her with some amusement.

'Rest assured, Mrs Hudson. Between us, Watson and I will take good care of him. Today, a watch is set and a man is posted at his door. Tonight, I intend to set a little trap. The men shall be withdrawn at dusk and Watson and I shall stand watch instead, as unobtrusively as possible. To all the world it will appear that Neale is unguarded, but if our villains attempt to strike we shall be ready for them.

If they have succeeded in tracking Neale to his new address, I rather feel that tonight shall see the dramatic denouement of our little mystery.'

Mrs Hudson nodded as she wrapped the muffler round my neck. 'Just as you say, sir. I imagine you are in for an interesting evening.'

'I hope so, Mrs Hudson, I certainly hope so.' He said it rather absently, and I noticed he was looking pensive. 'That story Watson told me last night, Mrs Hudson, about Neale and the flower seller. A peculiar tale, was it not? I didn't know what to make of it at first. But now...'

'Yes, sir?' Mrs Hudson met his gaze, and the great detective shook his head.

'Oh, it is no matter, no matter at all. Now, if you will excuse me...' He paused. 'Those flowers on the window sill... Carnations, are they not? Most attractive, Mrs Hudson. They cannot fail to catch they eye. Now I really must bid you good morning...'

No sooner was he gone than Mrs Hudson turned into a veritable tornado of energy, spinning this way and that as she rushed me into my outdoor clothes, issued orders, retrieved the candelabra and pulled on her own coat, apparently all in the same many-handed movement.

'Flottie, girl, forget the housework. I need you to find Scraggs and send him here as quickly as you can. Tell him to wait for me if I'm not here when he arrives. Then deliver the note for Mr Raffles that I gave you last night and the letter for Mr Rumbelow that you'll find in the drawer of the dresser. Then go to Whitley's in Grape Alley and tell him I've sent you for rags, your size, dirtiest he's got and plenty of 'em. When you've done all that, I want you straight back here for a lie down. We've got a long night ahead of us,

Flottie, and I want you fed, rested and sharp as a dandy's parting.'

In my haste, the day seemed to spiral away from me like water down a drain. Mrs Hudson had told me to be back by two o'clock but, although I jostled old ladies and dashed out under the hooves of horses, it took me two hours to track Scraggs to a vegetable stand in Exeter Market. He was trying to charm a young woman on the adjacent fish stand but he abandoned her rather rudely on my approach. His eyes widened when I gave him Mrs Hudson's message.

'Cor blimey, Flottie! Things is bad when Mrs H gets going like this. Give us five minutes to get someone to watch the stall and I'll be right along.' And he turned to pack up his things without any attempt at further flirtation.

The other errands were quicker but it was fully half past two before I was back in Baker Street with Mr Whitley's package under my arm. Finding Mrs Hudson had gone out, I obediently did as I had been instructed and went to lie down on my box bed. I even managed to doze a little and it was five o'clock and dark outside when Mrs Hudson woke me with a lump of bread and cheese.

To my surprise, we got ready in whispers. 'Mr Holmes is out already and Dr Watson is to follow him shortly,' she explained, 'but for now he thinks we're out on an urgent visit to my sister-in-law in Whitechapel, and that's the way I want it to stay.'

'What are we going to do, ma'am?'

'I have a bad feeling about tonight, Flottie. A man's life is at risk and although it's not my place to say so, I think he'll be best served if we keep a watch of our own. But since our gentlemen may not share that view, it's best to keep it to ourselves. And to make sure they don't find out, we're going to do a little bit of dressing up.' And with that she pushed the pile of rags to me across the table.

Half an hour later, Mrs Hudson turned to me with a grimace of satisfaction.

'I don't think the gentlemen will spot us now, eh, Flottie?'

Standing in front of me was the hunched and hideous wreck of a woman, her face deformed with a horrible rash, her nose bulbous, a half-empty bottle of gin sticking out from a filthy, stinking coat. The gin that was no longer in the bottle had been doused liberally over her person so that the smell she had acquired with the coat mixed alarmingly with the stench of cheap spirit. I, in turn, had been transformed into a sadder and more piteous figure than ever Fogarty had managed to make me. Despite so many layers of woollen undergarments that I could hardly walk, I was so hung with torn and tattered remnants of clothing that I gave the impression of being cruelly exposed to the elements. A surreptitious visit to the street had produced such a layer of grime over my face and hands that I looked like dirt come alive.

Mrs Hudson leaned forward and sniffed me, then stepped back with a demented cackle.

'Flottie,' she wheezed with a gruesome bronchial gasp, 'you are truly foul. Now to St Pancras, and God help anyone who gets too close to us!'

The streets were still busy, yet sad to say we passed unnoticed through them, limping and hunched and disgusting to touch. A light fog was beginning to creep up from the gutters, turning the world grainy and indistinct. Mrs Hudson looked around and sniffed.

'I feared the fog would come on tonight, Flottie. It bodes ill for Mr Neale. If it gets bad you could throw an army of watchers around his door and still have a child evade them. But we must do what we can. When we get there, we'll watch different sides of the street. Take this for if the fog gets bad.'

She slid something cold into my palm and my fingers opened to reveal a small tin whistle.

'If you see anything strange, give a light blow on that. And keep your ears open. Scraggs and I will be doing the same. One low whistle is a sign to be on your guard. Two is the signal to meet. That way we'll find each other however bad it gets.'

'Scraggs, ma'am?'

'I've left him outside Mr Moran's house, but he's to come and find us if he sees anything unusual.'

'You think Mr Moran is in danger too then, ma'am?'

But at that moment a policeman approached eyeing us dubiously and Mrs Hudson fell into a fit of disgusting, rattling coughs. When he had passed, I had another question ready.

'What should I be looking for, ma'am?'

'Anything odd, anything you feel doesn't fit. Anybody carrying a parcel or attempting to deliver a box.'

'Sumatrans, ma'am?'

This was greeted with an even noisier bout of coughing and an alarming rolling of the eyes which seemed to signal the end of our conversation.

The street where the guest house stood was a dark, shabby affair, wider than some of its neighbours but dirty and depressing nonetheless. It ran roughly from north to south, one end leading off towards the station, the other emptying into a seedy network of similar, friendless streets. A gas light towards each end stood for progress, but by the time we arrived the fog had thickened, blurring outlines and asking questions of your eyes. One side of the street was mostly blank walls, the backs of warehouses; the other, where one or two traces of light leaked from shuttered windows, a row of blank-faced dwellings. I knew some of the doorways must conceal rundown guest houses but the fog caught at the meagre light and hid their signs. The one we sought was in the darkest part of the street, most remote from the lamps. Although ill-lit and silent, the street was near enough to the station to ensure a slow trickle of pedestrians and, as the night took hold, it was all too easy for a pair of beggars to sink into the scene and disappear from notice.

We settled to our watch. I crouched in the shadow where the wall met the pavement and used my outstretched palm as an excuse to examine the muffled faces that passed by. It grew darker. Time and people passed, equally blurred, and the cold became the only constant. Somewhere a clock struck nine. A little after that an elderly gentleman stumbled past and pressed a coin into my hand. When the clock struck ten, it remained the only such offering I had received. Nothing then until half past the hour when a woman stopped and gave me a piece of paper. She told me it was the address of somewhere where they would give me food and pray for me. But it was too dark to read the narrow print. Occasionally I heard the horrible cough of Mrs Hudson or watched her shuffle down the other side of the street, mumbling to herself.

Then just before eleven, I heard a soft low whistle to my left. Turning towards it I saw a tall figure slouching towards me. I drew into the shadow and there was just enough light to make out a man in a naval uniform, half unbuttoned, his cap pulled down over his face. He was singing drunkenly to himself in an undertone so low I couldn't make out the words. Still slurring, he changed angle abruptly and tacked past me into the fog.

'What do you think?' croaked a voice close to me and I turned to see the lopsided figure of Mrs Hudson squinting at me out of the fog.

'Oh, Mrs Hudson! You made me jump. Is that the person we've been waiting for?' I asked, signally in the direction of the departing sailor.

'I don't think so, Flottie.' She seemed amused. 'Mr Holmes is many things but I don't think he's our murderer.'

'Mr Holmes?' I tried to recall the details of the figure that had passed me.

'That's right, Flotsam. He's passed me three or four times now and although he's taken a careful look I don't think he has any suspicions. So smelling this bad might not be a bad thing after all. Look up there, Flottie.'

She pointed to the one lit window of the house we were watching. It was a first floor window without shutters, about eight or nine feet above the street, its pale yellow light standing out very faintly in the fog.

'That must be Mr Neale's room. Every time Mr Holmes passes he takes a look up at it. If anything untoward happens, Flot, keep an eye on that window. And blow your whistle for all you're worth if you think anything's going on.'

I nodded and tried not to shiver. It was going to be a very cold night. For the next hour or so, things went on unchanged. A group of gentlemen in tails, slightly drunk, walked down the middle of the street. The drunken sailor appeared from time to time and then vanished just after midnight to be replaced by a priest caped in a huge, sinister cowl. Only when he passed very close to me as I crouched low in the gutter did a glimpse of naval trouser beneath his hem serve to allay my suspicions.

Then suddenly, just before one, the fog began to thicken. The light in the house we were watching seemed to flicker and go out. The far pavement disappeared, then the street itself, then the pavement I was sitting on. Neale's window became an almost imperceptible square of yellow grey that wasn't there when you looked at it but lingered on the edge of your vision when you turned away. Instinctively I found my other senses sharpening. My ears strained for any suggestion of movement and suddenly there seemed to be lots of it, as though the anonymity of the fog had breathed a pulse back into the dying street. A pair of steady, heavy boots approached from the south end of the street and a uniformed policeman passed within two feet of where I crouched. Two minutes later he passed in the other direction. Inspector Gregory wants to be certain, I thought.

The next footsteps to approach, no more than a minute after the appearance of the policeman, were hesitant and hard to follow, as if someone were moving forward only to stop, rethink, retreat a few yards and then continue forward. I drew back into a doorway, afraid the approaching feet would stumble over me, and for an instant in the swirling fog I glimpsed the features of Dr Watson, his collar up against the cold, looking desperately around him as though baffled as to how to find his friend. As he passed slowly away from me, the silence closed again. The fog smothered time with a damp hand and it became hard to guess the hour. The flow of pedestrians dried up. The policeman, Watson and the disguised Mr Holmes somehow contrived to avoid each other as if in some complicated *danse macabre*.

Just when I thought the moment must come when all three would coincide by chance on the same spot, the heavy silence of the fog was pierced by two urgent blasts of a whistle. The effect was dramatic. It was as if everyone in the street had stopped to hold their breath. Then just as I realised I should be moving towards the signal, another whistle sounded twice no more than two yards to my right. I paused, confused, and a figure leaned out of the fog and touched my arm.

'Flottie!' it whispered. 'This way, quickly!'

Mrs Hudson took my arm and tugged me urgently to the other side of the street, into a doorway I thought must be Mr Neale's guest house. I soon understood her reasoning. The second signal had produced the opposite effect to the first. After a fractional pause, footsteps began to converge from three sides towards the place where I had stood. It was only the confusion of the fog that prevented a collision, for once the sound had died away it became increasingly difficult to be certain where it had come from. The pair of heavy boots passed us moving southwards at speed. A second pair, lighter and quieter, set off in pursuit of them. A third set of footsteps, still hesitant, passed in the other direction. 'Holmes?' a small voice wondered in a whisper. 'Holmes? Is that you?'

No sooner had the doctor passed than I became aware of a new set of footsteps edging slowly towards us along the wall. Mrs Hudson pulled me hastily back into the doorway. Our faces now were no more than two inches apart and I could see her straining to listen. Below the sound of his footsteps, the approaching figure was humming ever so softly, and I saw Mrs Hudson's face relax.

'Friend, not foe,' she whispered to me. The shuffling footsteps stopped for a moment and then came forward with new certainty. When they reached the part of the pavement adjacent to our recess, Mrs Hudson shot out a hand and hauled in the pale figure of Scraggs.

'Phew, Mrs Hudson,' he whispered, 'it's a proper pea-souper and no mistake. You could march a brass band down here and lose 'em before they got half way.' He scrambled onto the step close to us so that our faces were almost touching.

'What's up, Scraggs?'

'Moran's gone, ma'am. He went out just after midnight. The lights had all gone out by then and I was just thinking nothing was happening when I caught a glimpse of him slipping out the main door. I followed him up to Maryle-bone but then the fog came on and he disappeared into it, so I came runnin' on here. Except the fog's so thick I ran past this street two or three times without seeing it, which is why I took so long.'

I could hear Mrs Hudson taking a long, slow breath.

'Moran's out in this fog, is he? And Mr Holmes's trap gone all awry because no-one can see their fingers in front of their noses. There'll be murder done tonight if we're not careful.'

She scratched softly on the door we were leaning against and to my surprise it opened a fraction. Standing up, Mrs Hudson whispered something into the darkness and the door opened a little wider, enough for Mrs Hudson to guide Scraggs through the gap. Then it closed silently behind him and we were left alone. My teeth had just begun to chatter when the policeman's heavy boots passed us heading north, towards the station. Close behind stole the lighter, softer footfalls. Not long afterwards Watson's hesitant footsteps passed us heading south. I leaned against Mrs Hudson and she put an arm around me.

'Cheer up, Flottie,' she whispered, 'at times like this Hudson always used to say...'

But before she could finish, she was brought to a halt by the heart-stopping sound of a human scream, swelling into the night with the serrated agony of terror. While it still hung jagged in the air, we were both up and running, cutting through the fog towards the station end of the road. No sooner had the scream stopped than it was followed by the sound of smashing glass, once, twice and again. We pressed forward but without sound there was no direction and within a few strides we had to stop to listen. At that moment, a few yards to our right, there erupted the sound of two men struggling. A punch landed with a hefty thud, then a cry and the sound of heavy bodies grappling. From the heart of the melee, a frantic voice yelled, 'Let go, man! There's a murder taking place!' while another, panting, gasped, 'Stop! Police!'

Miraculously, as though controlled by a higher power, the fog chose that moment to lift a little and we were confronted by the sight of Mr Holmes desperately trying to evade the grip of a burly constable who, as we watched, succeeded in pulling open the priestly cloak to reveal the naval costume beneath.

'You're no clergyman, Jack!' he grunted just as Mr Holmes, yielding to frustration, launched a straight left to his jaw. With an oath the policeman lurched backwards and the two of them rolled into the dark of an archway. I was aware of Mrs Hudson's grip on my arm tensing as she began to turn.

'It's a trick, Flottie! He's lured us all down here with that cry!' She let go of my arm and set off at speed the way we had come. I began to follow but ten yards on there was a sickening crump as two more solid bodies collided. The fog was still lifting and despite the dark I could make out two familiar figures wrapped in each other's arms.

'Dr Watson!' I heard Mrs Hudson exclaim.

'What? Who? What?' replied Watson, staring intently into the raddled, warty face that confronted him. Then his jaw sagged with astonishment and his eyes filled with recognition. 'Good Lord,' he exclaimed. 'Is that *really* you, Holmes? Bravo! Magnificent! I should never have guessed in a thousand years!'

Mrs Hudson grasped the initiative with commendable aplomb. 'Quickly, Watson,' she replied, dropping her voice a couple of octaves and signalling behind her to where the sounds of struggle were now continuing amid a chorus of police whistles. 'There's a policeman needs your help! Go quickly!' And she was off again, moving rapidly towards the guest house with me at her heels while Watson headed the other way with his stick raised purposefully and his moustache bristling with anticipation.

We sped on but as we reached the guest house another noise brought us to a halt. We heard breaking glass and from somewhere above us a startled cry. Looking up into the fog I was just in time to see a dark figure dropping to the pavement as if from nowhere. I let out a shout and the figure hesitated, trying to place the direction of my voice.

Then it was off, gliding like a dark spirit along the wall and into the night.

'There, Mrs Hudson! There!' I cried, waving my arms at the escaping figure, but she was groping intently along the fog-clad wall. Above us, a square of light marked the position of Neale's window. Mrs Hudson's hand closed on something.

'A drainpipe, Flottie!' Then turning upwards, she gave a booming shout of 'Scraggs!'

Only moments before such a shout would have attracted a great deal of attention but behind us, down the street, Mr Holmes's battle with the law was continuing. Renewed whistles and a cacophony of shouts and groans suggested that Dr Watson had now joined the struggle.

'Scraggs!' Mrs Hudson cried again and moving sharply to her right began to beat on the door. It seemed to open to her touch and I glimpsed a white-faced woman behind it. 'Upstairs!' she cried, gesturing frantically. 'Murder!'

And that's what it sounded like. As we leapt up the narrow stairs we could hear muffled sobs of fear from the floor above and then a crashing blow and the sound of splintering wood. Another blow followed before we burst through the door at the top of the stairs, Mrs Hudson first, her gin bottle raised to strike; behind her, panting, I was ready to throw myself into any fray.

It was a strange sight that greeted us. By the light of a greasy candle we saw a man huddled in one corner of the room, his cheek pressed to the wall and his eyes shut, whimpering to himself. In the middle of the room, brandishing a fire shovel, stood Scraggs, pale but triumphant. As we watched he raised the shovel above his head, stepped towards the window and brought it crashing down onto a low chest of drawers.

'Got it, Mrs H!' he cried, stepping back. Reaching his shoulder and following his gaze, I saw ghastly and distorted in the candlelight the hideous remains of a giant spider, its furred legs still twitching against the broken wood.

A Lesson

✝

It was a night that seemed to know no dawn. The fog turned slowly from black to grey without relinquishing its grip and the waking traffic trudged muted through an opaque half light. I was sleeping by the kitchen range when Mrs Hudson finally returned home. The process of calming Mr Neale had proved a lengthy one but with the assistance of Scraggs we had succeeded in bundling him out of the guest house before Gregory's men thought to detach themselves from the brawl outside. After some minutes of creeping through the fog, Scraggs had succeeded in conjuring up a cab and, while Mr Neale slept, we rolled in empty silence back to Baker Street. There Scraggs had left us and, after placing me by the fire, Mrs Hudson had disappeared into the night with the sleeping Neale.

Her return roused me and I made a sleepy effort to help her out of her things. The stinking coat had gone, replaced by a gentleman's cashmere overcoat.

'Mr Rumbelow's,' she explained. 'I could think of nowhere else to take him where he would be safe. There is no fortress so impregnable as an English solicitor's respectability. If there is one place in the Empire where you can be sure nothing untoward will occur, it must be at

Rumbelow's. Although I had warned him in my note this afternoon that some such action might be necessary, he was a little shaken by the hour of our arrival. Nevertheless, for a little while at least Mr Neale is as safe as the Bank of England.' She produced a sealed note from one of the coat pockets and placed it on the table. 'Between us we persuaded him to write this. It is a note for Mr Holmes from Mr Neale assuring him of his safety and telling him that he intends to lie low for a spell.'

'But Mrs Hudson, I can't make it all fit together. I don't really understand what we saw last night. Someone managed to elude us all and get as far as Mr Neale's window. But why did he stop there? There must be far surer ways of killing someone than by throwing a *spider* into the room.'

'And what do your instincts tell you, Flottie?'

'There is something *too* strange going on. Why not try to make sure of finishing off Neale there and then?'

'Well, Flottie, sometimes you can judge people best by what they don't do. I'm already confident I could tell you the name of Carruthers's murderer but wouldn't for the life of me be able to prove it. So for now, let's sleep. Tomorrow we set to work finding the evidence. And on top of that, Rupert Spencer is expecting you for a chemistry lesson.'

–

And so the fires were allowed to burn down and I slept. I stirred only once, when Dr Watson and Mr Holmes were returned to their lodgings by a chastened Gregory, and the grey morning had become an indistinct afternoon before Mrs Hudson woke me.

'Come on, Flottie, let's get you dressed.' As if in a dream, still heavy with sleep, I stood while Mrs Hudson recreated the neat young lady who had accompanied Dr Watson to Knightsbridge. My hair was neatly piled and pinned and another simple dress was produced. Again I found myself standing taller and straighter. I felt quite different. 'Is this really who I am?' I wondered. 'Or am I really the girl in rags taking coins from strangers?' The kitchen was warm and the muffled light that filtered through the fog made it all peculiarly unreal. Mrs Hudson paused with a hand on my shoulder and looked me up and down.

'You're ready, Flottie.' And handing me a dainty bag into which she had packed the two items intended for scientific examination, she led me out of the house.

Outside, the fog seemed to be turning to ice and the cold began to banish my sleepiness. As I began to revive, a little spurt of excitement surged through me. At that moment, in the yellow, choking air, with untold dangers at large all around me, life seemed unbelievably wonderful. I could walk tall with my head held up. I was on my way to a big house carrying crucial samples for analysis. I was going to watch and learn. And we were going to solve the mystery that Mr Moran had placed before us. I might pass for a young governess in these clothes, I thought; but the truth was far more exciting. What would the hunched passers-by say if they knew that my plain little bag contained a silver dagger and a dead spider bigger than my hand?

We crossed Bloomsbury Square, coughing in the fog, and as I went to pass to the rear of the big houses, Mrs Hudson stopped me.

'The front door on this occasion, Flottie,' she said firmly, and after a short wait the door was opened by a butler of almost unimaginable grooming. 'Miss Flotsam to see Miss Peters,' she announced haughtily, and we were ushered into a drawing room bigger than all our rooms in Baker Street rolled together. 'I'm not waiting, Reynolds,' she informed him. 'I was just escorting Miss Flotsam.'

'Very good, Mrs Hudson,' he replied with a sternly patrician bow of his head, then suddenly dropping his voice he added, 'If you were to call at the rear of the building in two minutes' time, Mrs Hudson, there is an exceedingly fine Tokay to be sampled that I think would interest you greatly.' And so with a mutual nod they parted company and I was left rather alone in the mirrored drawing room.

The young woman who burst in upon me a minute later was easily the prettiest I had ever seen. She was, I thought, barely nineteen, but she was such a slim, sprightly, vital vision in lace that it was absurdly hard to be sure.

'I'm Miss Peters,' she began, 'but you must call me Hetty. Everybody else does. I shall call you Flottie because that's what Mrs Hudson says everyone calls you.' She held out a tiny hand. 'Mrs Hudson says that I am to be your companion while you study with Rupert. Of course, not being very bright I've always thought what Rupert does in his laboratory most terribly dull. But when Mrs Hudson said someone must be found to accompany you, I realised it would mean spending simply *hours* with Rupert, so of course I leapt at the idea. Mrs H says you are terribly clever so you mustn't mind me. I shall be quite happy to sit and look at Rupert while you two do experiments and things. Of course, I know he will ignore me because he always does, but I like to think that eventually he will just give up and marry me to make me go away. If you come through here I'll show you to his laboratory. A horrible smelly place, though of course I know I must pretend to be frightfully interested in it...'

And in this blizzard of words, I was carried off to my first ever science lesson and to a world of new knowledge that in time would change my life.

Although it was hard at times to concentrate with Miss Peters fluttering beautifully by my side, I think it is fair to say that my first lesson did not disappoint. There beneath the microscope was a world I had never seen before, a whole continent of knowledge that I had never been shown. I saw the wing of an insect transformed into ridged gossamer, the fabric of a leaf into a mountainous landscape and a drop of my own blood into something foreign, rich and strange. While I looked at these and other wonders, Mr Spencer studied the items I had brought him. Miss Peters gave a little scream when Mr Moran's dagger was produced and threatened to swoon when the body of the spider was revealed, rendered all the more ghastly by the violent crushing wrought on it by Scraggs's shovel. Mr Spencer, ignoring her completely, looked at the spider and then at me.

'Remind me how this fits into your mystery, Miss Flotsam.'

I told him briefly about the watch at Neale's guest house, the figure on the drainpipe, the smashed window and the release of the spider into the dimly lit room.

'And this Neale is one of those said to be under the Sumatran curse?'

'Yes, Mr Spencer.'

'And are you and Mrs Hudson aware of the significance of this creature?'

'I think it's simply frightful!' put in Miss Peters. 'Of course I've adored Mrs Hudson ever since I was able to tie a bow in my hair, but I think it is most wrong of her to involve you in such gruesome activities, Flottie.'

I wondered for a moment what Miss Peters would say if she were to see me in the garments I had worn the previous evening but I put the thought aside and concentrated on the question.

'It's a very unusual murder weapon,' I replied.

'I feel it may be more significant than that. I shall make some inquiries tomorrow. Gregory has been persuaded to hand over the remains of the snake that killed Carruthers; when you next call, I hope I shall have some interesting things to report. Now, look at this. I have prepared two slides, one from the surface of the dagger you brought, the other from my silver paperknife. The first is the paperknife.'

I looked and saw a combination of different shapes, some dark and angular, others round and translucent.

'The solution contains everything I could lift from the surface of the knife. Dust, dirt, a little bit of grease. Now, look at a similar slide from Moran's dagger.'

The second slide seemed to contain nothing at all.

'You see, Moran's dagger is quite remarkably clean, almost as if it had never been used.'

'According to Mr Moran, they dip the knives in animal blood when they make the curse, sir.'

'There's no trace of that here. Of course, it may very well have been thoroughly cleaned since, but the thing is you would expect to see traces of *something*. This knife could be brand new.'

But by now my head was beginning to ache from the bombardment of new ideas and Mr Spencer was sensitive enough to my state to bring the lesson to a close. Miss

Peters sighed loudly as she accompanied me back through the house.

'Two hours, Flottie! I had no idea it would go on so long. But Rupert looks so wonderfully handsome when he's concentrating that I can't imagine why I never thought of doing this before. Now you must come back very soon for another lesson because it's good for Rupert to meet someone interested in the things that interest him. When he's with his friends from the club, he pretends to be interested in nothing but horseracing and cards. I'm sure it bores him enormously. That is why he will make such a *wonderful* husband; it will be so simple to dissuade him from going out. I shall make sure that I always have some disgusting creepy-crawlies around my person to attract his interest.' She burbled happily until we arrived in the hallway. 'Now I shall get Reynolds to hail you a cab.'

'Oh, no, Miss Peters, I should much prefer to walk. I pretty much always do.'

'Hetty, Flottie. You must call me Hetty.' She peered out of the window and eyed the fog dubiously. 'Well, if you really prefer...'

I assured her that I did and with many promises of a swift return, I stepped again into the glowering fog.

It was getting dark now and for a second night the city was being choked into a foggy paralysis. The streets were almost empty and suddenly Baker Street seemed a long way off, the safety of Mr Spencer's house distractingly close. But Mrs Hudson was expecting me back and I stepped out into the gloom and scurried forward across the square. In my haste, I became unsure of which street I needed to take and, choosing the first, I began to wonder if perhaps it shouldn't have been the second. I slowed a little and peered at the houses I was passing. Were they familiar? If this was the wrong street, the correct one must be parallel. If I took a right turn I should join it. Taking the next turn to appear on my right hand side, I skipped forward again; the correct road should be just a couple of dozen yards away... But after fully sixty or seventy paces the road appeared to be narrowing into an alley. There was no sight or sound to suggest it might be leading to a thoroughfare and I began to suspect that perhaps my original road had been correct after all. I retraced my steps cautiously but within a few paces the creeping fog revealed a fork in the road ahead. Which of the two had I come down? It was hard to tell. The fog imposed an eerie quiet. It was getting darker.

Choosing the right-hand fork, I ploughed on, my feet governed now more by a fear of stillness than by any certainty of direction. If anything, I seemed to be zigzagging, following left turn with right as the opportunity presented itself. Taking a sudden decision, I made myself stop. 'Keep calm,' I whispered, and the confidence born out of my new learning seemed to inspire me. I thought of where I had come from, of Mr Spencer's sure fingers on the microscope, his air of total confidence. It suddenly seemed a silly thing to get lost in a fog. I had stepped out of a calm, scientific world and I would not disgrace it. I would keep calm, would think my way forward and would absolutely not panic.

I proceeded with more care, and miraculously it seemed to work. I came to a corner where the metal name plate was not overlaid with soot and I recognised it as a quiet backstreet not far from Baker Street and home. I stood for a moment and attempted to get my bearings. I had just calculated that a left turn was needed when I heard the footsteps. Perhaps part of my mind had been aware of them before, clipping along somewhere behind me. But now as I took a pace forward and heard them start up again I realised that they had stopped when I had stopped. I took another three steps then paused. Three crisp footsteps sounded in the fog and then no more.

'Who's there?' I asked, turning to face the invisible, but my voice trembled a little in the heavy air and there was no reply. I began to back away very softly, almost silently. The fog was not so thick as on the previous night and despite the dark I could see that for five, six, seven yards, there was no-one. Perhaps now was the time to turn and run…

'No you don't, my girl!' snarled a voice from behind me and a dark figure stepped from the shadow. A hand caught my wrist and I was pulled hard into its arms. 'Nice to see you again, Flotsam,' spat Smale's voice, full of contempt. He twisted my arm behind my back and pushed my wrist up to my shoulder blades while his other arm wrapped round my neck so the crook of his elbow was at my throat and my cheek was pulled back next to his. As I hung there, pinned to him like a limed bird to a branch, the footsteps that had followed me moved slowly forward out of the darkness until Fogarty was revealed, sleek in dress clothes, his shoes and top hat shining in the traces of light that penetrated the fog.

'Flotsam,' he purred, stepping to within inches of me so that my face, angled back by Smale, looked straight into his. 'I had been expecting to hear from you. Your failure to report is most remiss.' He produced a silver case from inside his coat and very deliberately lit a cigarette. The lighted tip glowed brightly as he smoked, so close that I could feel the heat of the burning tobacco on my cheek.

'Perhaps these fine clothes of yours have put your brother out of your mind. I congratulate Mrs Hudson on the transformation she has achieved in you. Perhaps now that she is pimping you to the aristocracy, you wish to leave behind your blood ties?'

There was something in his tone that suddenly stilled my fear and replaced it with anger – flaming, violent anger at him and at his intrusion into a world that deserved better than him. The blood was rushing to my head and I began to pull and struggle in Smale's grasp.

'That isn't my brother, you liar! I never thought it was! I'd already checked for myself. My brother's dead!'

There was an awful moment of stillness. The enormity of the lie I had just told hung above me in the fog, and my struggles stopped as I raced to think of its implications. In my anger I had told Fogarty the last thing he should have heard and in doing so I had condemned the boy in his cellar to a dreadful fate. Until now, whatever the truth, he had a value to Fogarty. Now he was worthless. But much, much worse than this was a fear that made me suddenly cold – that now, thinking he had nothing to gain, Fogarty might tell me the truth.

He was watching me very closely, his eyes fixed intently on my face, weighing up the possibility of truth against the expectation of falsehood. Finally, after another draw at his cigarette, he nodded.

'I can see no reason for you to bluff, Flotsam, so let us be honest with each other. It is as you say. I'm not a complete liar, however. I did in fact check the records as I told you. I realised a real brother would be a great deal more valuable to me than an impostor. You can imagine my frustration when the registers clearly showed the child you arrived with all those years ago was already dead in your arms. Luckily for me, you seemed unaware of this fact, so I was able to revive him for another short – and I fear short-lived – cameo.'

He paused for another taste of his cigarette, his eyes still on mine. But I was no longer looking at him. A stillness had filled me to the very centre and I could see nothing but the night. So this was it. This was how it felt. I had feared this news all my life, more than I'd feared the night or the fog. Feared what I would feel when the truth was inescapable. Now I understood the emptiness I always felt when I thought of him and the detachment in me even as I felt for the pain of Fogarty's stand-in. And Fogarty, who had once promised to find him, had been as good as his word.

Sensing the change in me, Smale released his grip on me and for a moment I almost fell. Instead I balanced unsteadily between them in the darkness, my head hanging, waiting to be left alone.

'Tch, I see perhaps that was news to you after all. How very foolish of me to discard a useful card before it needed to be played.' Suddenly Fogarty's tone grew harsh and, reaching out, he tilted my head upwards to meet his gaze.

'What is Sherlock Holmes doing about Moran?' he demanded. 'What is he planning?'

'I don't know.' My voice was flat.

He jerked my chin higher. 'That's not good enough, Flotsam. There are urchins posted, watching Moran's house night and day. Why are they there?'

'I don't know. I didn't know they were there.'

Another jerk upwards and now his other hand was squeezing the back of my neck. 'Are they there to protect him? Or to watch him? What is Holmes thinking? When is he going to act?'

'I don't know what he's thinking! He's lost Mr Neale and he set a trap that went wrong and he may not know anything for all I know!'

The grip on my neck tightened. 'Don't insult me, Flotsam! He must be close to the truth. But as I would expect he seems to be playing a deep game.' Then, to himself rather than to me, 'Very well, if he will not act, I shall. This uncertainty does not suit my plans.'

He seemed to be about to turn away, but paused and took my chin between his thumb and fingers. He'd removed his glove and his fingers were cold as they pressed into my face.

'One last point. The brother I invented for you is worthless to me now. But you are a feeling girl and even without blood ties you may not want his final agony on your conscience. He shall be dead in a week, Flotsam. Without care he can hardly last longer. Before then, if you bring me clear information about Holmes's plans, you may take him away with you. I daresay some do-good doctor may be found to save him. If you don't come within a week, you should attempt to forget him forever – if you can.' He dropped his hand from my face. 'Come, Smale, let us leave her here to consider.'

I didn't look up as he turned and moved away in the direction from which he'd come but I became aware that Smale had not followed him. Lifting my head, I saw he was leaning in the shadows from which he had originally emerged. He came forward when he saw me looking and stood close in front of me in the position Fogarty had just relinquished.

'Just so you know, Flotsam, I shan't care if you don't do as he says.' Suddenly he shot his hand out behind my head and grabbed a handful of my hair. 'You see,' he hissed, 'if you fail him, you're mine. Fogarty has given you to me.' His breath stank in my face. Then he pulled his hand away with a sharp tug, bringing down the hair that Mrs Hudson had piled up a few hours before. 'Think of that, girl. 'Cos I like thinking of it. I think of it a lot. And until then I don't think you'll ever have seen the last of me!'

And with a curl of his lip, he turned and followed his master into the fog.

Smale would probably have been disappointed if he'd known how little his words affected me. For I was already too drained of feeling to fear him and now, alone in the street, I gave way to the weakness that had filled me since Fogarty had pronounced my brother dead. I sank to me knees and, too tired to care for my clothes, too empty even to cry, I let the fog creep around me like a mantle. Time and place seemed to have ebbed away when I heard footsteps approaching. Unsteadily I rose to my feet and a muffled male voice called, 'Flottie?'

The night must have filled my brain. For a moment my mind turned to the house I had come from. 'Mr Spencer?' I breathed.

Then the voice called again, followed by the form and face of someone achingly familiar, the form and face of Scraggs.

'Crikey, Flot! I lost you in the fog.' He paused, anxious, trying to read the damage in my tear-stained face. 'What have them sods done to you?'

'Scraggs!' I whispered, and for the second time in a week I was to be found in a night-filled street, encircled by fog, wrapped in a tender embrace.

The Night Thief

✝

Dear reader, if having read this far you are growing weary of my endless tales of fog, if you find yourself longing for a little clear air and a glimpse of the stars by night, then you can be no more weary, feel no greater longing, than that loose conglomeration known as Londoners when yet another day emerged stillborn, wrapped in a shroud of preternatural dusk. The gathering in Baker Street after breakfast could as easily have been nocturnal as matutinal so closely did the dark grey air press at the windows from the outside, so brightly did the lamps burn and the fires blaze within.

Mr Holmes and Dr Watson had been abroad making investigations all the previous day and this morning our rooms radiated a sense of optimism and cheerful companionship. At eight in the morning Holmes had taken up position by the kitchen range and had remained there through the morning, lavishly dressing-gowned and generously supplied with tobacco, as if the answers he sought were to be found through careful study of our glowing coals. For all his gaunt profile, it was a friendly silence – one that seemed to welcome the domestic currents that eddied around it. By the time the clock struck ten, even the activity of the kitchen had given way to a rare tranquillity. Opposite Mr Holmes, on the other side of the hearth, I was at work with needle and thread while behind us Mrs Hudson was folding laundry with intense concentration. It was thus that Dr Watson found us, his ablutions complete and his affable nature intent on seeking out company.

'Not intruding am I, Mrs Hudson?' he wondered from the door.

'Not at all, Dr Watson. Crowd yourself in by the fire and make yourself comfortable.'

'Indeed, Watson,' added Holmes, 'but since you are about to return to the study to retrieve something from the mantelpiece, may I trouble you to also fetch the telegram that I left behind the clock?'

'Certainly, Holmes! But how...?'

'Childishly simple, my dear Watson. I can see from the traces of tobacco still attached to your waistcoat that you have very recently filled your pipe. You have not brought it with you, so I deduce that you have not yet lit it, for you are not the sort of man to abandon a good pipe once it is lit. That being the case, past observation leads me to suppose that you have left it, already filled, beside the clock on the mantelpiece. As, in fact, you do most mornings.'

'Excellent, Holmes!' returned Watson reliably, and on returning from his errand he pulled up the kitchen stool and nestled between us by the fire.

'Since we are all here,' began Holmes, 'this would perhaps be a good time for us to summarise the position we have reached. I am ashamed to admit that I have made mistakes over the last few days. I have been led astray by my own assumptions. However, I feel I now make progress.' He nodded approvingly to himself. 'Unfortunately, in sharing my thoughts with Gregory, I fear I have provoked one of those rare flashes of imaginative thinking that are so dangerous when stemming from Scotland Yard. He believes the case is all but solved.'

'I say, Holmes!' Watson stirred with interest and I paused my needle. But Mrs Hudson, after a brief glance up, continued to fold placidly.

'Quite,' the great detective continued. He had settled comfortably into his seat and held his pipe in front of him. 'My first mistake in all this was eagerness to believe my own preliminary observations about Moran. Based only on his note, I made a number of statements to you about his age and situation. All of them were true except one. Unfortunately, observation of the man himself seemed only to support my initial analysis. The evidence of fever, the recent return from the tropics, the interest in fauna... I predicted all these correctly. But I had not reckoned on deliberate deceit on his part.'

Again I ventured a look at Mrs Hudson to see if she betrayed any sign of triumph that her own thinking was proved correct. But her face was impassive and had it not been that the pile of folded linen seemed to grow no larger I might have thought her unaware of what was being said.

'It was Mrs Hudson who put me on to the right track,' Holmes continued, with an acknowledging nod in her direction. 'When you were preparing to visit Neale at Brown's Hotel, Watson, Mrs Hudson happened to remark that it was one of our better hotels. A throw-away remark perhaps, but according to Moran's account, supported by those of his colleagues, the three had escaped to these shores penniless. *Yet both Neale and Carruthers could now afford to stay in the best hotels.* Moran too, when I traced him to his current lodgings, had clearly secured a reputable address.' Holmes shook his head. 'You see, his note to us was little more than a lie.'

Watson frowned.

'But, Holmes, Moran never actually stated in his note that he was in straightened circumstances.'

'That's true, Watson. Yet that writing paper was as much a deliberate falsehood as if Moran had told us he had come from the moon. It was all the more subtle for being unspoken. And I was, for a time, misled.'

'But Holmes, why should he wish to mislead us in that way?'

'Precisely the question I asked myself. We know from independent verification that the main facts of Moran's story are true – the mysterious deaths, the precipitous abandonment of their ventures – and there is no doubting from your own observations that his colleagues lived in fear. Yet if they really arrived penniless, as they claim, they seem to have commanded a respectable fortune within a relatively short time of their return. Why should this be a fact that Moran sought to conceal?'

'Goodness, Holmes!' Watson appeared suddenly enlightened. 'Were they evading the income tax?'

Mr Holmes permitted himself a smile. 'I hardly think that was their main concern, Watson. No, I am forced to conclude that their sudden flight and their concealed wealth are in some way linked.'

'These are deep waters, Holmes. I confess I cannot see…'

'Think, Watson! What happened in Sumatra immediately before our clients' flight?'

'A series of mysterious deaths, Holmes.'

'Aha! You are getting very warm, Watson. For some years their trading company has struggled to survive. Suddenly a series of inexplicable deaths take place and in no time at all Moran and his friends have the wherewithal to live extremely comfortably in London.'

Watson was alight with excitement and even Mrs Hudson seemed to be favouring Mr Holmes with an approving glance.

'But, Holmes,' Watson's mind was clearly thinking aloud, 'the victims were mostly natives and such like. None of them were rich. How do you explain it?'

Holmes shook his head calmly. 'All in good time, my friend. Meanwhile, as I mentioned, Gregory has found a theory of his own. Something to do with Chinese gangs. He reasons that there was a sizable Chinese presence in Port Mary. Had Moran and his friends crossed them in some way, perhaps in pursuit of some illegal venture, they may well have feared violent retribution, and perhaps it was this fear that led them to escape to London.

'But escape would prove harder than they thought. It might have become apparent to them that even in London they were not safe from those they had crossed. Finding themselves threatened, in their fear they turned to us.'

Watson was following intently. Mrs Hudson was arranging the folded laundry by colour.

'Of course, Holmes! And if they had been engaged in something disreputable, they wouldn't be able to tell us the truth, would they? Not without confessing their own murky activities.'

'Indeed, my friend. That is the beauty of Gregory's theory. Moran and his friends need help but they cannot explain why without raising awkward questions about their own behaviour. So they seize upon the native superstitions and use them to camouflage the truth.'

Holmes put down his pipe and stretched his arms above his head.

'The upshot of all this theorising is that Gregory has posted men outside Moran's rooms with orders to pay particular attention to any Chinaman seen passing the building. And yet for all Gregory's elaborations I cannot think this is the best advice, so I have promised Moran that you will drop in on him from time to time to check that everything is in order.'

Dr Watson nodded enthusiastically, but before he could reply Mrs Hudson had cleared her throat.

'If you will excuse us, gentlemen, seeing as you two are so cosy here, perhaps you will have no objection to Flotsam and I dusting the study?' And with some impressive bustling, she manoeuvred both myself and a large pile of dusters into the hall.

'Mrs Hudson, ma'am,' I asked as soon as the door was shut behind us, 'can all that be true? About the Chinese, I mean?'

'I think not, Flottie. Though Mr Holmes is certainly asking the right questions. All that sudden wealth, Flottie. How do we explain it? And why *are* we being told such improbable tales?'

But before I could answer, Mrs Hudson had opened the door to the study and revealed, to our joint astonishment, a tall, slim gentleman lounging casually by the fire. Seeing us enter he rose to his feet with languorous grace and a smile of semi-concealed amusement.

'Ah, Mrs Hudson!' he smiled. 'I'm slightly disappointed it is you, even though it is of course you I have come to see. Is old Sherlock in?' He was a darkly good looking man of about thirty and beneath clothes cut to the height of fashion he moved with the casual ease of an athlete.

'Mr Holmes is in the kitchen, Mr Raffles. I see you have let yourself in.'

'In the kitchen, is he? I hadn't picked him as the domestic sort. But perhaps he's looking for clues in the tea leaves or something.'

'Now, Mr Raffles, we'll have none of that. I know that you and Mr Holmes have never exactly seen eye to eye.'

'Well that's not entirely true, Mrs H.' The gentleman took a cigar from his waistcoat pocket and tapped it against the mantelpiece with studied care. 'I know he thinks I'm a frivolous ne'er-do-well, but the truth is we got on well enough once upon a time, until I ran him out at Lord's one summer in a match against the Gentlemen of Kent. I did it to win a bet of course, but Sherlock couldn't see the funny side. Lost his temper completely, resigned from the MCC and never played cricket again. Now he makes out he has no time for sporting pursuits. Damn shame, really. He could play the leg glance better than Ranji.'

'Mr Holmes is certainly a man of many talents, sir.' Mrs Hudson smoothed down her apron and allowed a glimpse of a smile to slip out from under her frown. 'It's good to see you again, Mr Raffles. It's been nearly a year. Now the two gentlemen were comfortable enough when we left them, so why don't we sit down here while you tell us what you've found out. I don't think we'll be disturbed for some time yet.'

'Of course, Mrs H. As you would expect, I've helped myself to a cigar. Not a very good one, I'm afraid, but the best I could find.' Before sitting down he leaned towards me with his hand extended. 'Mrs Hudson, you haven't yet introduced me to your charming assistant.'

She turned to me with another trace of smile. 'This is Flotsam. Flotsam, Mr Raffles. Since, like Mr Holmes, you don't read the sporting papers, you may not know that Mr Raffles has gained some small amount of fame as an amateur cricketer.'

'Oh, the very least of my talents,' he announced calmly. His handshake, although firm, was strangely delicate, rather as though his hand was weighing mine as he shook it.

'To business, Mr Raffles.' Mrs Hudson gestured me into the armchair usually occupied by Dr Watson and settled herself into the one opposite. Mr Raffles remained standing, leaning against the mantelpiece, smoking the purloined cigar with a series of long, laconic puffs.

'I received your note the day before yesterday,' he began, 'and business being a little quiet just now I thought I would act at once. It is always good to be able to return some of the many kindnesses you have shown me in the past.' Mrs Hudson replied with a small nod and Mr Raffles continued.

'Of course, there was no problem gaining entry to the place in Portman Street though the layout of New Buildings meant there was no option but to go through the front door. Moran and his dashed servant seemed to be mightily on their guard. In the end I had to wait till they'd gone to bed before slipping in.'

Mrs Hudson raised an eyebrow at him.

'Oh, it was easy enough, Mrs H, never fear. But it meant my examination was conducted in the dark, with consequences that were almost disastrous.'

I sat wide-eyed as Mr Raffles told his tale. I had imagined all sorts of ways Mr Raffles might have been helping us, but burglary had not been among them.

'If I may say so, Mrs H, my brief was rather vague. As you know, I generally have a very clear object in these sort of ventures. But I did what I could with the list of things you had asked me to look out for.'

He took another slow draw at his cigar while Mrs Hudson polished the arm of her chair idly with a duster.

'The first item on the list was easy. It was clear at a glance that there was nothing in the way of scientific equipment to be found there. I don't know what you hoped for, but it seems like a dead end. After that, it was a case of looking for papers and there were papers everywhere. However it was easy enough to find the ones he wanted to hide. There were caches of them in all the usual places – up the chimney, under the grate in the fireplace... People make these things tediously simple for the most part.'

He reached into his jacket and produced some neatly folded documents which he passed to Mrs Hudson. Beckoning to me, she began to spread them on the floor in front of the fire.

'There were only three that I felt were of any interest to you. That large one, as you can see, is precisely what you told me to look for. It's even stamped with the name of his company in the corner, and it seems to be plans for large-scale distilling equipment – stills, tubes and whatnot. I confess I was impressed by the accuracy of your prediction.'

'What they call a long shot, Mr Raffles. But it seemed to me likely that some such plans would exist somewhere.'

I studied them intently, trying to grasp their import. Stills? Did that mean whisky?

'The second document you can read at your leisure. It is a letter to Moran from someone called Carruthers. A very conciliatory letter. I thought you would find the passage I have indicated particularly interesting.'

We both turned to the letter in question, a tightly written sheet in blue ink. Mr Raffles had made a mark in the margin next to one of the later paragraphs.

'*The business has transferred remarkably well to London,*' it read, '*where the ignorant and desperate are to be found in greater numbers even than in the tropics. I confess we are making good money and our backer is delighted.*'

'Interesting…' mused Mrs Hudson, a small frown puckering her brow and her eyebrows pulling together into one straight line.

'The last document is quite intriguing,' Mr Raffles went on. 'My first instinct was to discard it but then it struck me that it may be of significance.'

It was a telegram addressed to Moran, dated November 10th. The message was brief in the extreme.

TASK COMPLETED PENGE

'The night Carruthers died,' murmured Mrs Hudson.

'I rather thought it might be.'

'Why? Were there any further indications?'

'Only one thing. A rather disturbing incident at the end of my visit.' Mr Raffles examined the glowing tip of his cigar with exaggerated interest. 'It was, I confess, a lesson to me and a lesson I thoroughly deserved. I shall be a great deal more discriminating in future. I was making my way to the door, feeling how nicely my mission had gone, when I was struck by an intriguing wooden jewel box on a table near the door. Now I know the purpose of my venture was purely altruistic, but in a moment of weakness I allowed my curiosity to get the better of me.' He paused and took another draw on his cigar. 'Once I was visiting an impoverished maiden aunt in Dorking and, on going through her things in a fit of idle curiosity, came across the finest amber necklace I had ever beheld. The incident made an impression on me and last night it was more than I could do to resist a peek inside that jewel box. The lid came off smoothly and I was just about to reach inside when a prickling at the back of my neck made me hesitate. Instead I turned my light on the box and what I saw gave me a nasty turn. I almost cried out – and I never cry out. But blow me if there wasn't a blasted scorpion scuttling around down there. It would seem that Mr Moran has something of a *penchant* for keeping exotic animals.'

–

In a few minutes more, Mr Raffles left us. After thanking him earnestly for his efforts on our behalf, Mrs Hudson seemed anxious to be left alone to think.

'Why, Mrs H, anyone would think you were ashamed of me,' he teased.

'Now, Mr Raffles, you know I shouldn't be entertaining in Mr Holmes's study. You let yourself out the way you came and be off with you.'

'Very well, Mrs Hudson. It is true I shouldn't stay too long. I have an appointment to view some rooms above a jewellers in Bond Street. And some wretched drip I was at school with is pestering me for an interview. I can't imagine why. I don't even owe him money.'

Taking his hat and coat from a table near the door, he bowed suavely. 'My very best wishes to you both, and the best of luck with the man who keeps scorpions. The sooner people like him are locked away, the safer the world will be for good citizens like myself.'

'Well, Flottie,' said Mrs Hudson once Mr Raffles had made a mysterious exit through Dr Watson's bedroom. 'What do you think of that, eh?'

My mind was still reeling as I tried to put everything I had just learnt into some sort of order. Possibilities were jostling each other in my brain like crowds in Piccadilly Circus, and on top of it all was the debonair Mr Raffles.

'Is he... well, is he a *burglar*, ma'am?' It seemed almost disrespectful to so label such an elegant gentleman despite the evidence of the last ten minutes.

'A gentleman crook, perhaps. He is, of course, an utter disgrace in many ways, but always charming with it. And by relieving the aristocracy of their excess jewellery he creates a great deal of employment for policemen, night-watchmen and the like, while at the same time preventing a number of terrible crimes against good taste.'

'But isn't that *wrong*, ma'am?'

Mrs Hudson smiled and put an arm around my shoulder. 'You're right, Flottie, it *is* wrong. But there's all sorts of wrong in this world and, for all our efforts, you and I won't be able to root up all of it. So while the likes of Fogarty are out there on the streets it would seem better to concentrate our efforts there rather than on Mr Raffles's rather cavalier approach to the redistribution of wealth.'

There seemed to be sense in that, but it seemed to raise other questions too. With a shake of the head I decided to store them away for another time when there were fewer mysteries to grapple with.

'So what about these documents, ma'am? Did you know they were there?'

'I hardly dared hope, Flottie. Mr Moran is going to have some explaining to do before long, but even these documents don't prove anything. They only confirm what I had already suspected.'

'But the scorpion, ma'am?'

'Ah, the scorpion. It's tempting to read a great deal into that – but how strangely uninformative it really is. I predict that before very long we may be less sanguine about the scorpion.'

'But, ma'am, surely it proves that…'

Before I could finish my point, the door opened and Mr Holmes appeared brandishing the telegram he had mentioned earlier. Behind him, in the hallway, Dr Watson was hurriedly pulling on his overcoat. Seeing us standing by the fire, still armed with our pile of dusters, Mr Holmes cast an approving eye around the room.

'Very homely,' he remarked. 'What a lot you have achieved while Dr Watson and I have been idling in the kitchen. I fear we scarcely deserve you. Indeed, such was the comfort of our surroundings that it is only a moment ago that I thought to open the telegram that arrived earlier. Fortunately the consequences of this delay have not proved serious but its contents are nevertheless highly significant. It is from Mr Moran in Portman Street. He tells us that yesterday evening he received a parcel similar to the one sent to Carruthers. Luckily we had warned him of what to expect and he exercised due caution. The parcel proved to contain a scorpion, Mrs Hudson. Now what do you make of that?'

'Mr Holmes, I can honestly say that developments in Mr Moran's case have long ceased to surprise me. I can see that this news has, however, left Flottie unsure what to think.'

Mr Holmes favoured me with a reassuring nod. 'Entirely to be expected. I know the fairer sex generally have a horror of such creatures. However, we cannot linger. We are off to assure Moran that he is safe. His house is being guarded day and night. Not a soul can leave or enter without our knowing it.'

As we watched the gentlemen depart, Mrs Hudson gave my shoulder a slight squeeze.

'You see, Flottie, it would be hard to prove whether the scorpion that so alarmed Mr Raffles was on its way *in* or on its way *out*. For the time being, we must suspend judgement. At least until we have had a good long conversation with Mr Neale. There are some things I want to ask him about his friend Moran.' She led the way back to the kitchen. 'It is tempting to do that today, but Mr Neale will wait for tomorrow. Both he and Moran seem safe enough for now. I think we might spend today tying up some loose ends. This afternoon would you be so good as to go back to Mr Spencer? I'm interested to know what he can tell us about the two dead creatures we sent him. In a hansom this time, I think, Flottie. That way you'll be sooner back.'

'Yes, ma'am,' I said with a little inner bounce. 'What will you do, ma'am?'

'I think the time is approaching when we shall need to visit Mr Moran in his lair. Before then I'd like to have a little look at how the land lies so we aren't in for any surprises. So this afternoon I shall conduct a little discreet reconnaissance. Let us agree to meet here by five, Flottie. That way you will not have to rush off rudely were you are pressed to stay for tea.'

Mrs Hudson's words proved invaluable in preparing me for what lay ahead, so that when just such an invitation was made by the radiant Miss Peters I found myself able to accept without the incoherent stammering that, I fear, would have been my instinctive response. Managing instead two or three mute nods of the head, I found myself, within five minutes of my arrival, seated nervously at a lace table-cloth.

'Rupert is still out, you see,' explained Miss Peters enthusiastically, 'but he left strict orders that I was to detain you if you called. He said he had *something hugely important to convey*.' She uttered the last words in a perfect imitation of Mr Spencer's voice, then laughed prettily. 'You see how privileged you are. I've known him since we were both too small to stand up but he's never attempted to convey anything of the least importance to *me*. Now, do you take milk? Lemon? Oh, I always take milk too. I can't bear all those tedious people who insist that milk ruins a perfectly good drink. Just because I haven't been to India and brewed my own tea at dawn on the banks of the Yangtze Kiang doesn't mean I don't know what's nice to drink and what isn't.'

Miss Peters made it all very easy, and gradually my nervousness subsided under the weight of words pouring over me. Those long-ago afternoons when Swordsmith used to show me how to take tea like a lady now seemed hugely important, but Miss Peters gave the impression that I could have drunk my tea standing on my head without appearing anything other than mildly eccentric.

In fact so comfortable did I become that I quite forgot about Mr Spencer until Miss Peters's chatter was interrupted by his return. He seemed delighted to see us both and he joined us at the tea table with a quiet grin.

'Is Hetty talking at you, Miss Flotsam?' he enquired with elaborate seriousness.

'Of course I'm not, Rupert. Flottie and I are just discussing the fashion in hats. We think women over forty who *will* wear those new French creations do so at great risk to their personal dignity.'

'Hetty is well-equipped to judge,' he confided to me, 'as someone who never felt the slightest hesitation in sacrificing all personal dignity if it meant that she could wear something French and fashionable.'

Miss Peters let out a little squeak and appeared to kick him under the table. Ignoring her with practised ease, he turned to me again.

'Since it's too late in the day for a lesson, Miss Flotsam, I assume you have called to find out about the specimens you brought me.' I noticed that his jovial manner concealed an air of considerable excitement.

'Rupert has spent all day touting that revolting squashed spider around the houses of funny little men,' put in Miss Peters. 'Sometimes I think he goes to *enormous* lengths to put me off him.'

'Hetty is quite wrong, Miss Flotsam,' he carried on. 'The spider was very easy to identify. The snake however was a different matter. You see, there's a lot of snakes about in the world and lots of them seem to look quite like each other. However, there's a chap called Michaels at the British Museum who's very keen on snakes. He got onto the case and fairly quickly he was able to tell me the little charmer that killed Carruthers is something called a blue coral snake. Only a baby, apparently. The grown-ups can be about four or five feet long and they lurk about on the fringes of the jungle and make a nuisance of themselves. He wasn't surprised Carruthers was dead. Highly venomous, apparently, and no known antidote to the bite. The chap seemed rather pleased with himself until I asked him where it came from. Then he went all vague on me. The thing is the little blighter could have come from any number of places – Sumatra, Borneo, even Siam. I was tempted to leave it at that but Michaels gave me a couple of other names and eventually I was pointed to an old chap called Mathers who had spent 35 years as a surveyor in the Colonial Service. Seems this chap is a manic herpetologist. Spent all his spare time studying snakes and such. Knows more about the snakes of the East Indies than anyone really needs to know.'

'Rupert, *please* tell me you won't want me to call on him,' interrupted Miss Peters with a grimace. 'Not like the man with the frightful beard and the collection of beetles?'

'Hetty, that was the Earl of Cleveland.' Mr Spencer gave her a look of exaggerated menace and carried on.

'I showed this chap Mathers the snake that killed Carruthers and it took him about two seconds to tell me what it was. He was very interested in the whole thing so I told him how I came by it and when I got to the bit about the Sumatran curse he interrupted me at once. "But Mr Spencer," he said as if it was obvious to anyone, "this snake isn't from Sumatra. This is rather a distinctive shade of dark blue. The Sumatran population is much closer to black. And the stripe is not so pale on the specimens you find in Sumatra," he insisted. "So where might

I be able to collect a specimen resembling this particular snake?" I asked. "Singapore would be the place," he told me. "There's loads of them like this one in Singapore." So there you go, Miss Flotsam, it's not a Sumatran snake at all.'

'Singapore! Where Mr Moran went when he left Sumatra! He could have collected it there.'

Mr Spencer nodded happily. 'I suppose it's technically possible that the priests might have got hold of a Singapore version of their local snake to send to London, but I can't for the life of me see why they should.'

'And did the spider come from the same place, Mr Spencer?'

'Oh, that's just it, Miss Flotsam. Everyone was unanimous about the spider. It didn't come from Asia at all. It's a tarantula spider from South America or Mexico or somewhere. I did a bit of investigation and found it's quite easy to buy one down on the docks. Sailors bring them back and sell them as curiosities. They drive up the price by saying they're terribly poisonous, practically man-eaters, and someone was obviously taken in. Because whoever it was who went to all that trouble to throw one at Mr Neale can't have realised that for all their loathsome appearance they aren't particularly poisonous at all.'

'So *neither* of the creatures used in these strange attacks was from Sumatra?'

He shook his head. 'Though someone seems to want us to think they are.'

'Moran!' I murmured under my breath. 'Someone who wanted us to believe in the Sumatran curse... You must both excuse me,' I told them abruptly, looking up at two intent, interested faces. 'You see, I simply have to get back to Mrs Hudson as quickly as I can.'

The Wisdom of Solomon

✝

Mrs Hudson was home before me. By the time I stepped out of the undiminished fog, the rooms in Baker Street were already glowing warmly and a rich smell of cooking promised a cheering supper. The strange calm of that morning had persisted into nightfall: Dr Watson was in his bedroom sorting through his collection of artworks, and in the study Mr Holmes had taken up his violin. The music, soft and surprisingly wistful, filled the air with a sense of drowsy thoughtfulness. Mrs Hudson herself was in the kitchen, sewing. The fire was banked up bright, and close to her chair stood a glass of the old Oloroso that had arrived the previous day with the compliments of Mr Rumbelow. While I changed my clothes she listened intently to my panting account of Mr Spencer's findings, nodding occasionally over her needlework, pausing occasionally to take a sip of sherry or to frown at the fire. When I finished, she lay down her work and signalled towards the seat beside her.

'Settle down by the fire, Flotsam. You were right to make haste with your news and I think you are right about its significance. But things are so arranged that I think we can afford to sit and reflect a little. Moran is under careful guard, Neale is safe at Rumbelow's and our two gentlemen are comfortably set for the evening. Pour yourself a glass of milk, fetch your mending and let's rest a little.'

Upstairs the hum of the violin swelled to a momentary peak, paused, then continued its slow musing.

'The gentlemen have spent the day with Mr Moran. I've not been told of what passed but there is something in Mr Holmes's face that suggests to me he's troubled. He has been playing that instrument ever since his return.'

'And what of Mr Spencer's news, ma'am?'

'It gives us something else to ask Mr Moran. But first we'll go to see Mr Neale. I rather think he may be ready to talk to us now. Our interview with Moran can wait till after that.'

She reached behind her to where a shopping list lay on the kitchen table. She turned it over and handed it to me. On the back she had sketched a rough floor plan of a building I didn't recognise.

'I've had a fascinating afternoon, Flottie. I was interested to have a look at the building Mr Moran lives in. If things develop in the way I predict, we may need to know how to get in or out in a hurry. However it was a great deal harder to achieve than I'd expected. With the various people watching the house and all the extra policemen patrolling, it's like Speakers Corner on May Day down there. I recognised Gregory's man straightaway. He was too busy looking casual to be anybody else. Then I spotted Mr Holmes's boy in an archway, lying low very commendably. I'd just decided that they were the only two I needed to avoid when I noticed a third, a scruffy child of about nine or ten. He was sauntering to and fro as if on the scrounge but whatever happened he was never more than a few yards away from Moran's place. Now I had fully expected *two* people to be watching, but the third surprised me. Who else has an interest in watching Moran, Flottie?'

I shook my head hesitantly.

'Exactly. And it made things a bit trickier for me because I didn't much want to be noticed. However, once I'd tracked down the caretaker for a quiet chat, I soon found out most of what I wanted to know. Let me show you, Flottie.'

She took the shopping list out of my hand and placed it on the floor in front of us so that we could both see it as we leaned forward. Her finger began to retrace the pencil outlines.

'New Buildings is one of those old mansion blocks. I don't know when it was new but it's certainly looking rather shabby now. And listen to this, Flottie. There are three different entrances and three different staircases. Moran's is reached from the left-hand staircase. That's the only one that concerns us here. His rooms are the uppermost of the three and – here is where it gets interesting, Flottie – the two below are both currently unlet and completely empty. Gregory's men have searched them and, just to make sure, they added their own padlocks to each door so no-one can get in or out.

'Next I checked the rear of the building. The apartments back onto an empty alley. Moran's windows are high up and there's only a rickety drainpipe to climb on. An athletic man with good nerves may be able to drop down *from* Moran's flat but he wouldn't be able to climb *up* to it. What this means, Flottie,' and here her eyes glinted keenly at me, 'what this means is that Moran's position is virtually impregnable. His door is watched constantly and that's the only way in. So we should know exactly where Moran and that servant of his are at all times.'

I nodded silently, intent on absorbing all the detail she had shown me in her pencil drawing. A week before I may have questioned the importance of such a diagram but the last few days had shown me that Mrs Hudson's instincts merited close attention. And I found myself remembering that desperate rush up the dark stairs towards Mr Neale's room when it seemed there was a murder taking place above us. Next time, I hoped, I would know where I was going and how to get there.

'Is Mr Moran there now, ma'am?'

'Philpotts the caretaker says he has scarcely left the house in the last two days. He must be wondering who has the papers that Mr Raffles lifted from under his nose.'

'I wonder if Mr Neale has been in touch with him.'

Mrs Hudson raised her glass to her nose in the suggestion of a toast. Behind the dark liquid her eyes sparkled.

'We can ask Neale that tomorrow, Flottie. Though I'd be surprised if he doesn't feel that one of the best things about being at Rumbelow's isn't the fact that it removes him totally from the reach of Mr Nathaniel Moran.'

–

The following morning we set off a little after breakfast, as soon as the gentlemen had left the house. Mr Holmes's violin had played long into the night and at breakfast that morning he continued deep in thought. Before leaving the house with Dr Watson, he put his head around the kitchen door. His pipe was unlit, but nevertheless he held it anxiously in his hand and on occasions chewed on it.

'Mrs Hudson, having considered deeply overnight, I worry that there are aspects of this case that still pose difficult questions.'

'Those Chinese gentlemen, sir?'

'Don't allow yourself to be distracted by them, Mrs H. It is possible there may be aspects of the case not yet revealed to us. You may perhaps begin to perceive that pure reason, however ably applied, has its limits. The truly great mind is aware of those limits and is able to identify unerringly the additional information needed to support its thesis. In this case, I conclude I need to find Mr Neale.'

His brow was still furrowed and he took another puff on his unlit pipe.

'Mrs Hudson, I perceive you are a woman of particular talents, and I am aware too that certain kinds of information may sometimes by more readily available to those below stairs rather than above. So if, by any chance, Mr Neale's whereabouts *were* to become known to you…'

Mrs Hudson wiped the table with slow, measured sweeps of her hand and nodded gently.

'Mr Holmes, if you allow me a few hours, I shall, at the end of that period, ensure that any information I have relating to Mr Neale is relayed to you forthwith.'

Their eyes met for a moment and Mr Holmes straightened. 'Very good, Mrs Hudson. And a very good day to you.'

'There you go, Flottie,' said Mrs Hudson decisively as the door closed behind him. 'As pretty a cry for help as you'll ever hear. The gentleman doesn't disappoint me.' She gave the table two or three emphatic swipes of the cloth, then straightened up. 'Now, Flotsam, gather up your wits and your woollens. We're off to visit Mr Neale.'

Mr Rumbelow, it emerged, was a resident of Kensington, and it wasn't until eleven o'clock that we alighted from an omnibus and made our way to his bright blue front door. The door was opened by a nervous housemaid who told us that Mr Rumbelow was not at home.

'We are here to see Mr Neale, child,' replied Mrs Hudson. 'Please be good enough to tell him that Mrs Hudson is here.'

'Mrs Hudson? Why, of course, ma'am. Please come in, ma'am, please.'

We were shown into a neat parlour furnished in what I could tell was discreet good taste. There, after a moment or two, we were joined by the gentleman himself. He was a tall, nervous-looking man, though no longer the shivering wreck I remembered from our night near St Pancras. A day or two at Rumbelow's had clearly done him good, for a slight flush of pink had replaced the deadly pallor of his cheeks, though when he spoke his underlying state was betrayed by the tremor in his voice.

'Mrs Hudson! I cannot tell you how delighted… I haven't yet thanked you properly…'

'Mr Neale, I fear we are here to ask you some very direct questions. Pray save your thanks for another time.' He gulped a little, as much at her peremptory tone as at the words themselves. 'Flotsam here was vital to your rescue the other night. You may trust to her discretion as you trust to mine.'

Mr Neale nodded at me faintly and waved me towards a seat.

'No, thank you, sir,' returned Mrs Hudson, seeing the gesture. 'We shall stand, if it's all the same to you.'

'Of course.'

His throat already sounded dry and his voice had fallen to little more than a whisper. The strong frame that Dr Watson had commented upon appeared to shrink a little.

'Mr Neale, Mr Holmes requires a full statement from you. A full statement, sir, laying out the whole history of this tawdry affair. You will appreciate he is a busy man. He has little time for those who have attempted to deceive him.'

For a moment I thought he would give in straightaway but from somewhere he found the strength to prevaricate.

'Really, madam,' he began, 'I do not understand you…'

'Mr Carruthers is already dead, sir. Must more lives be lost over this? There is no escaping the part you played. The plans for the distillery you built in Sumatra are as we speak lying on a table in Baker Street.' Her face was like iron. 'It is all over, Mr Neale.'

The effect of this was devastating. The man tottered slightly then seemed to crumple. He dropped into the chair behind him and covered his face with his hands. With a shock I realised he was weeping.

Mrs Hudson had stepped close to him to fire her broadside and now she stepped back. I made a move forward, towards the stricken man, but she caught my eye and, with a gesture neither unkind nor sympathetic, signalled me back.

'Mr Neale?' she asked.

'It wasn't me,' he sobbed from behind his hands. 'Mrs Hudson, I swear it wasn't me.' He dropped his hands and looked up desperately. 'Please, Mrs Hudson, I beg you, if I explain it to you, will you intercede for me with Mr Holmes?'

'You had best begin at the beginning, sir. We need to hear it all. What you added to the gin, for instance; how you came to be guilty of those terrible deaths; what you have been up to since coming to London.'

He nodded quickly and pressed his face with his handkerchief in an attempt to master his tears.

'It was Carruthers first,' he offered, continuing to wipe his nose. 'No, that's not true. It was my idea to sell gin to the natives. I'd seen in other places that spirits had an effect on the savages that rendered them helpless and easy to control. My idea was to use liquor as a way of winning them over and opening up the market. But Moran saw greater potential. He realised that we could manufacture our own gin and sell it all over the region. Postgate knew enough to construct a still so we set to work. We didn't really know what we were making but the natives knew even less and it all worked like a dream. Suddenly they were falling over themselves to trade with us.'

He shook his head as if remembering back to those days played out in the damp jungles of another land.

'The problem was that we were too successful. Postgate, one of our original group, ran the distillery. We threw in lots of local herbs and stuff to mask the terrible taste. Believe it or not, in the early days I was actually concerned about the taste. I wanted to take out a licence – had visions of a brand that people would drink throughout the tropics. But Moran and Carruthers didn't care for any of that. They wanted quick profit and when we couldn't keep up with demand they began to take risks. There is no law there – the nearest Dutch garrison is a hundred miles away – so we were free to do as we pleased. Carruthers decided the herbs we got from the Chinese were costing too much so he began to try out other things – God knows what he was putting in. He didn't seem to care, so long as it hid the taste enough for us to sell it to the tribes.'

I found myself imaging the scene, the steaming isolation of the island working gradually on the little group of Britons until it had stripped away the veneer of civilisation they had brought with them, the very thing they used to justify their contempt for those around them. I thought of them slipping into their damp beds at night, all their dreams reduced to this squalid act of profiteering and the sound of the rain on rusting iron roofs.

Neale's eyes were now fixed on the laced window as he talked.

'I knew things couldn't last and they didn't. There was one batch that went badly wrong. I don't know what we did. It must have been something Carruthers added. By then he was pretty much out of control. People began to have these fits that killed them. First it was Postgate, who was never above drinking his own poison. Then it was the natives. We tried to tell each other we weren't the cause but in ourselves we all knew the truth. We knew it as we watched them die.'

He was shaking as he remembered.

'It was terrible. It seemed to send them mad, writhing and screaming, screaming at visions only they could see. Unless their hands were bound they would tear out their own eyes, and all the time shrieking like demented souls.'

He looked Mrs Hudson in the eye. 'I don't know what did it. I've heard that wormwood in liquor can affect your mind – it must have been something like that. But far, far worse. I begged Moran and Carruthers to stop selling but by then we had a warehouse full of gin and no way of knowing which casks were sound and which weren't.

We carried on far longer than I believed possible, selling the stuff everywhere. I think we'd all gone a little mad ourselves. We sold to the natives, to sailors that put in, even to some of the Chinese. And we were getting away with it. No-one thought to blame us. Carruthers began to swear it wasn't the gin after all and Penge took his word for it. One night we found him writhing in agony on the veranda. He should have died – everyone else did – but we saved one of his eyes by tying him down and his remarkable constitution must have done the rest. But he was terribly altered in his head. Have you met him? Did you notice he never speaks, just looks at you with that one eye until you think you'll go mad?'

Neale was struggling to control his hysteria but around him the atmosphere was very still. A little carriage clock on the mantelpiece clicked softly to itself.

'Indeed, Mr Neale. I wondered why we hadn't been told about Penge's disfiguration. I see now that the loss of his eye didn't fit with the story Moran wanted us to believe. It would rather lessen the supernatural mystery if a survivor was on hand who could be questioned as to what had occurred. Now please go on.'

Neale continued, cooled slightly by her monumental calm.

'Penge had been Moran's servant since he was a child. I think that was the beginning of the split between him and Carruthers, though God knows they had been in it together as deep as could be. Anyway, after a couple of dozen deaths on the island, the game was up. The natives came for us and we got out as quickly as we could. Moran was down with fever and couldn't move. I wanted to take him with us but Carruthers wouldn't wait. We took ship for London and left him to his fate.'

A silence fell. His face was covered again but now that he had spoken he seemed more in control, as if confession had brought him resolution.

'And in London, Mr Neale?'

He rose to his feet and, moving to his left, leaned unsteadily against the mantelpiece.

'We had nothing when we arrived but some cases of gin and a diagram for the stills. Carruthers tried to sell the gin on the docks but he was picked up by one of the gangs who control that sort of thing. In fact that proved to be a blessing. Introductions were made and Carruthers, who could be plausible enough when it mattered, made a lot of promises about the money to be made.'

Neale was clearly calmer now and he paused to check his pocket watch.

'Go on, Mr Neale.' Mrs Hudson's face was blank but something in her voice spoke of a hard edge of excitement, as though she was reaching for something she was about to understand. 'You resumed your operations in London?'

'That's right. Until Moran came back from the dead. We'd never dreamed he might survive. But he did, and he came for us. Even when he reappeared he never threatened us, but we were frightened all right, I promise you, and not because of any curse. It was Moran we feared. We knew him well enough to be afraid.'

'And what happened to your operations in London?' Mrs Hudson's face was neutral but there was urgency in her tone.

But Neale shook his head. 'Mrs Hudson, you must forgive me. This has been a hard tale for me to tell and tomorrow I shall repeat it to Mr Holmes and accept my fate. I promise I will answer everything in full then, but in the meantime I would like to rest.' He took a deep breath and his exhaustion seemed almost palpable. 'I shall write to Mr Holmes this afternoon and arrange a time. Please excuse me until then.'

For a moment I thought Mrs Hudson was going to insist but instead she stepped back and dropped her head slightly.

'Flotsam,' she said quietly, 'it's right that Mr Holmes should hear this for himself.' She began to gather her things together. 'Until tomorrow then, Mr Neale,' she added with a cool nod of her head, before leading me to the door.

But even when we had reached the street, our excitement for the day was not yet over. We had gone no further than ten yards from Mr Rumbelow's door when a victoria-hansom pulled up beside us and there emerged from it the portly figure of Mr Rumbelow himself. But not the rather dapper solicitor with whom we were familiar. One glance was enough to see his usually fastidious dress sadly disordered, his carefully oiled hair woefully askew across his bald pate and what seemed remarkably like mud stains on both knees of his breeches.

'Mr Rumbelow?' asked Mrs Hudson and I together, with similarly disbelieving tones.

'Mrs Hudson…!' he began, his face pink with outraged dignity. Words appeared to fail him but he continued regardless, his mouth opening and closing mutely as if to give expression to an indignation that went far beyond mere language.

Mrs Hudson was the first to respond and taking my arm reversed our direction back to where the discountenanced solicitor stood.

'Come now, sir,' she exclaimed briskly. 'We can't have you standing in the street like that. Let us go inside and see if Flotsam and I can offer any assistance.'

The housemaid answered our knock and gave a nervous squeal when she caught sight of her employer. There was no sign of Neale, so Mrs Hudson bundled us all into the parlour. There she quickly identified a cabinet that contained brandy. Positioning an unprotesting Mr Rumbelow in the chair just vacated by his guest, she proceeded to fill one plump glass for him and, after an approving sniff, one for herself.

'Mr Rumbelow, sir, I've always maintained that the law's gain was a grievous loss to the wine trade.' She took a devout sip. The brandy, combined with Mrs Hudson's words, seemed to have a reviving effect on Mr Rumbelow.

'Merely a hobby, Mrs Hudson,' he replied, the power of speech returning. 'Absolutely no more than a hobby. Though I like to think my small cellar contains some items that would not be entirely out of place in establishments grander than my own.'

While Mrs Hudson had been dispensing restoratives, I had been using my handkerchief to staunch as best I could the flow of blood from a small graze on his hand, and now Mr Rumbelow smiled down at me fondly.

'Thank you, Flotsam. Your attentions are most kind.'

After some moments of brandy-fumed silence, he seemed to become more aware of his circumstances.

'Really, ladies, I fear I must apologise for my most melodramatic entrance. A quite unforgivable breach of good manners. The truth is I have had a most irregular experience this morning. *Most* irregular. I am not, as a rule, a man exposed to actions of a physical nature. Indeed you may say that mine is a line of business that does not, in general, require anything in the line of physical, er, exertion.' I could tell that, despite the brandy, he was still struggling to control his indignation. 'Really, I have been most damnably treated,' he finally burst out. 'It is an outrage!'

Mrs Hudson took another sip from her glass and her action seemed to divert his attention for a moment. A few more quiet sips of his own saw his shoulders relax with a little shudder.

'Dear me, sir,' soothed Mrs Hudson, 'what could have been the occasion for such a thing?'

Mr Rumbelow paused and began for the first time to look slightly embarrassed. 'Well, Mrs Hudson, I must confess that I was pursuing a line of thought suggested by the problem you placed before me. Indeed so. You asked me to consider the case of the small boy currently resident with one Mr Fogarty, butler to the Fotheringays, at their London residence.'

Mr Rumbelow produced a handkerchief of his own and began to dab at his extensive forehead.

'A most awkward case, Mrs Hudson. Flotsam's testimony makes it clear that the aforementioned child is being held as little more than a hostage. And yet the child has made no complaint and has no family to complain on his behalf. It is quite possible, since the child is not in a state to look after himself and since Mr Fogarty has been supplying him with medical assistance, that a court may consider the child's interest well served by the *status quo*. Mr Fogarty could well be commended for his charity.'

'But he's letting him die!' I exclaimed.

'Quite so, Flotsam. I believe you implicitly. But without a blood relative to make a complaint, it is hard to see why our claim to custody of the child should be one whit stronger than Mr Fogarty's.'

Mrs Hudson was looking at him with a very tiny gleam of amusement escaping from beneath her furrowed brow.

'You're not telling us, sir, that you have been so rash as to pay a call on Fogarty yourself?'

Mr Rumbelow's embarrassment reached its peak.

'I am, of course, only too acutely aware of your warnings on the subject, Mrs Hudson. It was most rash of me not to heed them. Yes, indeed, most exceedingly rash. I confess I harboured hopes that the, er, person in question, when confronted by a respectable member of the legal profession, might be persuaded to hand over the child without the need for litigation.'

'Sir,' Mrs Hudson's frown had grown into one of stern remonstrance but her voice was slightly more gentle. 'The person in question is one of the most hardened villains in Europe.'

'Quite so, Mrs Hudson. Quite so. Just as you warned me, in fact. I made the mistake of calling at the tradesman's entrance, not wanting my visit to be considered in any way official. In the course of a short interview the, er, individual in question was both dismissive and offensive.' Here Mr Rumbelow suddenly blushed hotly. 'He made, er, certain suggestions as to the relationship between Flotsam and myself that I found most objectionable. As indeed I told him. I made it clear that my next action would be to inform the Fotheringays of his abominable behaviour, at which he laughed most unpleasantly. He gave me to understand that any such action would have a most detrimental effect on the health of the child I was concerned with. He accompanied this with a most graphic epithet of a grossly personal nature and at that point, I regret to say, I may have crossed the strict line between professional conduct and personal satisfaction.'

'Mr Rumbelow! You didn't!'

'Mrs Hudson, I fear I did.' His eyes were engaged in elaborate manoeuvres to avoid ours. 'I attempted to strike the man in his own pantry. A most lamentable lapse and, I'm sorry to say, a most futile one. He eluded my blow with some ease and proceeded to throw me out. In the most literal sense. A process in which he was ably assisted by two large and unappealing individuals dressed as footmen.'

I confess that for a moment I was torn between laughter and applause. Instead, taking heed of the warning frown nodded in my direction by Mrs Hudson, I looked down demurely and endeavoured to compose myself.

'Mr Rumbelow,' the housekeeper replied gently, 'you may take consolation from the fact that there can be no-one more deserving of the blow you aimed at him than Fogarty. And from the fact that we are very far from finished with him and that child. Before long, I trust you will consider yourself avenged. But first, are you certain there is no legal proceeding that will serve our purposes?'

'I fear that any such attempt is only likely to endanger the individual it is intended to protect, Mrs Hudson.'

'Yes, I think that's true. Very well. In that case we shall have to play our other card.'

'And what card is that, Mrs Hudson?'

'Surprise, sir. Surprise backed up, if we must, by a good helping of physical force.'

Mr Rumbelow and I exchanged alarmed glances.

'Oh, yes,' Mrs Hudson chuckled to herself. 'Deduction and reasoning are all very well, but at the end of the day even Solomon, for all his wisdom, wasn't above smiting the Hittites.'

The Servant of Chance

✝

It soon became clear that Mrs Hudson was in the mood for action in other areas too. For the greater part of our return journey she muttered darkly about polishing, and on our arrival she pitched us into a frantic campaign of domestic duties, from scrubbing the floors to dusting the tops of the wardrobes. While I scuttled to and fro, Mrs Hudson towered above proceedings like Horatius at the bridge, never apparently engaging fewer than two jobs at a time, with her eyes already running ahead to where a third was lurking. Her face was fixed in brooding concentration and you might have believed her entire being centred on the elimination of household chores were it not for the occasional words mumbled under her breath when her physical effort was at its most intense.

'Introductions were made, were they?' she quoted to herself as, on her hands and knees, she scrubbed at the tiles around the hearth. 'I bet they were. If you touch pitch…' and she continued to scrub, with strong, soot-stained hands.

I was far too breathless to ask any questions but my own mind was working too. Neale's tale, and what it revealed about the casual ruthlessness of the people we sought to protect, preyed on my mind. What would happen to Neale now? By his own confession he stood guilty of crimes that had condemned scores of innocent people to a horrible death. I thought of Mrs Trent, all alone in Limehouse, mourning her lost son. There must be others out there, even among the untutored Sumatrans, who still sometimes gazed emptily ahead as they remembered a lost child's terrible last moments. Somehow the scene kept blurring in my mind until it became a memory of the small fair-haired boy as he twisted and turned in the damp bareness of Fogarty's cellar. I paused in my work. Mrs Hudson was polishing with controlled fury at the legs of Dr Watson's chair. Later the fires would be lit and the gentlemen would return with news of their day, Dr Watson blinking in the gas light, Holmes listening to his exclamations with a quiet good humour. But for now there was a floor to clean, and I threw myself into the task with some of Mrs Hudson's passion, suddenly glad of where I was and the people I was with.

'So, Flottie,' Mrs Hudson declared finally when we had retired to the kitchen with sore knees and necks. 'The place is sparkling like a guardsman's buttons and we are nearly at the end of this sorry affair. I think we can sleep well tonight. There shouldn't be any more unpleasant surprises.'

'Will you be able to explain everything to me after tomorrow, ma'am? There are still a few things I don't quite understand.'

'Of course, Flotsam. I would share my thoughts with you right now but I'm hoping that most of the explaining will be done tomorrow when Mr Neale finishes his tale. Let's hope that in this at least he can be trusted.'

And Mr Neale was as good as his word. Mr Holmes and Dr Watson arrived home shortly after dark and after changing into smoking jackets settled down with their evening mail. Not long afterwards came a decisive knock on the kitchen door and Mr Holmes entered with a letter in his hand and a quizzical gleam in his eye.

'Mrs Hudson, I see you have been busy today.'

'Good gracious, sir, I didn't expect you to notice. It was nothing more than a quick brush and a bit of polishing.'

'You misunderstand me, madam.' He held the letter up to his chin. 'This is another note from Mr Neale. He has broken cover and writes that he wishes to see us tomorrow. He adds the following…' Mr Holmes opened the letter and began to read.

'*Through the agency of your estimable housekeeper, Mrs Hudson, I have been persuaded that my only course is to place myself entirely in your hands.*'

Mrs Hudson flushed slightly and turned to the large pot bubbling on the stove.

'So you see, Mrs Hudson, your secret is out and I am in your debt. I begin to see you are a dark horse. Watson and I must look to our laurels.'

Mrs Hudson continued to stir the pot.

'Indeed,' the great detective continued, 'Mr Neale even extends tomorrow's invitation to you. That is, in my opinion, going a little beyond what is necessary but I'm pleased that he recognises your contribution.'

'Really, sir, it would hardly be our place for Flotsam and I to accompany Dr Watson and yourself on such a delicate visit.' I thought I detected a gleam in her eye. 'It would be most irregular, sir. What would people think?'

The words were well-chosen for they were greeted with a frown.

'Nonsense, Mrs Hudson! Dr Watson and I never stand on ceremony. We should be sorely limited in our investigations if we did. If it is Mr Neale's wish that you be present, however unconventional, I have no hesitation in urging your acceptance. Indeed I insist on your company.'

'Very good, sir,' responded Mrs Hudson very formally. 'If you furnish us with the address, sir, I'm sure Flotsam and I will both enjoy an outing.'

'That is decided then, Mrs H. We meet at one o'clock sharp at 84 Cavendish Street. Mr Neale is returning to the house he lived in before Moran's return from Sumatra turned him into something of a fugitive. I look forward to tomorrow. Oh, and Mrs Hudson…' He paused on the brink of leaving the room. 'Do not expect me ever to underestimate your talents in the future.'

'So Mr Neale plans to leave Rumbelow's, does he?' growled Mrs Hudson when we were left alone. 'Unwise, but perhaps inevitable. He must be wanting to put his things in order prior to an enforced absence.'

I had taken over the stirring of the pot and I watched as Mrs Hudson dipped a spoon for tasting.

'Oddly, Flottie, although I feel the danger is contained, I still don't like to see our pheasant flushed from cover. I shall make sure Scraggs is on Moran's doorstep from dawn. If Moran leaves his house, I want to know within minutes. And if he stays put, Neale is surely safe.'

She touched the spoon very delicately with her top lip and then pursed both lips together meditatively.

'Smart clothes tomorrow, I think, Flottie. And just a tiny bit more salt.'

Mr Neale's house in Cavendish Street proved smart and spacious and featured a great deal of marble. We were shown by a sharp-faced maid through a hallway into an airy drawing room. Beyond the drawing room was another door and it was at this she knocked to announce us. As the door opened, I saw that Mr Holmes and Dr Watson were there before us. The room we were ushered into was the sort sometimes referred to as a snug, although it bore no resemblance to those back rooms in public houses from which the name derived. It was furnished with self-conscious regard for comfort, with leather chairs, a desk and bookshelves that were a little too orderly to convey any sense of habitual use. Three armchairs had been drawn up into the centre of the room. Those occupied by Holmes and Watson faced into the room with their backs to the door, but the one intended for Neale faced us all full on so that he commanded a view of the whole room, even of the low bench behind the door where Mrs Hudson and I had settled a little awkwardly. Mr Neale had greeted us with a nod but no further sign of recognition, and he waited until we were all seated before he began.

'I would like to offer my thanks to you all for coming here,' he opened. His voice was much stronger than the previous day and his stance more determined, as if he had achieved a dignity in these last hours which in the past, when the option of flight remained, had always eluded him. 'I am a stranger to confession but I find that when one is ready to unburden one's soul there is a certain satisfaction in drawing together an audience to hear it. You mentioned, Mr Holmes, that Inspector Gregory of Scotland Yard may honour our little gathering?'

'Gregory will be here when he can,' replied Holmes. 'In the meantime, sir, I suggest you make a start.'

'I had also asked my solicitor to be present but a message was returned to say that the gentleman who has dealt with my affairs in the past is out of town. I understand that someone is to be sent in his stead, but in truth I feel that his absence is a blessing. He might wish to check me in my narration and I am in no mood to be cautious with my words.'

A silence settled on his audience as he began. He told from the beginning the story of his fateful venture in Sumatra. As he spoke I seemed to see even more clearly than before the rainy season lashing over the miserable collection of huts that passed for a town, the relentless tropical growth that ignored all attempts at clearance so that the jungle was constantly at their throats. The scene set, he proceeded to describe his suggestion of exploiting the natives' weakness for liquor, the growing contempt among his group for those around them, their descent into chaos and death. Holmes and Watson listened without interruption, Holmes's face impassive while Watson's betrayed an increasing sense of horror and revulsion. When Neale told of the decision after Postgate's violent death to continue their selling regardless, the doctor could stand it no longer.

'I say, sir! This beggars belief! I've never heard of such conduct amongst Englishmen!'

Neale smiled to himself.

'Dr Watson, I fear your experience of our countrymen overseas has been very different from my own. Your regimental spirit may well have survived the Afghan campaigns, but out beyond the edges of the Empire there is less scope for fair play. Out there you soon realise that the Empire won't protect you from the fevers and the flies. No-one will come to your aid when your money runs out in pursuit of a fairly-won fortune. And look around you. Back in London no-one asks about the means of your success. For seven years in the jungle I dreamed of a room such as this. Now, through dishonest endeavour, I have one. Did the army look after you so well, Doctor?'

Dr Watson seemed about to respond. His hands gripped the arms of his chair and his eyes burned with the indignant scorn of the honest man taunted for his honesty. But before he could launch into a reply, Mr Holmes had intervened.

'Steady, Watson. We came here to listen, my friend. Let us hear all there is to hear before we pass comment.'

'Very well, Holmes,' mumbled Watson, and he subsided a little in his seat. However, his usually placid gaze retained a simmering anger.

Neale continued with his tale, describing his last desperate days in Sumatra. I marvelled at his new-found calm. Although his hands worked as he spoke and I could sense the tension in his body, he returned the gentlemen's gaze frankly and his voice betrayed scarcely a hint of the hysteria that only the previous day had almost overwhelmed him.

He had just begun to describe his return to London with Carruthers when there was a fresh knock on the door, followed by the tentative entry of the maid. In one hand she held a silver salver on which rested a calling card.

'The gentleman from the solicitor's office, sir.'

Neale waved the card away. 'Ask the gentleman to wait out there in the drawing room, Gladys. I have no need of him at the moment.'

Again I was surprised by the decision in his voice, as though his days of being afraid of others were finally over. However, the interruption had broken his flow and Mr Holmes took the opportunity to ask a question.

'You were saying, sir, that you were able to continue your illegal activities in London. How could that be? There are surely a great many hardened criminals better versed in these things than yourselves?'

'You are right, Mr Holmes. In London our luck turned. Carruthers had been able to ship a small consignment of the remaining gin ahead of us. I don't know how he smuggled it past the excisemen, but he did. It was our only asset. But on trying to sell it we were taken in hand by a man called Melmoth. He was a gentleman by appearance but there was no doubt that he was the intellect behind any number of criminal activities. He had abrupt ways with people who tried to set up in competition and Carruthers and I thought we were bound for the bottom of the Thames that very night. But Carruthers talked fast, said he had connections in London whom he hoped to make use of. This man Melmoth seemed impressed when he heard we already had blood on our hands and he seemed even more impressed when he heard who Carruthers's contacts were. You see, despite spending most of his life at odds with his family, Carruthers had always been well connected. He was able to mention peers, Members of Parliament, even a bishop.

'Melmoth was clearly impressed. Suddenly he was our greatest supporter. He set us up with funds and premises, took charge of distribution and paid us well when the money began to flow. Soon we had little to do but sit back and enjoy the rewards, but we knew all along we were nothing to Melmoth but a front. If the Excise called, it was we who were incriminated. We didn't even know Melmoth's real name and we only saw him when he chose to call. We did exactly what he asked of us, took any risks, paid officials, gave jobs to anyone he named. He knew our guilty secret and would never have hesitated in sending us to the gallows if it suited him. But Carruthers did his part in making us indispensable, building on his connections in society until we were completely above suspicion.'

He paused for a moment to sip from a glass of water beside his chair. Holmes continued to regard him with unemotional intensity. From where I sat his strong profile gave him the appearance of a bird of prey, patiently marking his victim's movements. Watson's head was sunk low, as if in disgust. Mrs Hudson, who had listened quietly during most of Neale's exposition, had leaned forward intently when he began to describe his affairs in London. She stayed there, poised, waiting for something, when Neale continued his tale.

'I don't expect your sympathy, gentlemen, but for the first time since my departure for the tropics I felt that fortune was favouring me. Then everything changed. I learned that Moran was in London.' He shuffled uneasily. 'I had thought him dead. Or to be honest I had hoped him dead. For at the back of my mind I always knew that, if he had survived, a reckoning of accounts was inevitable. In London it began to seem impossible that he would ever appear again – but he did. He wasted no time in finding us. He told us we were in grave danger from the vengeance of those we had exploited, that there was a blood vendetta against us. He told us he intended to enlist your assistance in protecting us from our hunters. He told us that, if we lent him money, he had plans to travel to America. And through it all we believed nothing except that we were in great danger. Oh, we had no doubts! We could see the hatred in his eyes. We even left our homes and took rooms in hotels, believing ourselves safer in such public establishments. But still we were devoured by fear. Moran is relentless, sir! His heart is cold as stone and his hatred implacable!'

Something strange was happening to Neale. For the first time his voice was beginning to rise and waver. He stood up and moved to the mantelpiece. I could see his body beginning to shiver and the fear he spoke of seemed to be seeping into the room as though a dark angel stood at our door. I saw Watson look around uncomfortably and Mrs Hudson's hands grew tense as she sat gripping her knees.

'Is that your story, Neale?' Holmes's tone was flat, implacable, but a note of urgency suggested that he too was aware of the changed atmosphere. 'Is Moran responsible for Carruthers's death? For the attempts on your life?'

'I am sure of it, sir! I would stake my life that it is he alone I have to fear.'

'Calm yourself. Moran is at home. The police are watching his door and I have my own observer placed outside. If he attempts to leave his house, word would reach us within minutes. Now I have another question, one of the greatest import. What can you tell us of this man Melmoth who seems to be the very centre of an evil web of crime?'

'Melmoth, Mr Holmes? Why, yes. I will tell you everything. I have nothing to lose now. You see, by accident I was able to discover his true name.'

'You can only gain by sharing it with us. It will stand well with a court if you assist us in this.'

But at this point there was another knock at the door and again the maid advanced a step or two into the room.

'The gentleman from the solicitor's, sir. He's impatient to talk to you.'

For a moment all eyes were on Neale. From where I sat I could see the faces of Holmes and Watson turned eagerly towards him as he stood with his back to the mantelpiece, looking towards the open door.

As I looked, his expression began to change. His impatience at the interruption turned to mystification and then to a sudden, astonished disbelief. He seemed about to address the maid for his mouth began to open and then the sound of a shot exploded in our ears and Neale rocked backwards, a bullet hole drilled neatly into the centre of his forehead.

Almost before he hit the ground it seemed everyone was on their feet. Watson and Holmes were up out of the chairs and turning towards the door. Mrs Hudson and I were up and stepping forward, the open door hiding us from the assassin. Only the maid continued to look at Neale and it was her rising scream that masked the sound of the second shot.

This time it was Mr Holmes that crumpled, spinning to the floor as though clipped by the wheel of a speeding hansom. Two new cries went up and both Watson and Mrs Hudson leapt towards him. The maid was screaming uncontrollably now and Mrs Hudson had to push past her to reach the fallen detective. Watson was there first, striding over Neale's fallen body and tugging at Holmes's collar. Somewhere behind me running feet were escaping through the drawing room. I was in time to see the tail of a coat swirling out of view into the hall beyond.

'Stop him!' yelled Watson, looking up in time to see the hall door slammed shut. A thin voice brought us back to more pressing business.

'Neale, Watson! Look to Neale!' Mr Holmes was still conscious and gesturing with his left hand.

'He's dead, Holmes!' snapped Watson, still tearing at the buttons of Holmes's shirt. 'Dead before he hit the ground.'

At this the maid stopped screaming and appeared to faint, landing with a soft thud at my feet. So while my companions struggled to remove their patient's jacket, I fanned the fallen maid strenuously with my handkerchief. As I did so, crouched in the doorway, I was aware of a new figure advancing towards us across the drawing room. I recognised the tweed–clad figure of Inspector Gregory.

'Good God!' he cried. 'What has happened? The man I passed in the hall said Holmes was murdered!'

Dr Watson looked up, his eyes wide.

'The man you passed in the hall? Gad, sir! Why the devil didn't you stop him?'

'He was going for a doctor, Dr Watson. I...'

Realisation struck him like a blow and his honest face collapsed into despair. He began instinctively to turn in pursuit but Mrs Hudson stopped him.

'Too late, sir. Help us here instead. We should lift Mr Holmes into that chair.'

Within a few minutes, a semblance of order had been created amidst the carnage. A footman and a heavily blowing cook had been quick to the scene and had removed the quivering maid. Holmes, though pale, remained conscious and his wound, when revealed, proved to be no more than a cut to the flesh of his upper arm.

'You have been dashed fortunate, Holmes. Despite the bleeding there is little damage done. Once we have bound that wound properly, some few days of rest should see you well on your way to recovery.'

Holmes smiled at him grimly. His pale cheeks seemed to have sunk further into his face, making his features more gaunt than ever.

'Rest, Watson? This is hardly the time. Action is what is called for now.'

Nevertheless, he remained obediently in his chair while Mrs Hudson and I bound the wound with bandages provided by the cook, freeing Dr Watson and Inspector Gregory to examine the fallen figure of Neale.

'It's as I thought,' nodded Watson. 'The first shot killed him outright. Whoever fired must have taken good aim.'

In a few words he described to Gregory the scene we had witnessed. 'The villain fired from behind the maid,' he concluded. 'But why on earth should Neale's solicitor want to take a shot at him?'

'If you remember, sir,' came Mrs Hudson's voice softly, 'when we arrived Mr Neale said he had sent for his solicitor. But if I recall correctly, a message came back saying that gentleman was out of town and another would take his place. Could it have been that the original message was intercepted, sir, by someone who wished Mr Neale harm?'

'Good lord, Mrs Hudson! Could that be possible?'

'It fits the facts, Watson,' cut in Mr Holmes. 'I warn you that you underestimate Mrs Hudson at your peril.'

Inspector Gregory stepped into the drawing room and returned with the calling card that still lay on its silver platter.

'Hand-written,' he commented. 'And with signs of haste. "Lewis Monk, Attorney-at-Law",' he read. 'An alias, do you think?'

'Clearly,' Mrs Hudson and Mr Holmes said together, and then paused to exchange glances of mutual acknowledgement.

'Mr Neale wasn't particularly meant to see the card, you see, sir,' I piped up timidly. 'It was just a way of making sure the maid would open the door.'

Mrs Hudson raised an eyebrow at me in an approving way but Dr Watson looked unconvinced.

'A dashed risky plan though,' he pondered. 'How could he know he'd get a shot at him? Anything could have gone wrong.'

Mrs Hudson nodded gently.

'I think, sir, we are dealing with someone who is not afraid to take risks.' She tied a last knot in the bandage and Dr Watson examined her handiwork with approval.

'Come now, Watson. Enough of this fussing.' Holmes struggled to a more upright position. He was paler than ever but his eyes burned with determination. 'Neale is dead, Moran inescapably compromised. We must act quickly.'

'You think this is Moran's work, eh, Holmes?'

'I have just come from Moran, sir,' put in Inspector Gregory. 'When I left him he was repeating the tale he told you about Sumatra to one of my officers. I came here directly. It is inconceivable that he could have overtaken me.'

'Then that sinister servant of his. Could he be the guilty man?'

'Penge, sir? I'm afraid Penge left London for Cornwall on last night's express. My men followed him to the station and I received a telegram earlier today from the local constabulary confirming his arrival in Truro. His home town, apparently.'

'Then *who*, dash it?'

It was a question to which the policeman had no answer other than a shrug of bewilderment. Holmes, watching wryly from where he lay, turned to his companion.

'I'm afraid a joker has turned up from the pack to upset all our calculations, Watson. We can at least hope the maid had a good look at the man. When she is calmer she may be able to provide a description.'

Gregory blushed furiously at this reference to the assassin and to spare his feelings we all tried to look away, only to find that by doing so our gaze came to rest on Neale's paling corpse.

'Perhaps, if you're well enough to move to the drawing room, Holmes...' suggested Watson.

But Mrs Hudson had risen to her feet and was frowning at a spot of dust on the mantelpiece. 'This may of course be Mr Moran's work, sir, if he were acting through a proxy. But I am inclined to believe that Mr Moran himself might now be in great danger.'

Again Mr Holmes smiled.

'Ah, your woman's intuition, Mrs Hudson? Just when I thought we had converted you to more scientific ways of thinking!'

He rose unsteadily from his chair and Watson helped him to stand. 'You forget, Mrs Hudson, that Mr Moran is closely watched. His rooms are inaccessible except from the street and the entrance is under close guard. I think Moran is safe enough.'

'From what you've told me, sir, shouldn't I be arresting him for the other murder?' Gregory seemed anxious to atone for his earlier error.

'I would much prefer to speak to him first, Gregory, if I could prevail upon you to stay your hand for a few hours. We know him to be a villain but at the moment it is little more than Neale's word against Moran's. And Neale is not well placed to state his case.'

By now we had made our way to the drawing room and Gregory closed the door upon the grim scene in the snug.

'You are in no state to see Moran now, Holmes,' said Watson firmly. 'You need that arm in a sling and I insist you rest a few hours at the very least.'

'Very well, Watson. I shall call on him this evening. Moran will wait until then.'

But I could see from Mrs Hudson's tightly set jaw that this was a view of things she did not share.

'I beg you, sir. Perhaps I am wrong that Moran is in danger. But could we not take precautions? At least until you are well enough to call on him yourself, sir.'

Holmes considered her carefully. Perhaps it was the loss of blood or a reaction to the shock of his wound but his manner towards her seemed suddenly thoughtful.

'Very well, Mrs Hudson,' he said at last. 'There can be no harm in it.'

He turned to Dr Watson. 'I have already suggested to Moran that you will be sitting with him from time to time to reassure him as to his safety. Would you be so good as to go to him now? Given what we now know of him, I daresay your attentions will not be particularly welcome. But if you could stay there regardless until I have rested a little and can join you, I should be eternally grateful.'

Watson flushed with pleasure.

'Of course, Holmes. Happy to be of assistance.'

'I can think of no safer pair of hands than Watson's, Gregory,' said Holmes, 'and he will not put Moran on his guard as one of your men would.' Holmes turned again to Watson. 'Gregory's men will be on call should Moran try anything, but since he has no way of knowing of Neale's confession I can see no reason why he should.'

'In that case,' declared Mrs Hudson, 'I shall have no objection to Flotsam going with you, Dr Watson, in case you wish to send any messages back to Baker Street.'

Dr Watson smiled warmly.

'Excellent! I shall enjoy Flotsam's company greatly, Mrs H. We shall leave at once.'

Before we did, however, another small incident occurred. A knock at the front door was answered by the footman and a very small boy was ushered into our presence.

'Message for Mr Holmes,' he stated firmly as though it were an incontrovertible fact of existence.

'I'm afraid the gentleman is a little indisposed,' replied Mrs Hudson gently, indicating the bandaged arm. 'Allow Inspector Gregory there to take receipt.' So while Watson rooted in his pockets for a tip, Gregory opened the note and began to read.

'*My dear Mr Holmes*,' he began before breaking off. 'Are you sure you don't want to read this yourself, sir?'

'Not at all, Gregory. I receive no correspondence of a personal nature and the fact of this note being delivered here is of great interest in itself.'

Gregory nodded and continued to read.

'*My dear Mr Holmes,*

You must forgive me for the most unmannerly way in which I forced myself upon your acquaintance this afternoon. I would have chosen to meet under more agreeable circumstances. However, we are all the servants of chance and I regret that it was necessary to inflict on you a trifling wound. Rest assured that had I intended you any lasting harm, you would not now be reading this note. My restraint is a tribute to your reputation and to the hope that we may meet again in more propitious circumstances.

Necessitas non habet legem.

Melmoth'

'Melmoth!' exclaimed Watson. 'What damned impertinence!'

'And yet the neat hole in Neale's forehead suggests his boast may not be an idle one, my friend.'

Gregory was looking confused. '*Necessitas non* what?' he wondered aloud.

'Necessity knows no law, sir,' I informed him, remembering the utterances of my knife-grinding Latin teacher as he used to feast so liberally on Mrs Siskin's baking.

'Melmoth was the name used by Neale's mysterious collaborator,' Holmes explained to Gregory. 'The man is apparently guilty of more crimes than the one we have just witnessed. Neale was on the brink of revealing his identity when the blow fell.'

He turned to the boy who still stood determinedly in front of him, looking pointedly at Dr Watson's pockets.

'Who gave you this letter? There's a coin in it for you if you answer clearly.'

'The gent, sir.'

'And which gent was that, young man?'

'The gent what gave me the letter, sir.'

'That much logic cannot be faulted. Let me start again. Was this gentleman previously known to you?'

'Nivver saw 'im before. Came into The Red Lion, he did, asked the landlord if there was a boy to take a missage.'

'And what did the gentleman look like?'

The witness seemed a little taken aback, as though it had never particularly occurred to him that all gentlemen didn't look pretty much the same. However, he was not to be defeated and after a thoughtful pause he delivered his opinion.

'He were a dark gent, sir. He weren't fat at all. An' he had a black 'at on.'

Mr Holmes pondered for a moment.

'Thank you,' he concluded. 'That is an admirable description. I've known members of the professional force offer a great deal less. Gregory, since Watson appears short of change perhaps you could reward this child for his labours. Meanwhile, let us ready ourselves to depart.'

It wasn't until a cab was waiting at the door and Mr Holmes was about to step outside that Mrs Hudson stopped him quietly and drew him to one side.

'I wondered, sir, if you would have an opinion on this?'

I saw her pass him a marble ashtray which he took with his good arm and eyed intently.

'Tobacco ash, Mrs Hudson? I have written a monograph on just this subject.' He looked again, suddenly oblivious of the horses blowing noisily outside. 'Cigarette ash,' he said at last. 'And an expensive brand at that. Note the very fine texture of the ash. Egyptian, perhaps?'

Mrs Hudson let out a long slow breath. 'Egyptian, sir? I thought as much,' she said softly.

Holmes shot her a meaningful glance. 'You think this is helpful, Mrs Hudson?'

Mrs Hudson turned slightly and her eyes met mine.

'Oh yes, sir,' she nodded. 'I rather think it might be conclusive.'

The Errant Sentry

†

The November evening had begun to draw in around us long before we left Cavendish Street, and it was the far side of dusk before Dr Watson and I arrived at Moran's dwelling place. The drama of the afternoon had left us both drained and taciturn, and our journey took place in a heavy silence. Portman Street is a busy thoroughfare off Oxford Street and the milling crowds of London filled the streets. Street vendors manoeuvred their carts through the mud, heading south then westward where the business of the day was only beginning; and streams of shop girls and waistcoated salesmen made their way in the other direction, north and homeward towards streets where the gas burned less brightly. On dismounting from our cab, we were greeted with a salute by a uniformed policeman with a twinkle in his eye.

'Evening, sir. Evening, miss. Inspector Gregory sent ahead to say to expect you. That there door is Mr Moran's, sir. I'll show you straight up.'

'Thank you, constable, but I can find my own way. Is there anything to report?'

The twinkle in the man's eye grew markedly brighter.

'Well, you've missed all the fun, sir. We had a bit of a to-do here just a few minutes ago. Funniest thing I've seen all year. You see over there, sir?' He indicated towards where a man in a drab coat and shapeless hat lurked in a doorway. 'That there is O'Donnell. He used to work this beat before I did but he's been moved up to better things now. That's why he's in plain clothes, you see. The only difference between the two of us that I can see, mind, is that he's supposed to stand still and watch this door while I'm supposed to patrol up and down and watch it. But that's promotion for you. Anyway, about ten minutes ago a group of proper gay girls come heading down the street. Proper painted daisies they were, if you'll pardon the expression.' He looked a little shamefacedly in my direction.

'They must have been on the gin before their night's work because they were making a right noise, singing and shouting and all sorts. I was just going to move them on when they come up to where O'Donnell is. I can't say what they saw in him but suddenly they're all around him, patting his cheeks and such, saucy as you like. I could see he didn't know what to do and he was looking at me for help, and I was just thinking that perhaps for his extra pay it was up to him to get himself out of that sort of squeak, when suddenly they all come to blows.'

The memory clearly still filled him with laughter.

'A proper cat fight it was, with O'Donnell at the centre trying to get out and two girls scratching and tearing at each other while the others screamed 'em on. Well, it stopped the traffic, I tell you. Took me fully five minutes to get it all broken up and the crowds moved on. And when it was all done, I turned to O'Donnell and says to him, "That's right, lad. You just stand there quiet like and keep out of view, just like the sergeant told you." You should have seen his face, sir!'

But Dr Watson was clearly not amused.

'I'm afraid the humour of the situation escapes me, constable. Quite apart from the behaviour of these, er, ladies,' he stumbled, casting an embarrassed glance at me, 'the incident clearly diverted attention from the watch you were meant to be keeping.'

The policeman straightened his face into a mask of professional formality. 'Yes, sir. I mean, it was no more than a minute, sir. I shall go up now and check all's well.'

'There's no need for that now, constable. I shall go myself. Please keep close to hand and admit no-one until Inspector Gregory and Mr Sherlock Holmes arrive in a few hours' time.'

Dr Watson was still muttering angrily to himself as we climbed the stairs. 'I don't like it, Flottie,' he kept mumbling. 'It all smells very fishy to me.'

And if Dr Watson was out of sorts, it was soon evident that our host was in no better humour. The expression on Mr Moran's face when he opened the door to us betrayed a mixture of annoyance and mistrust.

'Ah, Moran,' opened Watson. 'Mr Holmes has asked me to look in to see that everything's all right. I trust you have had no unexpected callers in the last few minutes?'

'Callers?' He seemed on edge. 'Absolutely not. None but yourself.'

He made no sign of inviting us in.

'You will understand, sir, that it is Mr Holmes's express wish that I sit with you for a few hours on occasions when he feels you may be at particular risk.'

'Dr Watson, this is a most inconvenient time for me. I have some business matters to attend to tonight. Your presence would not be an assistance.'

The door was still open no more than a foot. Dr Watson's temper was beginning to fray.

'Damn it, sir, this is a poor welcome. Flotsam here is accompanying me should I need to send word to Mr Holmes. We have had a difficult day already and I do not intend to pass the rest of it parleying on your doorstep like a dashed tradesman!' Watson paused to give Moran a look of frank dislike. 'You may wish to know, sir, that Neale is dead.'

'Dead?' The news seemed to hit him as unexpectedly as a blackjack in an alley. He stepped back and allowed the door to swing open. 'You must forgive me for my poor hospitality, Dr Watson. My servant is away for a few days. I am alone here. Please, come in and tell me what has happened.'

He showed us into a dark living room lit by two green-shaded lamps and a leaping fire. On each side of the fire were green armchairs and between them a matching sofa. On a table to one side stood a decanter and glasses.

'Please, take a seat, I beg you. Doctor, let me pour you a drink. Is Scotch all right?' He ushered us most insistently into the armchairs but Dr Watson was not to be mollified.

'I note your anxiety is such that you are content to allow your servant to leave you quite by yourself.'

'Penge has been more than a servant to me, Dr Watson. I can hardly deny him a visit to his family when a bereavement dictates it.'

Dr Watson looked a little abashed at this but I could see that his distaste for Moran, engendered by Neale's tale, was not to be easily mastered.

'And you are quite alone now, Moran?' He looked around suspiciously. 'You have seen or heard nothing unusual in the last few minutes?'

'Nothing but a slight disturbance in the street. And I am quite alone, Doctor. A state I hoped would continue for a while longer.'

'What's beyond that door?' Watson indicated a second door that led from the living room to the rest of the flat.

'A dining room, bedrooms. Perhaps you would care to inspect them?'

Watson gave a short harumph and looked away, but Moran began to question us about the death of Neale, questions that for the most part Dr Watson parried with an air of puzzled stupidity that conveyed only the most grudging and minimal information. Moran seemed a little stunned by what he learned, as though he were struggling to make sense of it. Within a few minutes, confronted by Dr Watson's unwillingness to expand, the conversation petered out into a dissatisfied silence, broken only by the occasional crumbling of the coals on the fire.

Moran seemed to find it hard to settle.

'Really, Dr Watson. Your presence here strikes me as a little absurd. I am aware that there is already a policeman outside my door. I must ask you how long you intend to remain. You will understand that I have some business affairs to attend to.'

Dr Watson looked around pointedly. 'I cannot see how Flottie and I are currently in the way.'

'I must prepare some papers.'

'Feel free, sir.' He gave a wave of his hand at the table in front of him. 'I bought myself an evening newspaper on my way here, so I shan't need any entertaining.'

'Very well,' returned Moran stiffly. 'Please excuse me for a moment.' He stole from the room and returned a minute or two later with a newspaper of his own. In uncomfortable silence the three of us settled down to wait for Mr Holmes. Without the consolation of reading matter, I stared into the fire and tried to make sense of what I had seen and heard that day.

In the description of Melmoth it was hard not to see the scheming figure of Fogarty, with his Egyptian cigarettes and his passion for exerting power over others. If that were so, I could see why he might need to kill Mr Neale to protect his identity. But why was Mrs Hudson now afraid for Mr Moran? What connection was there between the two? Certainly the news of Neale's death had not appeared to frighten Moran. He had been genuinely surprised – perplexed even – but at no point did he seem in the least bit concerned for his own safety. Could that be an act? I looked at where he sat, apparently engrossed in his reading. He was clearly angry and impatient at our intrusion but it was hard to believe that any suspicion of danger lurked beneath his stiff exterior. If anything there was the faintest sense of triumph about him, a suggestion in his eyes that on the whole events were suiting him very well indeed.

Perhaps Mrs Hudson was wrong? Perhaps Moran wasn't in danger from Fogarty after all? In which case we shouldn't be sitting by the fire, allowing the pursuit of Fogarty to languish. We should be after him, trying to prove he had been at Neale's house that day, trying with every means at our disposal to bring him to book for his crimes. As I looked into the flames, a plan began to occur to me. It should surely not be beyond me to discover if Fogarty had an alibi for the day's dramatic events. If I could unearth something, just one telling fact about his whereabouts that day, it might make all the difference. I thought of the fair-haired boy. Was he really to die in squalor? One fact might be enough to save him.

I looked again at the scene around me. Dr Watson and Mr Moran were still engaged in silent contemplation of their mutual dislike. Outside Gregory's men were watching, and Mr Holmes was coming later. I could make little difference where I was, but out there…

My decision made, I gave a small cough and then leaned forward towards Dr Watson.

'I think, sir, I'd better be going. I'm feeling a little faint and some air might help.'

Dr Watson was all apologies. 'Of course, Flotsam. Not much fun for you here. I should have realised that…'

Mr Moran got to his feet when I stood up to leave and I gave him a formal curtsey. 'I'll show myself to the door, if I may, please, sir.' And with that I slipped out to the stairs and was gone.

Back in the street, I paused to look around. The crowds were only slightly thinner though it was darker now and the cold was flagrant in its attentions. On the far side of the street, the patrolling constable touched his hat to me. Somewhere, in one of the doorways, his rival would be scribbling my reappearance in a note book. I looked around again, impatiently, and then heard the low whistle I had been hoping for. Scraggs had stepped out of the shadow of an arch and was beckoning furiously.

'In here, Flot,' he whispered as I approached. 'Mrs H told me to keep out of sight. Which isn't easy with the street full of people watching the same doorway. We might as well get together and agree shifts.' He paused and looked me up and down. 'You look like a real lady in them clothes, Flot. I hardly recognise you sometimes nowadays. Are you off back to Baker Street?'

I shook my head. 'Listen, Scraggs, did you know that Mr Neale's dead?'

He nodded quickly. 'Yeah. Heard about it just now from the bobby over there. Who did it?'

'There's no telling for sure but I think I may be able to find out something that will help. Everything seems quiet here so I thought I'd chance it.'

Scraggs was looking doubtful. 'I don't know,' he said, rubbing his chin with the back of his hand. 'That hoo-hah down here earlier. It was all a bit too neat. It made me think something might be up after all.'

'Did anyone get into Moran's?'

He shook his head helplessly. 'I don't think so, but for a moment or two the crowd got in the way and I couldn't see the door.'

'Well there's no-one up there now. Look, I'm sure Mrs Hudson will be along here tonight. If you see her, tell her I'll be back soon.'

Scraggs pulled a face. 'I don't like the sound of that, Flot. You'll be off getting yourself into trouble and we've got enough of that as it is.' He looked around impatiently as if suddenly aware his hands were tied. 'I promised Mrs H I'd keep a lookout, and that's what I'd better do. But you know I'd be coming with you else, don't you, Flot?'

'Yes, I know you would,' and for a moment our eyes met quite seriously.

'Just look after yourself, then,' he grunted and before I could reply his eyes had turned back to Moran's doorway, and he let me slip away into the crowds without goodbye.

Sticking to the well-lit streets, I made my way east, moving as quickly as I could through the milling pedestrians. Although it was dark, the fog was not yet down and for a fleeting hour London would look like a city at play, crowds swaying past the theatres and music halls, tying into little knots around street performers, or spinning off the main current into the alleyways, where infinite possibility hung like a dark promise. By nine, the November fogs would take hold and turn even the most riotous celebrants into little more than muffled travellers struggling from lamp to lamp. But for now it was easy to pick my way and I made good time to the big square in Bloomsbury where Mr Spencer lived. The lights were blazing a welcome in every window of his house, but today I ignored the front door and carried on, in search of the next right turn. It led down a narrow passage to the back of the building. There I found the servants' door and rapped on it with all the force I could muster.

The door was opened by a housemaid in bonnet and apron who looked at my smart black dress and coat with some uncertainty. From behind her I could feel the warmth of the house stretching out to me.

'I need to speak to Mr Reynolds, please,' I told her firmly and at that moment the butler himself appeared at her shoulder. Although divested of both jacket and tie, he still looked more aristocratic than the average earl.

'My word!' he exclaimed. 'It's Mrs Hudson's young friend. What brings you round here at this hour, miss?'

'I need to find Miss Peters,' I explained. 'It's important, but I don't even know where she lives. I thought you might be able to help me.'

If this struck as an explanation that raised more questions than it answered, it was one that Reynolds seemed happy to accept.

'Of course, miss. Come right in and get yourself warm.' He led me through the kitchen, where a footman in his shirtsleeves greeted me with a startled bow, to a cosy back room busy with prints of racehorses. 'You see, miss, Miss Peters is the Earl's ward so she is here a great deal of the time. But she actually resides with her aunt, Mrs Gresham, near St James's. I believe however, being a high-spirited young lady, she is very rarely at home of an evening.'

He turned back to the door. 'James,' he called, 'could I trouble you for a moment?'

The footman appeared hastily and honoured me with another little nod.

'James, do you happen to know where Miss Peters will be this evening?'

'She's at the Fitzroys' this evening, Mr Reynolds. But she won't be there early if I know her at all. You might catch her at her aunt's for the next hour or so.'

'Very good, James. Do you know if Carrington was expecting to take out the Earl's carriage tonight?'

'I think there was some talk that Mr Spencer might be going out, but he's decided to study. With the Earl staying at his club, I should think Carrington is probably unharnessing the horses as we speak, Mr Reynolds.'

'Thank you. Could you catch him before he does and tell him he is to call for Miss Peters at her aunt's with a message from Miss Flotsam? The ladies will give him further instructions after that.'

'Very good, Mr Reynolds.' Accompanying a respectful nod in my direction with the slightest suspicion of a wink, James departed on his errand.

Mr Reynolds, having taken control, carried on as though such things were the merest commonplace.

'You will probably wish to call for Miss Peters yourself, miss, but I think it would be appropriate to send in a note on your arrival. Have you given any thought to what such a note might say?'

I had done nothing of the sort, but my rather unplanned scheme was going far better than I had expected and I felt wonderfully, vibrantly alert.

'Might I just tell her that if it were at all convenient I would very much like to speak to her?'

Reynolds appeared to weigh my words carefully.

'If I might make a suggestion, miss, having known Miss Peters for many years I feel a rather more forceful message might achieve better results. Far be it for me to compose on your behalf, but I suspect something along the lines of "High drama – come at once" would serve your purpose rather better.'

And so I composed my note, employing – in the spirit of Reynolds's suggestion – a very large number of exclamation marks. Reynolds settled himself comfortably into his chair and watched me write.

'Another one of Mrs Hudson's escapades, I daresay, miss. Ah, what an excellent woman she is! Although it's some years ago now, none of us have forgotten what a great help she was to the Earl when we had that problem with the pastry cook and the Dowager's will. Oh, yes, the Earl was quite a wild one in those days, though of course you'd never guess it now. Quite the Tartar nowadays. Mr Rupert is hoping the Earl will fund a proper laboratory for his work, but it's been made quite clear to him that any youthful high jinx and the money will all go elsewhere. So now the young gentleman hardly dares go out for fear of getting into some sort of scrape.'

And so a peaceful quarter of an hour passed during which time I was able to arrange my ideas in some semblance of order. By the time I found myself rattling towards St James's in the Earl's own carriage, I had a plan of sorts and too many thoughts in my head to leave room for worry. Miss Peters responded to my note precisely as Reynolds had predicted, bounding into the carriage with a whoop barely two minutes after it was delivered.

'Flottie!' she cried, folding me in an exuberant embrace. 'You *are* an angel! I've always *heard* about the things Mrs Hudson gets up to but I never expected to be allowed to join in! I always thought I was *far* too silly for anything like that. But here I am! I had the most gorgeous dress ready for the Fitzroys' but of course this is going to be much more fun! I should only have ended up dancing with the Walters boy who is so painfully dull, though frightfully good-looking, of course, and a quite marvellous dancer, as well as being a war hero and everything, which I think rather goes to show that getting medals is all very well, but it never made anyone good company, did it? Even Rupert is better to talk to, and he can be almost the dullest person alive, with all his formulas and things.'

She gave a little bounce on her seat and looked out of the window.

'Oh, we're still here! Shouldn't we be going somewhere as fast as we can? And where *are* we going? We can't keep Carrington sitting up there in the cold all night.'

I gave her the address of Fogarty's house and after some breathless words to our coachman the carriage rolled on again into the night.

'But isn't that the Fotheringays' address?' she asked with a little frown when she had settled back into her seat. 'Oh, Flottie, I can't *possibly* call on them. They are frightfully important and they hardly know me from Adam and I'm simply not dressed for it at all. Or should that be from Eve? I'm never sure. *Please* tell me it's not the Fotheringays, Flottie.'

Very calmly, speaking without pauses so as to ward off interruptions, I tried to explain my plan. After a while she began to listen quite seriously and it wasn't until I finished that she spoke again. When she did it was with genuine anxiety.

'Oh, but Flottie, I simply can't. I can't call on the Fotheringays. It would be most irregular. I should make a most frightful fool of myself. The Earl would have a fit!'

I paused to contemplate this setback. I had rather assumed that someone like Miss Peters knew everybody and would be as at home with the Fotheringays as she was with Mr Spencer. It had never occurred to me that it would be anything other than supremely simple for her to stroll into their drawing room and charm all the information I was seeking from the head of the household. I had imagined her sealing Fogarty's fate while a grateful household volunteered to bear witness against him. Now I had to rethink and, to make matters worse, the carriage was pulling to a halt a few doors away from our destination.

'You mean you really don't know them *at all*?' I asked desperately.

'Well, I've been at the same parties, but the Fotheringays are so *serious*, Flottie. Mr Fotheringay is always being called away to advise the Prime Minister on our policy towards Turkestan or Trinchinopoly or somewhere. They wouldn't have the slightest clue who I was even if I turned up on their doorstep and waved my calling card under their noses.'

An idea came to me.

'Then you could pretend to be someone else?'

She opened her mouth to dismiss this out of hand but somehow nothing came out. For fully five unprecedented seconds she said nothing at all, and when she spoke it was in rather a small voice.

'You know, Flottie, I suppose I could.' A thought struck her and suddenly her face lit up again. 'You know, I could pretend to be someone completely made-up! Someone a bit dotty and interesting, not like me at all! Of course, if they are at home they will refuse to see me but I would still be able to see if that awful man Fogarty answers the door. And if he doesn't, I shall... I shall interrogate the maid! It will be fun! Do you know, I've always wondered what it would be like to be one of those earnest women who call at the most inconvenient times to talk interminably about good causes. Nobody seems to think it strange behaviour at all, though I've often wondered why they don't get thrown out a good deal more often than they seem to. And if they can get away with it, why can't I?'

She made an impetuous movement towards the door where Carrington was waiting politely to hand her down.

'Wish me luck!' she cried dramatically and seemed about to disappear when she halted abruptly and turned towards me with a most serious expression on her face.

'Flottie, you don't think I should be a *suffragist*, do you?' Before she had finished asking, her face had begun to brighten again. 'No, of course not. I shouldn't have the *least* idea what I was talking about!'

I waited anxiously as she made her way down the street, half afraid that she would find the red front door barred against her. But it opened promptly at her knock and she disappeared into the light.

It was hard to measure the passing time in the plush silence of the carriage. Carrington had returned to his box and the horses' harnesses jingled softly from time to time. The fog clustered around the windows of the big houses as if it hoped to force its way past them, to smother the bright lights that burned there. Just as I began to grow restless, the door opened and Miss Peters reappeared, turning smartly on her heel with a little skip and clipping down the pavement to where we waited.

'Flottie,' she began excitedly as she bounced down beside me, 'I was an absent-minded philanthropist from Battersea! Isn't that splendid? Do you think it suits me? I was *ever* so convincing. I don't know where I learnt so much about good works and things. It can't have been from Daddy. And of course I'm not entirely sure where Battersea actually *is*. But I know she was most completely taken in.'

'Who was? Mrs Fotheringay?'

'No, silly. The *maid*. Mrs Fotheringay wasn't in. Nor was Mr Fotheringay. Nor was their butler as it turned out. Simply no-one was at home.'

'So what did you find out?' I found myself stressing the last two words very distinctly to make sure they got through. It was something I had noticed Mr Spencer did on occasions and before I had always thought it a little unkind. Now it seemed an absolute necessity. Miss Peters smiled sweetly and appeared completely unperturbed.

'Well, first I asked for Mrs Fotheringay and then I asked for Mr Fotheringay but the maid, who looked rather down-trodden, said they weren't at home, but in the way that means they really *aren't* at home, not the way that means they really are. Then I explained that I had called last week on behalf of the Society for the Propagation of Sacred Causes and I rather thought I had left my spectacles behind and she said she that she hadn't heard of anything left behind and I asked could I speak to the nice butler who I had met when I called. She seemed a bit surprised at that, as if she couldn't imagine him ever being called *nice*, and said that Mr Fogarty was away on other duties today and would I like to speak to the housekeeper instead? And I said, "What, away all day?" And she nodded, and of course now she'd told me one of the things you wanted to know so I really didn't need to speak to the housekeeper at all but I thought I should, just to keep up appearances, so we had a long chat about Sacred Causes, which she seemed to know even less about than I did, which frankly isn't anything at all. And then I left.'

She sat back with a contented sigh. 'I think I did ever so well, don't you, Flottie? I mean, I know you hoped that the Fotheringays would tell me exactly where their butler had been all day, but really I haven't been completely useless, have I?'

I gave her arm a little squeeze. Now that I knew Fogarty had not been engaged at the Fotheringays' that day, it was time to turn to the next stage of my plan. I gave Miss Peters another smile.

'Thank you. You've done wonderfully well. I'm going to slip away now. When I'm gone, get Carrington to take you back. I'll be able to get on with things by myself for a bit and after that I should be getting back to Dr Watson. He must be finding it a very long evening.'

'Flottie, darling, you can't believe for a *moment* that Carrington and I are going to leave you wandering in this fog. Carrington would be scandalised if we did any such thing. We shall be waiting here for you. I *like* waiting, I really do, and Carrington's ever so good at it. I shall be busy imagining the look on Rupert's face when he hears I have spent the evening talking about Good Works.'

Arguing seemed pointless and it was undeniable that the reassurance of an Earl's carriage behind me made me feel a little braver. Nevertheless, when Carrington handed me down and I stepped out into the night, I could feel the blood beating strangely hard in the sides of my head. With that rhythm accompanying me, I took a deep breath and made my way out of the big square and into the darkness at the back of the building.

-

The blue light over the area steps made the night seem colder and the fog thicker. The alley looked as dank and unwelcoming as the last time I entered it, and on this occasion I took good care to avoid the archway where Smale had been lurking. Lights showed in the servants' quarters, throwing squares of light onto the iron steps. At first they didn't hear my knock but after two or three further efforts I heard Smale's voice from somewhere behind the door.

'Who the 'ell's that? Get the door, won't yer?'

The door was opened by a pale girl a year or so younger than me. There was dread in her eyes as she did so, as if every task carried with it the inevitability of failure and of punishment. I might have been this girl, I thought, if fate and a stolen cabbage hadn't intervened.

Her eyes widened with surprise when she found herself confronted by someone female in a respectable coat and hat, as though such callers were beyond her experience. 'I'd like to talk to Smale,' I told her as gently as I could.

'It's a lady for you, Mr Smale,' she called out timidly, and with a curse Smale emerged from the back room into the light. He was in a soiled shirt with his sleeves pushed up untidily and he looked every inch the brute I knew him to be. He too blinked with surprise when he saw me standing there.

'Flotsam, eh? Decided to come back for a spot of work, have yer? Them posh gents not paying?'

'I need to speak to Mr Fogarty, Smale. I've got urgent news for him.'

'You do, do yer?' His surprise was replaced with his more familiar lecherous leer. 'And what might that be then?'

'That's between me and Mr Fogarty. Can I speak to him?'

He drew himself straighter and put one hand on the door frame a little above my head.

'And what's to stop me shaking it out of you right now?' He ran his eyes up and down me. 'Right smart you are again. I'd get a thrill giving a shake to someone who looks like a lady, even though I know there's gutter just under the surface.'

I looked at him with my face as still and expressionless as it had ever been.

'Mr Fogarty might feel he'd get more from me if I volunteered it. Where is he?'

'He's out.' Smale seemed a little unsure of himself, his instinct to bully curbed by his fear of Fogarty's wrath.

'Where?'

He smiled a smile of low cunning. 'That'd be telling. Why're you so keen to see 'im all of a sudden?'

'He wanted news about Moran's case and I've got it. Big news.'

'Oh, that.' Smale seemed to think he was moving onto safer ground. 'I get the feeling Mr Fogarty's a bit disappointed in you on that score, Flotsam. Told me he'd be sorting that problem out for himself. You weren't any bleedin' help at all.' Again his eyes travelled down my body. 'Shouldn't be surprised if he doesn't send for you soon to tell you so. Or he might send me round to give you a few lessons in friendly co-operation.'

I tried to look confused. 'What do you mean, Smale, "sorting it out for himself"? I've got something he needs to know. There's been a murder, you see.'

Smale pulled a face of mock surprise.

'Yer don't say! You'll have to do a lot better than that to get yerself off the hook. Oh, and you can forget all about that boy of yours downstairs. I'd give him two more days at most. Fogarty wants rid of 'im.'

'You know Mr Neale's dead?'

Smale hesitated, suddenly aware he might be giving too much away, but the habit of boasting was too strong for him.

'I've heard the news, I can tell you that much. Bit of a choker for Sherlock Holmes, eh? The bloke he's meant to protect catching a bullet right under his nose.'

A little thrill of triumph tickled my neck. How much more did Smale know?

'Mr Holmes has an idea about that murder. That's why I must find Mr Fogarty tonight. Where is he?'

But Smale was not as stupid as I'd hoped and expected. He was shaking his head.

'Sorry, Flotsam. Not good enough. Fogarty ain't got nothin' to fear from the likes of Mr Holmes. Like I said, he's sorting out his problem by himself. Tonight he's tying up the loose ends. Anything you've got to say can wait till tomorrow when he's finished.' He reached forward and put his hand round the back of my neck. 'Of course, you could come on in and wait inside…'

I shook him off and stepped back. My spirits were sinking again and Smale's touch filled me with disgust. I hated giving him the chance to gloat, but it was true that I'd relied on him giving away much more. Oh, I'd found out Fogarty had been away all day and that Smale knew how Neale had died, and that was proof of sorts. But it was nothing Mrs Hudson didn't suspect already. Perhaps she had been right about the threat to Moran. What were those loose ends Fogarty was tying up? It was time to get back to Dr Watson…

Seeing me about to leave, Smale couldn't restrain himself from one parting shot. So closely did it match the fears passing through my mind that at first I hardly took it in.

'Yes, Flotsam. You get along back to that fancy detective of yours. He'll be havin' a bit to do, explainin' to the newspapers how all three of his clients ended up dead.'

All three. All three. *All three.* A clock was striking nine. At the end of the alley the carriage was waiting. Was there still time? I turned and ran.

'Hetty,' I cried, leaping into the carriage before Carrington could get down from his box. 'We have to get back to Portman Street as quickly as we can. I've made the most terrible mistake.'

–

I had already discovered in the course of the evening that the irascible Earl of Brabham was blessed with sporting servants, and Carrington proceeded to prove the point. He responded gamely to my exhortations and drove his team for all they were worth. However, the Earl's lumbering carriage was not built for speed and the congested streets conspired to thwart his efforts. At times we waited in queues while unnamed obstructions ahead of us choked the streets to a standstill. Frustrated in their attempts to advance, the assorted cabbies and coachmen turned their ire on each other, shouting raucously, trading frank and unflattering epithets with their fellow strugglers. Eventually, somewhere in Oxford Street, Carrington gave up and shouted down to us.

'This is hopeless, miss. Some idiot up ahead tried to turn in the street and now we're stuck fast in all directions. It's these streets, you see. They weren't designed for all this traffic. They should say cabs and carriages only up here after five o'clock. That'd be a start.'

'How long to Portman Street?' I asked.

'Twenty minutes by carriage, miss, five minutes on foot. You'd be quicker to walk from here, and that's the truth.'

I turned hastily to Miss Peters. 'I'm going to leave you, Hetty. I have to get back to Dr Watson as soon as I can. Thank you for being so good to me tonight.' Her reassuring squeeze of my hand as I slipped out of the carriage went a long way towards fortifying me for the ordeal to come.

Out in the street, I was able to make good progress and I was panting by the time I reached Portman Street. When I was still thirty yards short of Moran's door, I glimpsed through the crowds the solid figure of Mrs Hudson approaching from the other direction. She was walking briskly with a large basket on one arm, and the crowds seemed to part for her like water round a battleship. Although I quailed at the reception I would receive when she learned I had deserted my post, my heart gave a little leap at the sight of her. Surely Moran was safe after all. Perhaps my old fear of Smale had distorted my judgement and had allowed his taunt to take on a significance it had not deserved.

Mrs Hudson raised a questioning eyebrow when she noticed my approach.

'Flottie?' she asked when I came up to her. 'Aren't you supposed to be upstairs looking after Dr Watson? What has happened?'

Still out of breath, I poured out my story, how I had left my post in pursuit of clues about Fogarty, and how Smale's last words had brought me rushing back. As I spoke I could see clouds of anxiety gathering on her forehead until her face was set in its sternest expression.

'Come inside, Flotsam. There's nothing to be gained by us freezing out here.'

Inside, at the foot of the stairs that led to Moran's rooms, she paused to take stock.

'I don't like this, Flotsam. I have a bad feeling about tonight and it's getting worse as the evening goes on. Scraggs has just told me about the scuffle in the street earlier. He thinks it was all put on. But you say Moran was well enough when you left him? I hope Dr Watson is safe, Flottie. I wish you'd stayed with him.'

Our conference was interrupted by a small commotion in the street outside caused by the arrival of Inspector Gregory and Mr Holmes, the latter's arm neatly bound in a sling. Before stepping in they heard reports from O'Donnell and his uniformed colleague, and through the glass in the door we could see Holmes shaking his head gravely. When they finally entered the hallway, Mr Holmes did not seem surprised to find us waiting for him.

'Ah, Mrs Hudson!' Holmes declared. 'I perceive from your basket that you have delivered supper to our two sentinels.'

'Not yet, sir. I've only just arrived. We were just about to go up.'

'There's no need for that now. I can take the basket. You may both get back to Baker Street for a well-deserved rest.' He peeped under the gingham cloth and nodded approvingly. 'I'm sure Watson will appreciate this greatly. He is probably thinking about supper even as we speak.'

An unlucky prediction, for even as he spoke a shot rang out from somewhere above us. Mrs Hudson was the first to move, dropping her basket and leaping to the stairs with surprising agility. Holmes was after her in an instant, and overtook her on the first floor landing, his face working with anguish. Gregory followed them three steps at a time and I, the slowest to react, pursued him grimly. For all my efforts I was still toiling on the last landing when I heard Holmes reach the upper apartment. The front door banged open and I heard him shout his friend's name, his voice trembling with fear.

As Gregory and I reached the door, Holmes spoke again, but this time his tone was suddenly different, his voice bland with confusion.

'Great heavens!' he exclaimed, and I saw he had come to a halt in the frame of the door that led away from Moran's sitting room into the rest of the apartment. Coming up to where he stood, Mrs Hudson at his side, I looked into the room beyond and the sight I saw brought me to an abrupt and shocked halt.

For stretched out on the carpet, eyes fixed open and shattered skull pouring blood, lay the body of Nathaniel Moran. And standing over it, a revolver clutched in one hand, was the dazed and swaying figure of Dr Watson.

The Sealed Room

✝

For one fraction of a moment there was complete silence. The four figures in the doorway gaped mutely at the scene before them while the doctor looked at us in total confusion. Suddenly he dropped the weapon onto the rug and stepped back, away from the body.

'Holmes,' he cried desperately. 'Holmes, what has happened?'

Seeing the gun fall, Gregory moved forward smartly and picked it up while Holmes followed Mrs Hudson to the stricken doctor. While Gregory tried to find a pulse in Moran, Mrs Hudson pulled out a chair and with Mr Holmes's help lowered the doctor into it.

'Watson, my dear friend!' he whispered. 'Speak to us. Tell us what has passed here.'

But while Watson was still shaking his head silently we were joined by the uniformed force in the shape of the constable we had spoken to earlier. Close behind him, from his vantage point across the road and still breathing heavily, came O'Donnell, the much put-upon plain clothes man.

Gregory, still kneeling by the body, was quick to take charge. 'Search these rooms, men! I want to know for certain if anyone is concealed here.' They leapt to the task with alacrity but Watson, watching them go, continued to shake his head.

'It's no good, Gregory. There's no-one else here. It was just Moran and me.'

'Hush, sir,' responded Mrs Hudson soothingly. 'You've had a shock and you should just take a moment to recover.'

'Quite right,' agreed Holmes, who remained crouched anxiously by his friend, his hand on the doctor's arm, while the search of the flat was carried out around them.

My experience at the St James Hotel on the night Carruthers died must have taken a deep hold, for while the others looked to Mr Moran or Dr Watson, I found myself taking a detached inventory of the room where the body lay. It was furnished as a dining room and one half of the room was taken up by a dining table and its attendant chairs. The table was laid with the remains of a meal for two, dirty plates and crockery still lying where they had been abandoned. A bottle of claret stood half full in the centre of the table and an empty glass stood by each place. The other half of the room was spread with a dark rug, where Moran now lay dead. Two further doors opened from the room, one apparently to the bedrooms where the searches of both policemen were now concentrated. The other, standing open, revealed a tiny, rudimentary kitchen and a window facing out to the back of the building. The position of the kitchen meant the dining room had no window of its own, relying for light on a dirty skylight above our heads. Heat from the kitchen range filled the room, making the atmosphere doubly oppressive.

Any further study of my surroundings was halted by the return of the two policemen.

'There's no-one here excepting ourselves, sir,' reported O'Donnell. 'We've been through the place inch by inch, like. There's nowhere much to hide though. There's no attics or trapdoors, nothing.'

'Very well.' Gregory was again displaying the energy that I had witnessed at the scene of Carruthers's murder. 'O'Donnell, I want you to check the flats below. The doors should have been secured. Go and take a good look at them and see if they've been touched or tampered with.'

As O'Donnell parted with a salute, Gregory rose and went into the little kitchen that looked over the blind alley at the back of the building. The window was open and, leaning out, he scrutinised the scene below. Then he joined us again and addressed the remaining policeman with crisp decisiveness.

'Jenkins, this afternoon I placed a man at the entrance to the alley behind this building. Fetch him up here as quickly as you can.'

While this exchange was taking place, Mrs Hudson left Dr Watson to Holmes's ministrations and took a shrewd, appraising look around her. I watched her repeat Gregory's visit to the kitchen where she too looked out of the window. Her curiosity satisfied she returned to the dining room, but not before she had examined the kitchen thoroughly and had sniffed interestedly at a pile of pans that had been left lying next to the tiny sink. While Gregory returned to his examination of the body and while Holmes and Watson conversed in low tones, she crossed the room and joined me.

'This is an unusual little apartment,' she commented. 'It really is neither one thing nor the other. These are gentlemen's rooms and it was never intended that there should be a kitchen here at all. At some point someone has seen fit to modernise and at considerable expense has created that cramped and impractical little room. The arrangement is most irregular and I imagine it was intended to allow a gentleman's gentleman to prepare very simple meals.'

Before I could nod wisely at these domestic observations, the two policemen returned together, accompanied by another uniformed member of the ranks.

'This is Flynn, sir. He's been on duty in the alley since four o'clock,' Jenkins reported briskly.

'Thank you, Jenkins. Now, Flynn, I want you to answer very carefully. Has anyone been in or out of the alley in the last hour?'

'No-one, sir. I'd stake my life on it.'

'And could anyone have been concealing themselves there at any point during that time?'

'No, sir. There's nowhere to hide, sir.'

'Did you hear the shot from where you were?'

'No, sir. I must have been up by the main street, sir, where there's a bit of noise.'

'And there has been no other disturbance to divert your attention at any point? I'd rather have the truth, man, even if the truth is that you may be in error.'

'On my life, sir.'

'Is there any way anyone could have entered or left the alley without passing you?'

'No, sir. The facing wall is the back of the old stable block. There was a bad fire there last year, sir, and now all the doors are boarded up. I checked them myself when I came on duty. Apart from these three flats, sir, there's no other windows or doors opening on to it.'

'And no-one could possibly have dropped down to the alley from one of these windows without you noticing?'

'No, sir, most definitely not.'

'Thank you, Flynn. I want you and Jenkins to go back to that alley and search it again. I want to know of absolutely anything that seems suspicious.'

As the policemen shuffled out, Mrs Hudson watched them thoughtfully.

'Of course, Flottie,' she remarked, apparently at random, 'every cook knows it's no good boiling the water after you've made the tea.'

While she continued to look slightly worried at this perplexing thought, Gregory was carrying on briskly.

'Now, O'Donnell, tell us about those doors.'

'Sealed as tight as a Dutch purse, sir. Padlocked from the outside. Police locks. No sign of tampering.'

'Hmm…' Gregory began to look worried and he cast a nervous glance in the direction of Dr Watson. 'Tell me exactly what happened when you heard the shot just now, O'Donnell.'

The policeman contorted his face in thought. 'Well, sir, from where I was you couldn't be sure it was a shot. I heard a bang from somewhere and I was just wondering what it was when I saw Jenkins here charging towards the door. He being much nearer to the shot than me, you see, sir.'

'Yes, quite. Go on.'

'Then I didn't waste any time, sir. I rushed over the road, straight through the outer door and up the stairs. I'd caught Jenkins up by the time we got up here, sir.'

'And did anyone come out of the outer door after the shot?'

'No, sir.'

'There's no possibility you might have missed somebody in the hallway or on the stairs as you came up?'

'None, sir. You've seen it for yourself, sir. There's nowhere to hide.'

'Thank you, O'Donnell.' Gregory paused, at a loss for what to ask next. 'I'd like you to remain downstairs for now. Don't let anyone in or out.'

As the policeman departed, a tense hush fell upon the room. Watson, his colour a little returned, was looking at Holmes who had begun to pace the edge of the rug, parallel to where Moran lay. Mrs Hudson, seated beside me near the dining table, appeared to be examining the pattern on the dirty plates.

'Well, gentlemen,' Gregory began. 'It seems the problem is a simple one after all. Since we know there is no-one else in the building, and no-one has left since the shot was fired, it is clear that Moran has taken his own life. He did, after all, have a great deal on his conscience. Presumably, Dr Watson, you came into the room on hearing the shot and picked up the gun from where he had dropped it?'

Dr Watson, still puzzled and anxious, shook his head. 'I'm sorry to say it, Gregory old man, but there's one difficulty. As you say, I was seated next door by the fire. Moran had cooked us a bit of supper and had just stepped back in here. He said something about tidying up a few things. I was just thinking that another drop of Scotch would go down well when, blow me, a blasted gunshot goes off next door. Well, I hauled myself out of my seat and got in here as fast as I could and, when I got here, there's Moran spread out like that and I think to myself, 'The coward's shot himself.' So I got down to see if there was anything I could do to save him for the gallows but it was pretty clear right away that it was all over. It was only then I realised. *There was no gun.*'

Gregory stared at him, his face a study of mystification. Beside me, Mrs Hudson, after running her forefinger across one of the dinner plates, nodded slightly.

'Go on, Watson,' prompted Holmes.

'Well, Holmes, it all happened a lot quicker than it takes to tell. At first I thought the gun might have fallen from his hand but one glance told me it wasn't nearby. I stood up and looked around, and there it was – placed carefully on the edge of the dinner table at least three yards away. I'd just picked it up when you came rushing in.'

'But Dr Watson,' cried Gregory, 'how can we possibly explain that?'

'I've no idea, I'm afraid. I may be a bit slow sometimes but I knew straightaway that what I was seeing was impossible. Moran couldn't have put the gun there after he shot himself. But who else could have done? I'm afraid it will take a better brain than mine to explain it all. I do know it looks dashed black for me, though.'

'Chin up, Watson!' Holmes thumped him vigorously on the shoulder. 'None of that defeatist talk. This has been quite a shock to all of us but I shall now bring my faculties to bear on the problem and I'm sure we shall have an answer in no time.'

There followed half an hour of strange unreality. Mr Holmes produced two magnifying glasses of different sizes and proceeded to subject each room to the most minute scrutiny. Working with only his uninjured arm, he examined each wall from the skirting board to the picture rail, clambered on a chair to study the skylight, and even descending the stairs to check the doors to the lower apartments. He too examined the view from the kitchen window into the alley below. While all this went on, Dr Watson circled around the whisky decanter and occasionally helped himself to another glass of Scotch. Mrs Hudson, after a careful sniff at the decanter, decided to join him and, after some desultory wanderings through the bedrooms returned to her station next to the dinner plates. Gregory, now thoroughly deflated, went through the motions of investigation for a short while and then joined the rest of us in the dining room, staring morosely at the whisky glasses. All this was watched by the sightless eyes of Moran from his final vantage point in the middle of the room. The fire in the kitchen had gone out and the room was beginning to grow cool.

Finally Mr Holmes rejoined us, his eyes still hazy with concentration. He stepped over Moran without apparently noticing him and pulled out a chair from the dinner table. The rest of us watched him settle down and waited in silence.

'This case presents certain difficulties,' he announced at last.

'Well, Holmes?' asked Watson eagerly. 'Can you put us all out of our misery?'

Holmes had taken out his pipe and was contemplating it so carefully he appeared not to hear the question.

'I suppose, Gregory, that all your men are to be trusted.'

'I can see no reason why not, Mr Holmes. O'Donnell and Jenkins are certainly honest and while I don't know Flynn so well, all his brothers are in the force and they are all generally well spoken of.'

'Hmm. I feared as much.' Holmes took out a small pouch and, holding his pipe between his knees, used his good hand to stuff it with a dark, rather pungent tobacco. 'As I say, the case presents certain difficulties. Gregory, when you entered the kitchen to look out into the alley, did you happen to notice if the window was already open?'

'Yes, Mr Holmes, it was. At first that struck me as important. But, on reflection, the heat from the range made that little room uncomfortably hot so the open window was only to be expected.'

'Hmm. You will notice that the only other windows that give onto the back of the house, those in the bedrooms, are secured from the inside. It would be fanciful to consider the windows at the front of the house as a means of egress as they are high above a busy thoroughfare and, besides, Dr Watson was in the living room from the moment the shot was fired until he entered the dining room and found our assailant vanished. Similarly, my scrutiny of the skylight confirms that it has not been opened or interfered with for many years. We ourselves were at the bottom of the stairs when Moran was shot, so can testify that no-one left the building that way. So we are left with the kitchen window as the only possible means of escape.'

Gregory nodded wearily.

'Yes, sir. And the drainpipe that runs down the back of the house might be reached from that window. It would be a hazardous descent but a daring man might make it. Yet Flynn was on guard in that alley until some minutes after the shot was fired and the alley offers no place of concealment. I can't see how the window helps us, sir.'

Again there was a silence. Everyone was looking at Mr Holmes expectantly, with the exception of Mrs Hudson who was licking the tip of her finger thoughtfully.

'Have you another theory, Gregory?' Holmes asked.

'Well, sir, if there was no way in or out, perhaps the shot was fired from outside. The roof of the old stable block across the alley overlooks these rooms and if the window were open…'

Holmes and Watson both sprang to their feet. Holmes took up a position in the centre of the room, his feet on each side of Moran's body. Holding his pipe at arm's length and pointing it at the open window, he closed one eye and squinted down the line of his arm. Watson stood slightly behind him, stooping so that he too could follow the direction in which Holmes was pointing.

'My word, Gregory,' commented Holmes after a moment of consideration, 'it is possible that you have excelled yourself. Your colleagues at Scotland Yard are not noted for their imagination but the scenario you suggest, although unlikely, is actually possible. If Moran was of roughly my height and was standing about here, then a marksman hidden beside those chimneys would have a clear line of fire. And, purely by chance, his bullet would pass through the open window.'

'It would be a damned fine shot, Holmes,' said Watson, still peering into the dark, 'but I've known Pathans out in Afghanistan who could shoot the face off a penny piece from a distance not much shorter than this one.'

For a moment all three men seemed to swell with shared gratification until a small cough from Mrs Hudson brought them back to the scene of the crime.

'Excuse me, sir, but how does that theory explain the revolver on the dining table?' She had risen from her chair and out of polite curiosity was also examining the line through the open window that had so excited Mr Holmes.

'Well, Mrs Hudson,' he replied, 'there is nothing to tell us for certain that the fatal shot came from that gun.'

'Of course not, Holmes,' added Watson. 'If Moran was nervous for his safety it is highly likely that he should have armed himself with a revolver. He might have been carrying it all along and happened to place it on the table the minute before he was shot.'

'Do you have a better idea, Mrs Hudson?'

'Well, sir, if I may be so bold I should like to ask Mr Watson a little more about how he spent the evening.'

'With Moran, you mean, Mrs H? There's very little to tell. Just sat around and waited for Holmes, don't you know.'

'Perhaps if you could indulge me with a little more detail, sir?'

'Certainly. If I can. Let's see. When Flotsam left, Moran made another attempt to persuade me to leave. He seemed extraordinarily keen to keep his own company. But he soon saw I was having none of it and he became quite cold. "Am I to understand I am under house arrest?" he asked. Told him not to be so damned silly. Pointed out that he'd asked for our help and now he was jolly well going to get it. Then I turned my back on him and settled down to my newspaper. Fascinating item about a fellow called Phelps who claimed he shot the last quagga in the Cape. Thought he might have been the father of a chap I was at school with. Must have been reading for half an hour or more before I remembered the chap I was at school was called Phillips, not Phelps.'

'And did Moran stay with you all this time, sir?'

'Absolutely, Mrs Hudson. He wasn't happy though. I noticed how jumpy he was, looking around at the slightest sound. I suppose he was still worried about those Sumatrans.'

'And then what happened?'

'At about eight o'clock I suppose we were both feeling a bit peckish and Moran suggested he get a bit of supper together. I thought he meant to go out for it at first, but he assured me that if I gave him half an hour or so, he'd see if there was anything in the house he could scrape together. To be honest it was a relief to have him out of the room. Since I'd been shown the true nature of the man, I found it rather uncomfortable sharing a space with him.'

Mrs Hudson was listening very intently now, one round arm folded across her bosom, the other resting on it to support her chin.

'As you can imagine, I wasn't particularly looking forward to breaking bread with the blighter, but as it happens he served up a remarkably tasty little meal. Potatoes, greens and the best cheese soufflé I can remember tasting. Good bottle of claret too.'

'And he produced all this from that kitchen?' asked Mrs Hudson, pointing.

'Well, I can't see where else it could have come from, Mrs H. Obviously I didn't stand over the fellow while he worked.'

'Did he serve the food to you while you were seated at the table?'

'Really, Mrs Hudson!' interrupted Holmes. 'I understand your interest in such matters but surely the dead man's serving arrangements cannot be relevant here?'

Mrs Hudson's eyes never left Dr Watson. 'Did he, sir?'

'No, Mrs Hudson. It was all laid out on the table when he asked me to come through.'

'Of course it was,' said Mrs Hudson to no-one in particular. 'And the kitchen door, Dr Watson, was firmly closed for the entire time you were dining?'

Dr Watson was looking concerned now, as though he feared these questions were designed to undermine the theory that appeared to exonerate him.

'Yes, Mrs Hudson, it was,' he admitted after a pause.

Gregory was quick to leap in.

'I don't think, Mrs Hudson, that the position of the door *while they were eating* has any bearing on my suggestion of what happened here. Granted, if the door were shut our marksman would have less opportunity to get Moran in his sights, but when Moran opened the door to begin tidying up, that obstacle was removed.'

'Ah, yes. "Tidying up…" I believe, Dr Watson, that was the phrase Mr Moran used when he left you in the sitting room shortly before he was shot?'

'Something like that, Mrs Hudson. "Excuse me while I go and tidy up a few things." I think those were the words he used.'

'Mr Moran was clearly something of an ironist, Dr Watson. Thank you, that is all I wished to ask.' And to everyone's surprise she lowered herself back into her chair with an air of finality.

Holmes and Gregory exchanged glances.

'And where exactly does that leave us, Mrs Hudson?' asked Holmes, his pipe and one eyebrow both raised.

'The assassin, sir, is a man of more than average height. Earlier today he murdered Mr Neale. This evening he was concealed in the kitchen all the time Dr Watson was dining. He passed the time smoking a rare brand of cigarette. If you want confirmation of this, I suggest that Inspector Gregory sends his men to search directly below the kitchen window. They are likely to find the remains of at least one Egyptian cigarette identical to that found at Neale's house.'

A silence fell more profound than any that had preceded it. Watson and Holmes both stared at Mrs Hudson in astonishment. Inspector Gregory frankly gaped. I, for all my faith, found myself trembling at the audacity of her assertion. Finally Dr Watson sank back on to his chair with a deep escape of breath.

'I can't see how you work all that out, Mrs H, but I'm very pleased to hear you say it.'

Holmes lowered his pipe and smiled quizzically. 'Mrs Hudson, I confess you astonish me. Could we ask you to share with us the reasoning behind this startling theory?'

'Indeed, ma'am,' added Gregory. 'Until you have explained some very baffling details, you will forgive me if I remain a little sceptical.'

'Of course, sir. Why don't you gentlemen sit down. It's hard to be comfortable seated around the unfortunate gentleman here, especially on these chairs, but there's no harm in our trying.'

There was a moment of subdued settling down, Gregory clearly still incredulous, Holmes having finally succeeded in lighting his pipe with one good hand, showing in his smile signs of amusement at the policeman's discomfiture. Watson was leaning forwards intently, his honest face turned hopefully to where Mrs Hudson sat, unperturbed by the attention she suddenly commanded. She gave herself a little shake from side to side as if to form a better contact with the narrow dining chair and, after a little cough to clear her throat, addressed herself to Mr Holmes.

'There were, sir, two particular things that told me a third person was present in these rooms when Mr Moran met his end. As a housekeeper by profession, I can only sit back and marvel at the way you search so systematically for scientific clues that would mean nothing to me. But in domestic matters I've had years of experience that you gentlemen don't have, so it's hardly surprising I see things in a kitchen that are beneath the attention of your investigations.'

Holmes nodded slowly as she spoke, his pipe unattended in his hand.

'And to what particular details do you wish to draw our attention, Mrs Hudson?'

'If you will allow me, sir, I suggest you take a close look at the state of the oven.'

'The *oven*, Mrs Hudson?'

'Of course, sir. As I pointed out to Flotsam here, the kitchen here is rather an unusual domestic arrangement. These being bachelor's rooms you wouldn't expect to find a kitchen here at all. But at some point in the past someone decided it was necessary and created that tiny kitchen as we see it now, in the process robbing this dining room of its only window. A most unsatisfactory arrangement, if I may say so. The range is small and awkward and seems unnecessary for a place like this. Indeed it's clear that the oven has rarely been used. You can see from a glance inside that, unlike the top of the stove, it shows signs of rust and old marks that suggest it has not been in use – or properly cleaned – for some years before tonight. Penge may have been using this stove to prepare breakfast but his ambition clearly hasn't extended to baking or roasting.'

'Mrs Hudson, I fear I'm failing to see the significance of all this. But go on. What is the second detail to which you wish to draw our attention?'

'To the peculiarity of the cheese soufflé that Dr Watson enjoyed this evening.'

'But Mrs Hudson,' exclaimed Watson, 'there was nothing at all wrong with the cheese soufflé. It was quite perfect.'

'That, Dr Watson, is the peculiarity I find so interesting.'

A short silence followed this extraordinary utterance. The doctor looked completely baffled and Gregory suddenly tutted impatiently. Holmes however had an eyebrow raised and was eyeing Mrs Hudson with extreme attention, as if her words were opening up important lines of thought in his brain.

'Indeed, Mrs H. A fascinating concept. I only wish I had thought of it myself.'

'Eh, Holmes?' Watson's perplexity showed no signs of untangling itself. 'I'm sorry. You'll have to make it all a great deal clearer for me, I'm afraid.'

'My apologies, gentlemen.' Mrs Hudson was leaning back with eyebrows trembling slightly as if she were enjoying herself enormously. 'I fear I am being quite unnecessarily cryptic. A most objectionable habit, I'm sure. And I am running ahead of myself. I shall return to these details in a moment. I only mention them now because they confirmed for me what I already believed – that there was a third party present here throughout the evening. Since Dr Watson didn't kill Moran and Moran clearly didn't kill himself, the murder must either have been done as you suggest, by someone outside the building, or by someone who was here all along. Now you must forgive me if I find

255

your manly grasp of angles and lines of fire magnificent but just a little unlikely. Quite possible, of course, but how much easier if the murderer was simply hidden in the kitchen.'

'But, Mrs Hudson...!'

'I know, Inspector. I'm aware of the difficulties. But I look at it like this. There has only been one opportunity this evening for anyone to enter this building without our knowing about it, and that was during the highly contrived disturbance in the street outside. That occurred just before Dr Watson and Flottie's visit. So anyone who entered then would have been seen by them on the stairs – unless he had already entered these rooms before they arrived.'

Dr Watson raised his hand. 'But how could he have entered without Moran knowing? It's simply not possible. Yet when we arrived Moran was adamant that he was alone.'

'Yes, sir. You made the mistake of assuming that Moran was as afraid of intruders as he pretended. In fact he had no sense of danger. This was a welcome caller, someone he *wanted* to meet. From his anxiety to be rid of you, it's clear he was extremely eager to attend to his guest.'

Dr Watson lowered his hand thoughtfully and Mrs Hudson continued.

'Now, let us imagine events. While those observing the front door are distracted, a mystery visitor – let us call him Melmoth – slips inside. Moran welcomes him in and is eager to speak to him. The pair are, however, almost immediately interrupted by the arrival of Flottie and Dr Watson. There are clearly reasons – almost certainly criminal ones – why Moran and Melmoth do not wish to be found in conference. So Melmoth slips into the dining room and waits for Moran to show you the door. Imagine their consternation when you will not be persuaded to leave at any price. Moran is in a difficult situation but, under the pretence of fetching his newspaper, he is able to appraise Melmoth of the situation. The pair agree to wait until the obstinate guests take their leave.'

Heads were nodding now. Even Gregory seemed to feel this sequence of events made sense.

'Now if Melmoth had called with the idea of murder already formed – and I believe he had – why did he not do so at that point, when he was briefly alone with Moran? Why wait so tediously? Perhaps he was not yet certain that Moran had to die. Or perhaps a cunning scheme was forming in his brain. When he was informed that the inconvenient visitor was none other than the renowned Dr Watson, what better than to make his mystifying escape in such a way as to throw suspicion onto the doctor? So he waited, sir. And the longer he waited, the more convinced you became that you and Moran were alone.'

By now we were all listening with intense concentration. A little shudder ran through me at the thought of murder so coldly calculated. Mrs Hudson gave another shuffle in her chair.

'When Moran excused himself on the pretence of investigating supper, he was probably doing no more than looking for an excuse to confer further with his new accomplice. By now Moran may have been worrying, rightly, that your continued presence was the prelude to a visit from Mr Holmes and possibly the police. He left the room to explain his fears to Melmoth.

'At this point it is only fair to explain that I have my own ideas about Melmoth's true identity. The man I have in mind is quite capable of seizing upon the opportunity that presented itself. He liked the supper idea. It gave Moran an excuse to absent himself from the sitting room and so enabled the two to talk without arousing Dr Watson's suspicions. Furthermore, by entertaining in the dining room Moran would cement in Dr Watson's mind the idea that the rooms beyond the sitting room were unoccupied. So while the two of them got down to the discussions interrupted by Dr Watson, Melmoth prepared supper.'

Gregory opened his mouth to interrupt but Mrs Hudson silenced him with a stern glare.

'I am aware, Inspector, that this is all speculation, which is why the domestic details are so important. We know the oven was not commonly used. Tonight someone used it. It is *possible* that Moran, liberated by the absence of Penge, decided to experiment with new levels of culinary creativity. But it is surely unlikely. Dr Watson also testifies to the perfect soufflé. To create such an object on such an awkward range attests to a highly skilled hand. It is possible that Moran has long concealed a talent for soufflé. But again, surely unlikely. These details prove nothing in themselves, you see, but they are enough to convince me of the presence here tonight of one Maurice Orlando Fogarty.'

The effect of this declaration was dramatic, startling her listeners like a sudden flash of lightning. I felt a little surge of pride at their astonishment.

'Maurice Orlando *who*?' muttered Watson.

'Never heard of him!' added Gregory.

Mr Holmes laid down his pipe on the dining table.

'Let me get this clear, Mrs Hudson. You are telling us that as well as knowing *how* this murder was committed, you also know the identity of the murderer?'

'Oh yes, sir.' Mrs Hudson seemed surprised at the question. 'I've known that all along. It was finding ways of demonstrating it that was the difficulty. Even now I'm afraid I don't have actual *proof*. Not proof that would hang the man. But enough for my own satisfaction, and that is at least something.'

'But who is this man Fogarty?'

'There will be plenty of time to tell you all about Fogarty later, sir. For now, suffice it to say that his soufflés have been praised from Madrid to St Petersburg. His fish soufflé once turned the head of a minor, though quite substantial, Bourbon princess. But tell me, sir, before I go on, don't you think something should be done for Mr Moran? It seems wrong to leave him here very much longer.'

'Presently, Mrs Hudson. When you've finished.' Holmes waved aside her query with his pipe. 'Now let us suppose this Fogarty was here tonight. Let us agree with your remarkable contention that Watson's supper is itself proof of his presence. Let us even set aside for the time being the question of *why* he committed this remarkable crime. How do you propose to explain his disappearance into thin air?'

'But that is surely quite simple, sir. We know he must have left through the kitchen window. There is no alternative. When Dr Watson was seated comfortably next door, Fogarty shot Moran, taking care to place the gun on the table so that a verdict of suicide could not be an option. He was out of the window while Dr Watson was still rising from his armchair. He had of course taken care to plan his escape long before he paid his visit. Mr Fogarty is the sort of man who likes to know the whereabouts of the back door before he calls at the front.'

Inspector Gregory looked as though he was in danger of exploding.

'But, Mrs Hudson, you heard my man swear that there was no-one in that alley at any time. How could he have escaped?'

'He simply walked out of the alley, sir. Calmly so as not to excite suspicion, I imagine.'

'Then you think Flynn was lying?'

'Oh no, Inspector.' Mrs Hudson seemed appalled at the thought. 'Flynn wasn't there.'

'But he claims he was there all afternoon and evening.'

'No, sir. Shortly after the murder you asked him to come up here. I imagine Fogarty anticipated something of the sort. He's generally clever that way. He knew the chance would arise.'

Gregory's tone began to contain a hint of desperation.

'But he was out of that window before Dr Watson could cross the sitting room. Flynn was still there at that point. And he could hardly have failed to notice a man dropping to the alley.'

'Of course not, sir. But why do you assume he dropped to the alley straightaway? Why do you assume the only way out of the window is down?'

The beginnings of a ghostly pallor began to show in Gregory's face.

'You mean he…'

'Yes, sir. The drainpipe leads *up* as well as *down*. Now, it's not very firmly attached, but if you take another look you will see that a man with a good reach might succeed in clambering from the window up to the roof without relying on it. That is why I suggested he must be above average height. From the roof he would have a good view of the alley. When he saw your man withdrawn, he made his escape. Of course, he was prepared to wait there for as long as it took, guessing rightly that the police would be slow to undertake a search of the rooftops.'

'But if you knew…' Gregory seemed lost for words. 'If you had told us this before, surely his escape could have been prevented?'

'I did think about that, Inspector. But he is a ruthless man, sir, not afraid of desperate measures. I feared that if I raised the alarm earlier you gentlemen would have insisted on heroic pursuit and he would not have hesitated in shooting at least one of you dead. A very masculine sequence of events but what an unnecessary waste it would have been. Fogarty will not escape forever, sir. For now I thought it better to wait.'

'Bravo, Mrs Hudson!' Mr Holmes rose smiling from his seat and slapped the speechless Gregory firmly on the shoulder. 'Inspector, see what a study of my methods can achieve? I too had wondered about the rooftop. But is it really possible that you withdrew the *only* observer from the alley?'

Gregory's face looked grey and his eyes glassy.

'I'm afraid so, Mr Holmes.'

'It never occurred to me you would have been so short-sighted. Thankfully Mrs Hudson has less confidence in Scotland Yard than I do.' He slapped Gregory's shoulder a second time. 'Cheer up! Watson is proved innocent and you will be able to show Lestrange and your other colleagues the mechanics of a singularly daring murder. All that remains to us now is to hear from Mrs Hudson about why this Fogarty character was so determined to kill Moran.'

'Why, yes!' Some animation began to return to Gregory and he looked eagerly across at Mrs Hudson. 'And it may not be too late to make an arrest!'

A knock at the door prevented her from replying and the sturdy figure of Jenkins entered the dining room.

'Please, sir, just to report that Flynn and I have gone through that alley inch by inch. No sign of anyone hiding there, sir.'

'No, Jenkins, I'm afraid we're too late for that.'

'There was one thing, sir. There's a drainpipe runs down the wall from just about here. Flynn noticed that the section at the bottom has come away from the wall a fraction. He's not sure, but he doesn't think it was like that before. We thought we should mention it, sir.'

Gregory looked slightly sick. 'Good work, Jenkins,' he muttered. 'Is there anything else?'

'Only these, sir.' He held out his hand and revealed three or four dark objects lying in his large, pink palm. 'We found them by the drainpipe, sir. Looks like someone was having a smoke.'

We crowded forwards to look closer. The cigarette ends, though damp from the cobbles, were strikingly familiar.

Mrs Hudson picked one up and held it thoughtfully. 'A number of gentlemen smoke Egyptian cigarettes. And there's nothing to show these were smoked in this kitchen. I'm afraid, Inspector, there is nothing here to justify an arrest. The man you seek will have taken care there is not.' She turned to the assembled company.

'If you will forgive me, gentlemen, I see it is already after midnight. There is nothing I can add to what we've all seen tonight and nothing more to be done. Flotsam here has scarcely had a night's sleep in the last two weeks and Mr

Holmes is still pale from his wound. I shall be delighted to explain all my ideas about recent events tomorrow, but now I think it's time for us to head home. It's been a difficult day.'

'Mrs Hudson is right once again, gentlemen,' Mr Holmes concluded happily. 'But before we go, Mrs H, I want your promise that tomorrow evening we shall gather at Baker Street to hear what you have to say. That is agreed? Excellent! Very well then. Until tomorrow!'

The Hittites' Revenge

✝

The next day was a Sunday and the persistence of the church bells left the city in no doubt of the fact. Mrs Hudson, who was a surprisingly irregular churchgoer herself, clearly felt that after I had been exposed to such naked transgression of the Sixth Commandment it was vital for the good of my soul on this particular morning that I should attend. So, leaving the gentlemen undisturbed, we ventured smartly into the mist-shrouded morning where the successful completion of much organised standing, kneeling and sitting left us wide awake and with a ready appetite. We returned as pale sunshine was attempting to break through the mist to the streets below. Mrs Hudson seemed peculiarly bashful about her performance of the previous evening, changing the subject whenever, frequently, I returned to it.

'Flotsam,' she said eventually, 'I wish I could share your sense of enthusiasm. But there's a man dead who should still be alive if I had been a little quicker of thought and a little less willing to think well of myself. And Fogarty will be walking the streets this morning as free as he ever was, with nothing to be done about it.' The thought seemed to cast her into deep gloom and her lips pursed into a worried grimace.

Despite her words and regardless of the efforts of the Church, I found it hard to mourn Moran. For now the air was bright, people in the streets were smiling and I was full of pride in the solid figure who walked beside me. It seemed like a day to be happy.

'And you're forgetting something else, Flotsam.' It was as if she had divined the frivolity of my thoughts. 'It's four days now since you last met Fogarty. That's four days since he threatened to let that boy of his die. Now the little difficulty with Moran has been sorted out, Fogarty has even less use for your help and even less reason to keep the boy.'

'But, ma'am, if he feels everything is settled now, won't he just throw the boy out? What can he gain now from carrying out his threat?'

'Fogarty thrives on power, Flottie. You have let him down and it is important for him to punish you. He saw you felt pity for the boy. It will amuse him to let you feel the guilt for his death.'

Suddenly the day seemed a good deal less bright and the places touched by the sun seemed only to accentuate the cold of the shadows.

'What's to be done, ma'am?'

'As I said to Mr Rumbelow, we must take action. Fogarty will not expect that from the likes of us, and I'm reluctant to allow him to win every trick. Tell me, Flottie, do you think you could find the boy again if you went back to that house?'

I hesitated, trying to recall the twists and turns I had taken when I had followed Fogarty on my previous visit.

'I think so, ma'am. It's all a bit confused in my mind right now, but I think if I was actually there…'

'Good. That gives us a chance. Though we shall need to enlist some assistance. I wonder…'

And she descended into a deep, contemplative silence that persisted until we were back at Baker Street.

Perhaps to make sure that I didn't dwell too much on the triumphs of the previous evening, Mrs Hudson made sure that there was plenty to do that morning and it was not until Scraggs arrived in the early afternoon that I had a chance to stop and look around.

'Hello, Flot,' he said warmly, perching himself on the kitchen table. 'I just thought I'd pop in and see what's up.'

'I'm up to my neck in hard work, that's what. Did you hear about last night at all, Scraggs?'

He nodded. 'Friend of mine has a brother in the police. I hear old Mrs H showed them all a thing or two.'

'It's not *old Mrs H* to you, Scraggs,' came a stern voice from down the corridor, followed by the appearance of the woman herself. 'We'll have a bit of respect when you're in this house, young scallywag. Nevertheless, for all your cheek, I'm glad to see you. I need someone to take a message to Mr Spencer.'

'I'm your man, Mrs H,' he chirped brightly, bouncing down from the table. 'It's my pleasure to serve the old and wise.'

Mrs Hudson scowled. 'You are an insufferable young ruffian, Scraggs. More of your cheek and I'll take my business elsewhere. Which isn't to say you didn't do good work last night. Stuck to your post like glue. Unlike some people.'

I felt myself flushing but, at the crucial moment, Mrs Hudson's frown at me wobbled slightly in a way that rendered it useless for purposes of serious intimidation. 'Now, Flottie, you go and take those tea things in to Mr Holmes while I give Scraggs that message.'

If I wondered at all what Mrs Hudson was plotting with Mr Spencer, I was able to form a pretty shrewd guess that very evening. For when at seven o'clock we were called by Mr Holmes into the study, it soon became clear that Mrs Hudson had no intention of satisfying his curiosity there and then. As she stood before the two gentlemen, her face was assembled into a look of deep perturbation.

'Why, whatever is the matter, Mrs Hudson?' asked Dr Watson. 'I've never seen you look so glum.'

'Watson is quite right,' added Holmes. 'If there is something troubling you, you mustn't hesitate to share it. It would be a privilege to be of assistance.'

'Well, Mr Holmes,' began Mrs Hudson hesitantly, as if unsure whether to proceed. 'It relates to the gentleman I was talking about last night.'

'This man Fogarty?'

'Yes, sir.'

'All the more reason to tell us everything. If he is the villain you say, something must be done.'

And so Mrs Hudson allowed them to draw from her the story of my past encounters with Fogarty and the perilous situation of the child he had attempted to pass off as my brother. As the tale unfolded, Watson's horrified reactions were enough to reassure me that the help Mrs Hudson had talked of would be forthcoming. If anything, the cold, set face of Mr Holmes as he listened, his injured arm still hanging in a sling, revealed even more determination to strike a blow for justice. When she had finished her tale, it was he who spoke first.

'You are quite right, Mrs Hudson. Something must be done and there is not a moment to lose. Anxious though I am to hear everything you have to say about this man, I am happy to postpone your full explanation until tomorrow.'

'But what *can* be done, sir?' asked Mrs Hudson with a most unlikely display of uncertainty. 'Mr Rumbelow says the law cannot help us, and of course physical force is not to be contemplated...'

'Nonsense, Mrs Hudson!' Dr Watson was on his feet and quivering with determination. 'It sounds like the only language this devil understands. We must snatch the boy away! Between us, I'm sure Holmes and I...'

He tailed off as he became aware of Mr Holmes's arm in its sling.

'Precisely, my friend. I fear I am not best able to assist. Nevertheless, your instincts are right. But perhaps before we resort to brawn, we should employ our brains a little. What would we need to do to make such an audacious raid possible?'

Mrs Hudson cleared her throat quietly. 'Well, sir, one thing did occur to me...' I noticed her eyes travelling to the clock on the mantelpiece as though she were anxious to keep an appointment.

'And what was that, Mrs Hudson?'

'The boy is being kept below the servants' quarters at the rear of the house. I thought that some sort of diversion at the *front* of the house might give us an opportunity.'

'Hmm, yes.' Holmes passed his hand over his chin. 'I wonder how we might achieve that...'

At that moment the clock struck the half hour and almost simultaneously there was a knock at the front door. Mrs Hudson was on her feet in an instant and returned a minute later, her face impassive, with a calling card on a tray.

'A gentleman to see you, sir.'

'A Mr Rupert Spencer,' read Holmes. 'I wonder what this is about? Show the gentleman in Mrs Hudson.'

Mr Spencer bustled in with his usual air of irrepressible energy. He sailed past Mrs Hudson as if he had never seen her before and if he noticed me standing at the edge of the lamplight he didn't for a moment show it.

'Mr Holmes, so good of you to see me. I have been meaning to call before this, ever since I heard that an old acquaintance of mine is in your service. But tonight I happened to be passing...'

'I fear, sir, that you find my household engaged in an important matter that concerns us all. Perhaps if you could return another time...?'

'Of course, Mr Holmes. At your convenience. You see, I'm something of a scientist myself and I'm hoping to persuade my uncle to fund a laboratory for research. I thought a good word from you...'

'I say, sir!' It was Watson who interrupted him. 'Your name's Spencer. Is it possible that your uncle could be the Earl of Brabham?'

'Indeed, sir. Are you acquainted with my uncle?'

'The Irascible Earl? No, I regret to say I am not. But the presence here this evening of the Earl's nephew is remarkable timely, is it not, Holmes?'

'Watson, you excel yourself! Come, sir, take a seat. Please excuse our presumption, but an important issue has

269

arisen in which all of us here have an interest. An innocent life is at stake and we need assistance. As the Earl's nephew, I assume you are acquainted with the Fotheringays?'

'The Fotheringays? Rather! My uncle used to whip old Fotheringay regularly when they were boys. That sort of thing forms a bond.'

Holmes greeted this with the faintest lift of his eyebrow.

'Sir, I am aware that we are presuming upon the shortest of acquaintances, but it is in your power to help us greatly.' In a few short sentences he sketched out the situation regarding Fogarty and the boy.

'Despicable!' declared Mr Spencer when he had finished. 'The man is a monster! How like the Fotheringays not to notice that they have a monster for a butler!'

'You will understand, sir, that we need someone to cause a disturbance at the Fotheringays'. Do you feel you might be able to oblige?'

'Absolutely! What a remarkable coincidence my calling just now!' He looked around the room innocently. 'I shall be delighted to help. As it happens, I am accompanied this evening by the Earl's ward, Miss Peters. She is waiting in the carriage as we speak. Something tells me she may be the perfect person for this situation.'

'So what's the plan, Holmes?' asked Watson excitedly.

'Simple, Watson. The excellent Mr Spencer here will create some sort of uproar at the front of the house such that all able-bodied men in the servants' hall will be called upon to assist. While they are absent, you and I, guided by Flotsam, will retrieve the boy and make our escape.'

'But, Holmes, your arm! You can't possibly risk yourself in that way. You are still weak and if we ran into any difficulties you would be a liability rather than an asset.'

'Nonsense, Watson!'

But Mrs Hudson sided with the doctor and in truth Mr Holmes still looked a shadow of his usual self. I had already noted that he stayed seated more than his wont and lost his colour quickly when he stood for more than a few minutes. Eventually, when it became clear the opposition was implacable, he turned to Mr Spencer and said, 'You see, sir, how I am fussed over. It seems that the excitement will take place without me.'

'Mr Holmes, if Miss Peters and I play our part, Dr Watson will have to do nothing more than carry out the patient. Let us hope that is the case. The Earl's carriage is at your disposal, Dr Watson. Shall we set off at once?'

And that is how the strangely assorted grouping of Mrs Hudson, Dr Watson, Mr Spencer and myself all came to be crowding into the Earl's carriage at eight o'clock on a dark winter's evening, bound for the lair of a master criminal. Miss Peters gave an excited squeak as we crushed in, and up on the box Carrington surveyed the scene with some bemusement. But Mr Spencer shouted the address before squeezing in beside Miss Peters and, before I'd time to think about what would happen next, we were on our way.

The journey was not a comfortable one.

'Rupert, darling?' asked Miss Peters plaintively once appropriate introductions had been made. 'I know I insisted on coming, and I know that I'll need to be frightfully intrepid and everything, but *must* you sit on my dress like that? It's not that I mind about the dress, you understand, it's just that I don't know what you want me to do yet and if it's something where I need to look my best then having a dress that looks as though it's been sat on by a camel will simply ruin *everything*.'

Mr Spencer shifted awkwardly until he was crushing Dr Watson's hat instead.

'Listen, Hetty, I think you're going to excel at this. Remember how you called on the Fotheringays the other day? Well, we're going back there. I'm going to tell old Fotheringay you're the patient of a friend of mine and you suffer from delusions, and the delusion you are suffering from at the moment is that you're married to him or something. Then, before we have to explain exactly why we've come, you have to throw a complete fit and scream the house down. What do you think?'

Miss Peters looked aghast. 'But, Rupert, they'll have me locked away! Mr Fotheringay will make sure I'm committed forever. And even if he didn't, I'd become a social outcast. Even the Walters boy won't dance with a known lunatic. I'll never be able to go out again. Rupert, you haven't thought this up as a way of getting rid of me, have you?'

Mr Spencer seemed to think about this. 'It's an excellent idea for the future, Hetty, but on this occasion I'll make sure no-one locks you up. As soon as you've got all the servants up there trying to restrain you, I'll rush you off muttering about a sanatorium.'

'But that's terrible, Rupert! I'll be man-handled by footmen and however exciting that may sound, it's *quite* unladylike and even rather undignified, and when you've seen me like that you won't *ever* want to marry me. And then think what the Earl would say!'

'The Earl won't ever know.'

'He'll know when Mr Fotheringay meets him over dinner and tells him that his favourite ward has tried to seduce him in his own hallway.'

'Hetty, my dear, I promise you that old Fotheringay is far too busy worrying about the Balkan question to recognise you again. So long as you don't say anything against Servia he'll have forgotten the whole incident before bedtime. He's got no idea what's going on in the real world at all.'

Miss Peters seemed to find this comforting. Her face began to brighten. 'Actually, it might be rather fun to throw a fit. But how can I make sure they call the servants? Why wouldn't a big brute like you just bundle me out all by yourself?'

Mr Spencer considered. 'I know. You'd better hit me.'

Her eyes opened wide with joy. 'No, Rupert, not really? Well, if I really must…' She turned to me, bubbling with excitement. 'You see, Flottie, I *told* Rupert that I was good at adventures. And now I can show him for myself!'

Mrs Hudson, meanwhile, was conferring earnestly with Dr Watson and the carriage had long since pulled out of Baker Street. None of us were aware of events behind us, where a pale figure in a cape was attempting to hail a cab with the one good arm at his disposal. As the Earl's carriage lumbered into the night, a hansom carrying a small, neatly suited gentleman pulled up in a flurry of hooves and harness.

'Mr Holmes?' queried the passenger in the hansom.

'Ah, Mr Rumbelow!' replied Holmes. 'I perceive you are bound for the Fotheringays.'

'Well actually, Mr Holmes, I was looking for Mrs Hudson.'

'Precisely! And she is bound for the Fotheringays. Move over, sir, or we won't fit in. We have plenty of time to catch them.'

The night had closed around the city like a black glove and when Carrington pulled to a halt the alley leading to Fogarty's lair lay still. Without thinking why, our voices sank to whispers as we finalised our plan. Mr Spencer had become serious and urgent as he addressed us.

'Dr Watson, set your watch by mine. In three minutes, Miss Peters and I will knock on the front door. Allow us three more minutes to create a distraction, then you and Flottie can go in. If the door's locked, smash a window. We'll try to keep the household occupied for as long as we can. If things go well, we'll all meet back here.'

At that point a hansom pulled up beside us and Mr Holmes and Mr Rumbelow got down.

'Good evening, my friends,' grinned Holmes triumphantly. 'I felt it was my duty to accompany Rumbelow here, who appears to have taken a very strong dislike to the man Fogarty. How can he and I be of assistance to you?'

Mrs Hudson eyed him reproachfully. 'I wish you hadn't come, sir. But since you are here, perhaps you would remain by the coach and keep an eye on our line of retreat. Mr Rumbelow, you can accompany me. We'll wait outside while Flottie and Dr Watson fetch out the child, just in case any extra help is needed.'

Mr Rumbelow came to attention, his head shining delightedly in the gaslight.

'At your service, Mrs Hudson,' he confirmed.

'In that case, let's make a start. Good luck to you all.'

And with a sudden lump in my throat I allowed Dr Watson to hand me down from the carriage and into the waiting night.

Dr Watson and I were in position at the servants' door within two minutes. Through a crack in the shutters I could see into the main servants' room, where three tough-looking footmen were lolling idly. As I watched, they were joined by Mrs Flegg the cook, she who had once conspired with Smale to make my time in that household misery without relief. The room they sat in was one we should have to pass through to accomplish our mission. If Miss Peters and Mr Spencer failed to attract all four of them, our task would be impossible. Dr Watson and I counted the seconds go by and watched anxiously.

Suddenly the four turned and looked at a point above them. One of the footmen was about to speak when some new urgency was communicated, for all exchanged puzzled glances and rose to their feet. In an undignified rush, the room was emptied and our path lay clear.

I was through the door almost instantly, leading the way down a short corridor and across the main servants' room towards the door beyond. Dr Watson followed gamely. Above us we could hear hysterical screams interspersed with a wild, manic cackle as Miss Peters got into her stride. Then we were through the door, onto a flight of stone steps that led down to the cellars below. At the bottom I hesitated. Three doors led away from the bottom stairwell and, while I was sure Fogarty had taken me to the right, two of the doors seemed to lead in that direction.

'This one!' I gasped and flung myself against it, only to come to an abrupt and painful halt. I scrabbled desperately at the handle. 'Locked!' I cried.

Doubt enveloped me. I tried the other door and it opened smoothly into a familiar-looking corridor, lined with stained and flaking paint. The only light came from behind us, leaving the far end of the corridor lost in gloom.

'This way,' I called again and plunged forward. 'It's one of the rooms on the right. Try them all!' And while I attempted the first one, Dr Watson pushed past me to the second.

I found the first door locked and after tugging at it once or twice I gave up and moved on. Dr Watson had flung open the second door and was peering in.

'Broom cupboard,' he grunted and followed me to the third door. This also opened with a turn of the handle and revealed a curtain of darkness. Dr Watson tugged at his waistcoat pocket for a light and when he held up the match we saw a room empty but for a bare iron bed.

'Is this the one, Flot?' he asked tersely, sensing my disappointment. I was about to say yes, that we were too late and our mission was lost, when I sensed something different. Surely the other had not had that gap where the plaster had fallen away from the damp bricks? I fumbled at my memory in panic.

'No, sir! It's like it, but I don't think it's the one.' I saw him look at me doubtfully.

'This is the last door, Flottie. The corridor's a dead end.'

'Back to the stairs, sir. This must be the wrong corridor. Let's see if we can try the locked one.'

Dr Watson was first back to the stairwell where he eyed the locked door coldly then met it firmly with his shoulder. The door stood defiantly firm. Stepping back, he tried again with extra determination and to my surprise the door burst open, sending him sprawling to the ground. 'Just like my rugby days,' he grunted as he picked himself up, but by then I was past him and into the darkness. Again there were three doors and again they yielded nothing. The first two rooms were empty even of furniture and devoid of any sign of recent habitation. The third opened onto narrow wooden stairs that led down to a wine cellar.

'That's it, Flotsam. We've tried them all.' Dr Watson was peering at his watch in the gloom. 'We can't be found down here, you know. It's time to go.'

'One more, sir. Please! There was that locked door in the first corridor. Can we try it again?'

Silently he moved past me, back to the original corridor. I could hear his breathing, heavy and irregular, as he paused to size up the door. 'Into touch, then!' he growled, and charged it with his shoulder. With a splintering of wood it sprang open.

This time there was no need for a light. A cheap candle still burned faintly in one corner, illuminating the scene I remembered. A boy no more than a child lay gaunt and still on the bare bed. His arm, flung out, was dangling towards the floor.

'He's dead!' I moaned, feeling for a moment a terrible faintness pass through me, but Dr Watson already had his fingers to the boy's neck, feeling for a pulse.

'No, Flottie. We're in time.' He lifted the boy in his arms with a grunt. 'Can you find the way out?'

Suddenly, for the first time, fear of being caught gripped me. I sprang up the stairs at double speed and it was not until I reached the proper light of the servants' room that I paused for Dr Watson to catch up. It was while I was looking back to where he trailed behind me that the door at the other end of the room swung open. Dr Watson stepped into the light at precisely the same moment as the first of Fogarty's footmen. By the time speechless surprise had been registered on all sides, all three footmen and Mrs Flegg the cook were lined up opposite us, barring our way.

'Well, what have we here?' began Mrs Flegg, and one of the footmen began to roll up his sleeves in a manner full of menace. Dr Watson looked at me helplessly but at that moment there was a rustling in the doorway behind the line of footmen.

'Over here, sir!' boomed Mrs Hudson's commanding voice and in perfect synchronicity the four who faced us turned to see who had come up at their rear. Never has surprise been more effective. As the tallest of the three men turned, someone small and impeccably suited burst through the doorway, head down, and butted him at maximum velocity in the stomach.

'Mr Rumbelow!' I yelped, but before I'd finished speaking Dr Watson had seized his opportunity. With the child carefully shielded in his arms, he repeated the manoeuvre he had employed so successfully on the doors downstairs, this time on the back of one of the footman. The impact of his shoulder sent the man crashing into the door post. Meeting it solidly, he sank slowly to the ground while momentum carried Dr Watson forward, through the line of the opposition and into the corridor beyond. I hastened to Mrs Hudson's side through the gap he had created.

The third footman stood still in bewilderment, gazing dumbly at his fallen colleague, until Mr Rumbelow, in attempting to disentangle himself from his first opponent, fell awkwardly against the back of his knees and pitched him forward.

'Oi!' Mrs Flegg suddenly found her voice but as she began to move her eyes fell on Mrs Hudson who was peeling back her sleeves with an awful deliberation. Mrs Flegg looked at those forearms and stepped back smartly.

So rapid had been our victory that for a moment we hesitated. Then Watson, seeing the way ahead unbarred, let out a roar of encouragement and all four of us were blundering onwards while the fallen footmen were still struggling to their feet.

The night welcomed us into its arms but the iron steps were narrow and awkward in the darkness. I was the last to the top and it was clear from the sounds behind us that our opponents were re-forming and intent on pursuit. Before I could think what to do, a cool male voice sounded at my shoulder.

'To the carriage as quickly as you can, Flotsam. This should hold them.'

Beside me stood Sherlock Holmes, brandishing an iron bar in his left hand.

'Don't wait,' he added before plunging down the steps, and I didn't hesitate to take him at his word. The panic of flight had seized me and I scuttled towards the waiting carriage without a backward glance.

Mr Spencer and Miss Peters were there ahead of us and Carrington, game as ever, was ready with the doors open. In the carriage, wrapped in a tense, sickly silence, Dr Watson was examining the boy. For a moment no-one spoke. Then the doctor raised his head, his eyes gleaming.

'We're in time!' he cried. 'I'm sure of it!'

Miss Peters let out a breathless hurrah and suddenly everyone was piling noisily into the coach, squeezing around the patient as best we could.

'Quickly!' Dr Watson shouted to the coachman. 'Baker Street as if your life depended on it!'

Carrington needed no second urging and with a whoop of joy he shook the reins and sent us rattling into the darkness.

Headlong flight breeds panic and panic is a contagious disease. Only Mrs Hudson seemed immune. While she tried to restore some order, the rest of us became convinced that our pursuers were on our heels and capture was imminent. Dr Watson made things worse by persisting in shouting 'Faster!' in his loudest voice whenever he looked up from his patient.

'Whoa, sir!' Mrs Hudson countered, unheard. 'We are clear of pursuit and out of danger.'

But before this message had communicated itself to Carrington, we heard an oath from his box and the carriage juddered to an alarming halt. Peering out of the window, the reason became obvious. In our headlong flight, we had come face to face with a speeding hansom cab and only excellent horsemanship on the part of both drivers had spared us a collision. As we paused for Carrington to recover himself and to sooth the horses, there was an angry shout from outside. A distinguished-looking gentleman of about seventy was descending the steps of his club, gesticulating violently.

Something in his voice had a galvanising effect on the occupants of the carriage. Mrs Hudson, Mr Spencer and Miss Peters all put their faces to the window and Carrington, now back on his box, let out a nervous groan.

'My carriage!' exclaimed the distinguished gentleman.

'My uncle!' gasped Mr Spencer.

'The Irascible Earl,' explained Mrs Hudson to those in the carriage who harboured any doubt. Before she could say more, he had recognised her face at the window.

'Mrs Hudson!' he roared.

'Indeed, your lordship,' she replied calmly, lowering the window. 'You'll be relieved to know that all's well. We shall explain later. Carrington? Drive on!'

–

It was an exhilarated and talkative group who finally tumbled out onto the pavement in Baker Street. In the course of the journey, Dr Watson had found space to reassure us again that the unconscious boy, though malnourished, was not in immediate danger. This news, following the narrow escape from Fogarty's and our brush with the Earl, bred a euphoria that touched us all. Mr Rumbelow, squashed between Mrs Hudson and Miss Peters, beamed pleasantly as plaudits were rained on him for employing his legal brain with such great effect, while I, wedged rather tightly between Mrs Hudson and the window, told anyone who would listen about Dr Watson's prowess with his shoulders. A few feet away I could hear Miss Peters taking gaily at Dr Watson and Mr Spencer about her mastery of the hysterical state.

'Hitting Rupert proved such a spectacular success that it seemed obvious to try it again. So I looked Mr Fotheringay in the eye and hit him too. And do you know, I rather think that took his mind off the Balkans for a bit.'

'My dear Miss Peters…'

'Oh, it's all right, Dr Watson, I didn't hit him *nearly* so hard as I hit Rupert, did I, darling?'

Mr Spencer grimaced.

'Tell me, Hetty, just where did you learn so much about the activities of fallen women? Your ravings on the subject were very persuasive.'

281

'Well, do you know, Rupert, I rather think that must have come from Daddy...'

It was only on our arrival that Dr Watson looked around and asked a question that had seemed obvious to me for some time.

'I say, Mrs Hudson, where's Holmes?'

There was a little pause as everyone looked around, taking in his absence.

'Yes, Dr Watson, I have been a little worried about that myself. I understand it was his intention to bar the door behind us. His instructions for us to complete our escape were quite clear and it didn't seem a sensible thing to argue. Mr Holmes can be a very stubborn man.'

I quickly told them what I had seen of Mr Holmes actions and said that I thought he must have succeeded in barring the door.

'In which case, Dr Watson, I'm sure he will be on his way home to us,' added Mrs Hudson reassuringly. But I could see that Dr Watson was concerned, and while Mr Holmes's absence continued the good doctor's sense of triumph remained slightly dimmed.

We were a merry gathering for all that. The boy was put to bed in my cupboard room and Dr Watson sat with him for some time before rejoining the rest of us. Meanwhile Carrington was dispatched home with a note for the Earl composed by Mrs Hudson.

'That should do the trick,' she commented as she sealed it up. 'I have reminded the Earl of the day in '63 when Macaroni won the Derby. Tell Carrington his lordship will be quite all right once he has read that.'

The rest of us were gathered around the newly awakened fires and Miss Peters and Mr Rumbelow were debating whether champagne or brandy should be opened when we heard a sharp knock on the front door.

'Holmes at last!' declared Watson happily and I was sent off downstairs to let in the errant detective with all speed.

On opening the front door, however, I found the doorstep empty. A dark cab waiting on the far side of the street, its driver wrapped against the cold, was the only sign of life. Concerned that it might contain the weakened Mr Holmes, I had just stepped towards it when a rough hand closed tightly over my mouth.

'So here we are again, Flotsam,' hissed Smale's voice in my ear. 'And this time you come with me. It's time for you to be taught a lesson or two.'

Struggling furiously, grunting and squealing as best I could, I was dragged towards the waiting growler, whose driver was dismounting with a cruel smile. Between the two of them they forced a gag into my mouth and thrust me roughly onto the floor of the cab. Smale climbed in behind me and began to knot my hands tight behind my back. I thought I heard a cry from somewhere down the street as the door was slammed shut and then the carriage jolted forward, carrying me away from the warm study and into the heart of the night.

–

Unseen by me, it was Scraggs who raised the alarm. Slamming frantically through our open front door, he burst upon the celebrating company with a cry.

'Mrs Hudson! They've just taken Flottie! They've taken her away in a growler! Come at once!'

Mrs Hudson and Mr Spencer were first down the stairs, reaching the street a few seconds ahead of Dr Watson and Miss Peters, just as two empty hansom cabs passed the door.

'*Driver!*' boomed Mrs Hudson, bringing both to a halt. 'Have you seen a growler pass?'

'Yes, ma'am. Going at some lick, he was. As if he had the devil behind him.'

'Catch that cab!' commanded Mrs Hudson, signalling the start of a chase that is talked about to this day in cabbing circles. The two cabmen, fired by a sense of right and the prospect of a guinea apiece, jostled with each other for position as they rattled through the cobbled streets, shouting for reports to their colleagues on other cabs when the trail seemed to be going cold. In this way they were able to keep in touch with their quarry, following Smale's progress by word of mouth as he and I were carried southwards, towards the river and the dark streets beyond. In Piccadilly a startled policeman pointed Mrs Hudson's cab south and even in the tangle of cabs around Trafalgar Square the pursuit was maintained, flying with a whoop into the Strand amid a riot of police whistles and the startled fists of choleric gentlemen.

It was after Waterloo, where the crowds began to thin, that the scent was lost amid the stench of rubbish and the competing invitations of numerous dark streets. The two cabs slowed while the drivers looked for someone to consult. A small boy looked blankly back at them when asked, and there was no-one else to question.

It was Mrs Hudson who kept up their momentum. 'That way, driver!' she commanded. 'Back down there and work back towards the river. They're in there somewhere.'

Mr Spencer looked at her in astonishment. 'But, Mrs H, how can you tell? They could be anywhere!'

'Indeed, Mr Spencer. But we won't help Flottie by stopping here. Besides, I have a feeling. Drive on!' And Mrs Hudson, her lips clamped tight, set her face towards the on-rushing night.

–

While my would-be rescuers blundered into the tangle of dark wharves and warehouses that spread along the river like an infection, my own plight was becoming desperate. At first Smale had been too anxious of pursuit to turn his thoughts to me. At one point, after I had felt us change direction a dozen times, we had stopped abruptly and I heard him lean out of the window and curse.

'Bloody cab drivers, blocking the road like that! Go and sort him out, man!'

He returned to his seat and I felt the vehicle lurch as our driver got down from his box. A few moments later he returned to his place with a grunt and our journey continued. Now I felt Smale begin to relax. I still lay on the floor of the cab, my hands tied and my mouth gagged so tightly that my first fear was of suffocation. That, however, was soon replaced by worse as Smale turned his attention to me for the first time. He reached down and began to stroke my cheek with his thick, clammy fingers.

'So, Flotsam, it's true. You really are mine now.' He continued to stroke, slowly, without tenderness. The icy menace in his voice was unmistakable. I remembered it from years before, from the moments before his most calcu-lated acts of cruelty. Suddenly he grabbed my hair and pulled me up so hard that I was lifted, gasping with pain, onto the seat beside him.

'I'm taking you to a quiet place, Flotsam. Not even your Mr Holmes will be able to find us there. And we'll stay there until you learn to be agreeable.'

With a laugh that flecked my face with saliva, he pushed me back to the floor and began to give directions to the driver. I'd seen enough from where I lay to know that we had turned off the main thoroughfares and were plunging into a world of unlit streets. I thought I could smell the river.

Eventually Smale called on the driver to stop.

'This is good enough,' he shouted up. 'I want to walk the last bit so my friend here can see there's no place to run. So get yerself out of here and I don't want to see your face till dawn. Pick me up then at Cable Wharf. The warehouse by the river. You know the place. I'll be waiting.'

He pulled me out of the carriage without a glance at the driver and from there we went on by foot, Smale pushing and shoving me in the direction he desired. Our progress was slow. More than once his pushing made me stumble and fall. But the pain of his kicks and blows was nothing to the pain caused by my helplessness. My hands were still bound fast. There could be no escape.

After more twists and turns than I could remember, Smale pushed me into a narrow street, in reality little more than a gap between two old warehouses, that ended abruptly with a drop to the river. I could see a small dark doorway in the wall of one of the warehouses, right up by the water's edge, and it was towards this that Smale prodded me. We were still a few yards short when the sound of horses reached us, moving at speed and coming closer.

'Mrs Hudson!' I thought and felt a warm rush of hope. But the sounds were still streets away and with a sudden loss of heart I realised she couldn't be in time.

Smale realised too and his voice was triumphant.

'This is the place. No-one's going to find us in here, you know.'

He pushed me to within a few feet of the door then stepped past me, reaching into his pockets for a key.

'How right you are!' came a voice from the doorway. Before I had time to focus properly a tall figure with his arm in a sling stepped out of the shadow and, with a straight left to the jaw, sent Smale spinning away from me and crashing to the water below.

–

Mr Holmes and I were still peering into the murky water when the pair of hansom cabs arrived somewhere behind us and began to disgorge their passengers into the alleyway. The two drivers, having been converted completely to my cause, were quick off their boxes and began to advance menacingly on Mr Holmes until Dr Watson's assurances persuaded them back to their cabs. Mrs Hudson, mean-while, advanced to where we stood and eyed us both thoughtfully.

'Mr Holmes,' she began.

'Oh, it was nothing, Mrs Hudson,' he replied loftily, examining his knuckles.

'Mr Holmes,' she continued, 'you are in disgrace. Your wound is bleeding, you look a fright and if you survive the night at all it will only be because we're taking you home this instant.'

In reply the great detective swayed a little, gave an embarrassed smile and dropped in a faint to the cobblestones.

The Clear Light of Day

✝

That morning, as we rattled homewards, the fog lifted and for the first time in days a blinking city looked dawn squarely in the face. Before it did, while the night still lingered on the street, we had reached our rooms in Baker Street. The effect of his exertions, coupled with his earlier loss of blood, had rendered Mr Holmes insensible for most of the journey, but once brandy had been supplied and he had been laid in Mrs Hudson's big chair by the kitchen fire, it soon became clear that no damage had been done that a strict regime of rest would not cure.

'Really only a scratch,' he murmured as Watson bound the knuckles of his left hand. 'It was the timing that did the trick, Watson. I wish you could have seen him fall. As sweet a blow as you'll ever see, eh, Flottie?'

'Indeed, sir.' I was leaning against Mrs Hudson on the other side of the fire, shivering with cold and relief. Mrs Hudson, having denied me brandy, was in the process of warming blankets and wrapping them around me in ever greater numbers until my shape had disappeared altogether and I was as round as a winter sparrow. Crouched between Mr Holmes and I, on the low stool, Scraggs was tending the fire, watching intently as the coals hissed and the flames leapt for the chimney. Behind us, in chairs carried off from the study, Mr Rumbelow and Miss Peters wallowed in the warmth, the latter muted by exhaustion and yawning rather beautifully whenever unobserved. Behind and above them, Mr Spencer perched on the kitchen table and swung his legs like a schoolboy.

'But tell us, Holmes, how the devil did you come to be there tonight? It defies belief!' Dr Watson puffed out his cheeks in bafflement at his companion's dramatic reappearance.

'It was far simpler than you would imagine, my friend.'

'Simple? That's typical of your modesty, Holmes. Simple! Huh, I've never known anything like it!'

'Perhaps if I were to explain...' He reached for his pipe with his bandaged hand and Watson helped him with a light. 'Thanks to the timely arrival of Mr Rumbelow, I was able to join you in your little raid on Fogarty's quarters. I was lucky enough to be able to secure your retreat with an old length of iron railing. After that I made my way here as quickly as I could on foot.'

He paused to draw deeply on his pipe.

'I was just turning into Baker Street when I first noticed the carriage. Those of you who know my methods will be aware I have honed my powers of observation to a unique pitch and it was without great thought that I observed the driver had a tattoo of an anchor on one cheek and one of a mermaid on the back of his left hand. I paid a good deal more attention when I observed the carriage stop at our door and a figure dismount. Imagine my alarm when, still some seventy yards away, I witnessed the brutal abduction of Flotsam. The whole thing was too quick for me to prevent but as they sped away I was close enough to hear the kidnapper address an instruction to his driver. I was able to catch the word 'wharf' but nothing more. But of course that, coupled with the nautical theme of the tattoos, allowed me to form a very fair idea of their destination.'

'Incredible, Holmes. And your reasoning proved spot on!'

'Alas not, my dear Watson. My guess was entirely wrong.'

'But, Holmes!' Watson seemed at a loss.

'I decided that desperate men with nautical connections might well be heading east, out to the pool of London, where all manner of lawlessness still prevails. As soon as I could hail a hansom, I set off with the vague hope that by heading south towards the Embankment I might gain on them, for a hansom is faster than a growler, especially in these crowded streets. It was, however, entirely fortuitous that our paths crossed rather literally just by the Haymarket. Of course, from then on the rest was child's play.'

'You followed them?'

'Really, Watson! That would have been a singularly illogical reaction. If, as I surmised, they were bound for places where the law stands for nothing, I should hardly have been assisting Flottie by accompanying her there, alone and one-armed. No, it seemed more prudent to instruct my driver to pull directly into their path.'

'Into their path? Good lord, Holmes! And what happened then?'

The detective examined his bandaged left hand with a satisfied air.

'A certain amount of confusion ensued, leading – as I had hoped – to that blackguard of a driver stepping down from his box. He was clearly no pugilist. A simple upper cut quite removed him from calculations. Finding him too craven to take further punishment, it was the work of a moment to divest him of his cape and take his place on the box. The substitution went unremarked, as I knew it would, and for want of a better plan I headed for Trafalgar Square. I confess the ride was a wild one for my control with one arm was not all it might have been. That policeman on the Strand was perhaps fortunate to avoid serious injury.'

He smiled happily to himself, then considered his pipe before continuing.

'Had my control been greater, it was my intention to pull up safely in a well-lit area, but it was not until we were across the river that I was able to assert myself and by then the ruffian below me was shouting instructions. Deciding that in those dark streets surprise was my best weapon, I followed his orders. He made it easy by telling me precisely where he wished to be collected. With Flottie all tied up and moving slowly, it was the simplest thing to get there ahead of him and spring my little surprise.'

Watson's eyes glowed with admiration. 'I say, Holmes, that really is the most splendid thing. Your brilliance at its very best.'

'Really, Watson, you quite embarrass me.' Holmes gave a self-deprecatory wave of the hand and smiled broadly.

Then a thought seemed to strike Watson. 'But I'm forgetting, Holmes. I still don't have the slightest idea who it was you sent into the river, or why he was after Flottie. In fact,' and here he ran his eye around the assembled company in mute appeal, 'I have to say there's quite a lot about our recent adventures that I really don't understand at all.'

Mr Holmes turned to Mrs Hudson with an apologetic flap of his sling.

'I know that everyone here is waiting for an explanation but I find myself still a little weak. Mrs Hudson, perhaps *you* would be so kind as to put our friends out of their misery and give them your own views on what has been going on?' He turned to the rest of us. 'I am convinced that Mrs Hudson's grasp of events is scarcely less complete than mine. I recommend that you trust her account as if it were my own.'

'Hear, hear!' added Watson. 'Greatly appreciate it if you spill the beans, Mrs H. Shouldn't be surprised if you know just about everything.'

A murmur of concurrence rose around the fire and all eyes turned to the stern figure of the housekeeper.

'Very well, sir,' she replied with a slow nod of her head. 'I'm happy to tell the story from the beginning, if that's what you wish.'

'Oh, goody!' squeaked Miss Peters, now thoroughly awake again. 'I do love a story! I hope I understand it, Rupert. You know how awfully *clever* Mrs Hudson is.'

'I think this calls for the old tawny, Mr Rumbelow,' decided Mrs Hudson, deftly ignoring her. 'You'll find it next to the laundry cupboard. I took the liberty of decanting it earlier, in anticipation. Mr Spencer, the correct glasses are on the dresser... One for Flotsam too, I think, if you'd be so kind.'

A tingle of excitement ran along my shoulders as, furnished with port, we settled back into our places and Mrs Hudson began the explanation I had waited so long to hear.

'I think you all know a little about the events that led us here tonight,' she began cautiously, her voice a little gruff, her forehead drawn into a frown as she sought a starting place. 'It all really began on our first night in these rooms, when Flottie was so alarmed by the delivery of a letter by a one-eyed servant who slipped away into the darkness.

'My suspicions about Mr Moran were aroused from the very moment Flottie told us how his letter had been delivered. All that cloak and dagger nonsense… well, really! A simple call one morning would have sufficed. And if there's one thing I can't abide it's drama for the sake of it. So, while I couldn't find any reasons to contradict the conclusions Mr Holmes drew on that first evening, my instincts were telling me that Mr Moran was a man not to be trusted.'

'But, Mrs Hudson,' struck in Dr Watson, 'all the observations Holmes made about that letter seemed to be spot on.'

'Indeed, sir. And very brilliant observations they were too. But it struck me that all of them were open to more than one interpretation. You see, sir, Mr Holmes is a detective and he looks at things from a certain angle. A detective gathers things together and then looks to see what he's got. But when a cook goes shopping she already has an idea of what dinner she's going to prepare. Since my instinct was to distrust Moran, I decided to look for facts to support my theories rather than the other way round. To my surprise, they were rather thick on the ground.'

Mrs Hudson took another sip and signalled to Scraggs with the lift of an eyebrow that it was time to replenish the glasses.

'My very first step was to find out more about Mr Moran's whereabouts. From his notepaper I knew he wished us to think him poor, so I instinctively concentrated my search in the better areas of the city. I commissioned Scraggs and a few of his fellows to make enquiries on my behalf. Scraggs and his friends see a great deal. If they weren't already aware of a tall, scarred, one-eyed servant, recently arrived at a good London address, then I didn't think the information would be very hard for them to elicit. One of Scraggs's colleagues called that very afternoon with the news that a gentleman with a servant fitting that description had recently taken rooms in New Buildings on Portman Street. I took the precaution of confirming the fact with Moran when he called that evening and he was unable to deny it.

'So by the time Moran arrived in this house, I already knew him to be, if not a liar, then at least someone deliberately intent on misleading us. What I didn't know was why. Why the charade with the cheap paper when he could clearly afford much better? What motive could he have for wishing to foist this fiction upon us? I felt sure that the answer would lie in the story he was to tell us. I awaited his appearance with considerable interest.'

I recalled Moran's arrival, his nervous air, his alert, watchful eyes as he surveyed the company before him. Mrs Hudson cleared her throat and went on.

'So what were we left with once he had told his tale? Thanks to Lord Ponsonby, I was quickly able to ascertain that Moran had indeed been in Sumatra; that his company had failed; that the terrible and fatal blindings Moran described did occur, and that the natives of Sumatra felt a very great hostility to Moran's company at the time of its collapse. All that was in the official report of the Dutch authorities. In addition I knew – whatever the true explanation of those events – that Moran wished us to believe a fanciful tale of a malignant curse and vindictive spirits.'

'Now, Mrs Hudson,' Watson frowned, 'why on earth would he want us to do that?'

'Obviously, sir, his tale was a deliberate smokescreen to distract us from the true sequence of events. But again, *why?* No-one appeared to be asking any questions about those events. If any crime had been committed it was under Dutch jurisdiction rather than our own. And if anyone over here had ever wondered about the unfortunate deaths in Sumatra, their concerns were now surely forgotten. Moran had avoided bankruptcy and had no stain on his character more damaging than a failed business venture. Yet for some reason he now felt it vital that Mr Holmes should believe that he and his colleagues were under threat of death from a band of remote and primitive tribesmen.'

'Absurd!' snorted Watson.

'Quite,' added Holmes, very intent on filling his pipe.

'I sat down and thought about it. If Moran, for some reason I couldn't yet fathom, wanted us to believe that Sumatran tribesmen were poised to murder him on the pavements of Oxford Street, he had to provide us with a motive for their obsession. The motive he gave us was the insults to their sacred spirits, a rather thin tale which never rang true for a moment. And yet it was clear from the Dutch intelligence reports that there genuinely *did* exist a great resentment on the part of the local people for Moran and his company. Moran was clearly going to great lengths to hide the true reason for that resentment.'

Dr Watson, who had just raised his glass to his lips, lowered it again and opened his mouth as if to speak. Then he closed it again. 'It's beyond me, Mrs H,' he concluded sadly.

'Well, sir, clearly the true reason did not reflect well on him or the company and needed to be concealed. I felt if I could discover what it was I would be some way towards understanding the mystery we were meant to be solving. What was Moran's company doing that was so much worse than a hundred other trading companies up and down those coasts? I'm sorry to say it, but there are many unscrupulous traders in those parts, many who trick and cheat and bully in the name of trade. But although resented, sometimes even threatened, they are rarely forced to flee their quarters, leaving their fortunes behind, in fear of their lives.

'Then things began to happen quite fast. I had recognised the name Matilda Briggs, a vessel that plies the East Indian routes and which was to come to our attention again. An old friend of mine had lost her son at sea from that very vessel. I remembered vaguely that he had been unwell before he died. On checking I found that at the time he was lost he was suffering all the symptoms of the fatal illnesses that had been reported in Sumatra. Once I had heard his mother's story again, the connection was made. *Her son was given to hard liquor.* That was the link I sought.

'Moran had given us all the clues himself, perhaps from carelessness, perhaps from a desire to bolster his fiction with genuine facts, or perhaps from that tiresome over-confidence that men so often have when they aren't telling the truth. He told precisely what possessions were found beside the first victim – no food or clothes, only his weapons, some lucky charms and *bottles of liquor from Port Mary*. Again, when describing the white settler who died soon after, Moran told us he came into Port Mary to trade skins for gin. So was that the cause of all these horrors? Was it the spirits they were drinking? Some gruesome failure on the part of the distillers? It was impossible to be certain, but I was sure that Moran's fiction was designed to obscure his role in this wretched, shabby episode.'

From behind me Rupert Spencer coughed politely.

'Is that all you had on which to draw your conclusions, Mrs H? I can't help thinking it's all a bit tenuous...'

'Oh no, Mr Spencer, there were other ways in which Moran betrayed himself too. For instance, in an elaborate attempt to sustain the illusion of an evil curse, Moran told us a *second* dagger had been cursed and dispatched to him. Well really, sir! Why would they think to perform the curse *twice*? I could see how a second dagger, sinisterly delivered, added to the drama of Moran's tale. But wouldn't *one* deadly curse generally be considered sufficient? To curse the same person twice is to use two eggs when the recipe only calls for one.

'Moran also mentioned that the second dagger had arrived on the ship Matilda Briggs. At about the time he told us this, a certain Mr Norman called on the ship's owner and told him an alarming tale of supernatural malevolence on a recent passage from the Indies. Here I recognised another attempt to introduce themes of the exotic and supernatural where none existed. Nathaniel Moran... Mr Norman... Mr N Moran...' She smiled at me. 'It doesn't take someone with Flotsam's flair for word games to see a connection. And sure enough, when I prevailed on the ship's owner, Mr Winterton, to accompany me to Portman Street, he was able to observe Moran from a distance and confirm that Norman and Moran were indeed the same person. You see, it was easy for Moran to bribe the Lascar crew to support his tale; much harder for him to refrain from over-cleverness in his fictions.

'But here again I seemed to run out of steam. I felt convinced in my heart of hearts that Moran's greed had been behind the deaths of a dozen or more people. Horrible, painful deaths. Yet guilt would be hard to prove. The incident was closed and would surely stay closed. What possible motive could he have for bringing it all to our attention again?

'If I had been quicker to answer that question, I may have been able to save Carruthers from an agonising death. My only consolation is that Carruthers, Neale and Moran were all equally responsible for the experiment in Sumatra, and all to a certain measure deserved their fates. The first clue was when Dr Watson told us of Carruthers's great terror. I began to feel it might be inspired by something more tangible than a remote Sumatran curse. What could it be that Carruthers and Neale both feared so greatly?'

Dr Watson stabbed the air with his pipe. 'That devil Moran!'

The housekeeper nodded sagely.

'Precisely. They knew they had betrayed Moran and they knew he was a man to take violent revenge. Of course, with Carruthers's death everything became clear. The absurdly melodramatic method in which it was brought about made it obvious to me that the perpetrator was trying to make us look abroad for our assassin. And which individual was already trying to direct our attentions abroad? Mr N Moran. Once a murder had taken place, it became clear that his tale had all along been intended to distract us from the truth. Moran arrived in these shores with the explicit intention of murdering his former colleagues. It was the problem of how to kill both men without incurring overwhelming suspicion that led him to create his fictional story. If he could make the world believe a hideous curse was being worked out by native assassins he became a pitied victim – and if he subsequently chose to disappear from sight completely no-one would think it anything other than a very sensible precaution. All his fictions – and his request for your aid – were smokescreens to conceal his own murderous intentions.'

'Duped!' murmured Watson and frowned furiously to himself.

'Go on, Mrs Hudson,' prompted Mr Holmes. 'I'm confident you've grasped all the salient points.'

'One problem, sir, was to prove that Moran's motive for following his friends to London really was pure hatred. But I understand his manservant Penge has now confirmed this. As a result of a telegram I suggested to Inspector Gregory, Penge was arrested in Truro this morning. He throws all the blame for the murders onto Moran. He claims it was hatred roused by his companions' behaviour in Sumatra that was driving him. They had taken a solemn vow, remember, to stand shoulder to shoulder until their fortunes were made. Yet Neale and Carruthers lost their nerve and abandoned Moran to almost certain death in Sumatra. Moran was not a man to forgive that. So he travelled to London to take his revenge.

'The challenge at this point was to gather enough evidence to hang Moran for the murder of Carruthers while preventing the murder of Neale. Flottie and I were able to intervene to prolong Neale's wretched and guilt-wracked existence for a time. I thought we had succeeded in our task, but I reckoned without the entry of another character into our drama, a criminal mind far greater, far subtler, far more sophisticated than Moran's...

'Sir, it was my misfortune to know no small amount about Maurice Fogarty before I joined your service. I shall be happy to tell you all I know of his past when Inspector Gregory arrives, though I fear no crime that has occurred this week will be successfully laid at his door. For now suffice it to say that, although corrupt to the core and motivated by a desire to control and manipulate others, he is nothing if not daring. Indeed there are areas in which he could be considered brilliant. Flottie was known to him in the past but he showed no interest in continuing their acquaintance until shortly after Moran called on us. Then he attempted to convince her that her brother was in his power, although his investigation had already shown the boy was dead. Flottie had the intuition to see through this fiction and the great good sense to find out what he wanted. It became clear that Fogarty was interested in Moran's affairs and in Mr Holmes's assessment of them.'

Dr Watson looked puzzled. 'Eh? I'm afraid I don't see the connection, Mrs H.'

'Nor did I, sir. But suddenly the pieces began to fall together. Carruthers and Neale's choice of hotels suggested they had come into funds. How? Did they make their fortune in Sumatra or had they found a way to get rich on their return? If the latter, you could be sure it was not by legitimate means. Through an old acquaintance I was able to lay my hands on certain papers that put things into sharper focus – plans for distillation equipment and a conciliatory letter from Carruthers to Moran alluding to the success of his ventures and mentioning a mysterious sponsor who was well pleased with the outcome of his investment. I know Fogarty to have a hand in every sort of illegality. The link between Fogarty and Moran began to become clearer.'

'Of course!' muttered Watson. 'Cheap gin!' His eyes widened as a thought occurred to him. 'I suppose you could say it was evil spirits at work here after all, eh, Mrs H?'

'As you say, sir. The papers from Moran's flat confirmed that in Sumatra the three associates had been involved in unlicensed distilling, which is not an evil only confined to foreign shores. All the papers are in the dresser drawer, sir, behind the jelly moulds, should you wish to examine them.'

'I'm sure that can wait, Mrs Hudson,' allowed Mr Holmes with a regal nod.

'I begin to understand!' Dr Watson exclaimed. 'This Melmoth-Fogarty chap struck a deal with Carruthers and Neale and used their knowledge and connections to circumvent the Excise.' His voice dropped. 'But why should Fogarty be concerned about *Moran*? Why not just ignore him and carry on as he was?'

'Because, Doctor, Neale and Carruthers left Fogarty in no doubt that their cosy situation was likely to be severely disrupted by Moran's arrival. This didn't suit Fogarty at all. Carruthers's respectable connections were of value to him. He didn't want Neale or Carruthers panicked into any indiscretion. He warned off Moran but Moran was intent on his own agenda of revenge. In the normal course of things, Fogarty wouldn't have hesitated to eliminate an annoyance like Moran, but before he could do that he discovered that Moran had called here to consult Mr Holmes.'

'That spiked his guns, eh, Mrs H!' chortled Watson.

'It certainly made him hesitate, sir. He couldn't be sure what had passed here. Had Moran, in a fit of revenge, explained everything to Mr Holmes? How much did Moran know and how much had he passed on? Fogarty wanted to know. So he approached Flotsam in the hope of finding out if his own name had been in any way implicated. When he had found out how things stood here, he would be better able to plan his next move.

'The situation changed drastically when Moran murdered Carruthers. It left Neale in a fatally compromised position. Moran was already intent on his murder and suddenly, without Carruthers and his connections, Neale was of no value to Fogarty either. If I had understood how peripheral Neale was to Fogarty's schemes, I would have realised the danger. But I assumed that Neale, as an ally of Fogarty's, was only at risk from Moran. While Moran was being watched, I thought Neale was safe. By the time I learned otherwise, it was too late.

'Neale's murder was a typical example of Fogarty's daring. Neale had now become a danger to him – a weak man who knew too much. Fogarty's course was clear. His interception of the messenger and the way he turned that circumstance to his advantage – these things are typical of the man. I should have anticipated such an attack but instead I allowed Neale to break cover and return to his own quarters for one last time. I fear I did him a poor service.'

Mr Holmes shook his head pensively. 'Don't torment yourself, Mrs Hudson. It takes a rigorously trained intellect to see the full picture on every occasion.'

'Thank you, sir. You are very comforting.' Mrs Hudson turned to the rest of us. 'There is very little more to tell. Immediately after his attack on Neale, Fogarty paid a visit to Moran to settle the score. In order to ensure a welcome, I imagine Fogarty had written to Moran and offered to cut him into the profits of his operation in some way. Certainly Moran seemed eager to talk to him on that last evening, until Dr Watson's arrival interrupted them. But Moran had defied Fogarty's warnings, killed off a valuable business venture and, worst of all, he knew more about Fogarty's dealings than Fogarty was comfortable with. Fogarty had already planned a diversion in the street to allow him to visit Moran unnoticed but he never planned to talk business. I feel sure that Fogarty knew all along that he would kill Moran that very night.'

'The man is an ogre!' exploded Mr Rumbelow, unable to contain himself any longer. 'Am I to understand that he has been responsible for two murders, the imprisonment of a child and countless other outrages, and yet absolutely nothing can be done about it?'

'I fear it is as Mrs Hudson says, sir,' returned Mr Holmes. 'What you have heard tonight can leave none of you in any doubt as to the true sequence of events, yet what evidence is there? Some cigarette ends, an identification by a nervous maid… A man such as Fogarty will have taken steps to ensure he can account for his movements at all times.'

'But we can hound him out of town, Holmes!' Watson was looking fiery. 'My word, if I have to go to Fotheringay myself, we can make sure he is smoked out of that nest of his!'

'No need for that, sir,' replied Mrs Hudson calmly. 'With Sherlock Holmes and the police both taking an interest in his affairs, I suspect Mr Fogarty is likely to disappear of his own accord. It is usually his way. But I fear, sir, he will be back.' She gazed at her port, apparently lost in thought.

'Oh, yes, he will be back.' And I knew she was thinking of that time in the future and promising herself she would still be here, waiting for him.

'And what of Flottie's abduction?' chirped Miss Peters. 'Isn't anyone concerned about that?'

'It was someone called Smale,' I told her. 'Someone who used to bully me. But he's gone now. Into the river. I've nothing to fear from him again.'

'Bravely said!' declared Watson. 'On my honour, Flottie, I swear we shall never let you come to any harm.' A declaration that I blush to say was warmly drunk to on all sides.

And so the evening passed and conversation became more general. Mrs Hudson promised Mr Spencer that the Irascible Earl would be appeased by her message but refused to be drawn, regardless of the mellowing port, on any of the details of Derby Day in 1863. Disappointed, Miss Peters took to yawning again.

'I think it is time you carried me off, Rupert,' she announced happily. 'Of course it's now *so* late that in the eyes of Society I'm already completely compromised. So I think carrying me off is the very *least* you can do.'

For once Mr Spencer made no attempt to protest but went himself into the street to hail a cab.

'I cannot help but notice,' commented Mr Rumbelow sadly when he returned a minute later, 'that everyone here gets a cab the moment they want one. That never happens to me.' He poured himself another glass of the old tawny in recompense. 'Quite so,' he concluded.

The departure of Miss Peters and Mr Spencer reminded Dr Watson that the night was gone and the dawn already well set. With an impressive show of determination, he supported the drooping Holmes from his chair and to his bed. A few moments later he returned and put his head round the door for a last word.

'Mrs Hudson, it's been a great pleasure. Dashed fine!'

'Thank you, sir,' said Mrs Hudson simply.

And then there was only Scraggs and Mr Rumbelow left. For a while the four of us sat in silence looking at the fire, but eventually the glasses were drained and Mrs Hudson rose to her feet.

'And thank you all,' she told us softly. 'Now we should all get to our beds for an hour or so. Because as Hudson always used to say, there's no knowing what will happen tomorrow.'

So while Mr Rumbelow looked for his coat, I walked Scraggs to the door.

'I was keeping watch tonight, Flot. I'd seen that bit of slime watching you before this. I was trying to keep an eye on him. Thought you'd be all right if I was watching. But I was too far off to stop him.'

'Thank you, Scraggs. For looking out for me.'

'Is it all right, Flot? Me looking out for you?'

I thought about it.

'Perhaps I should be looking out for myself.'

He looked at me.

'Yes, I think you'll be good at that,' he said slowly. 'Goodnight, Flot.' And he turned to the street and stepped out into the new day.

I watched him out of sight and turned to find Mr Rumbelow approaching from the stairs.

'Ah, Flotsam!' he bumbled. 'Just off, I am.' He paused on the doorstep. 'You should stick close to Mrs Hudson, young lady. She's a very fine woman. A very fine woman indeed. Indeed. But that is not to say she isn't by nature independent. Oh, yes. Fiercely independent.' He sighed sadly to himself. 'I must remember to replace the bottle we drank tonight. I have some very fine Madeira that might fit the bill.'

So he made his departure muttering of vaults and vintages, and I bolted the door and made my way up to the kitchen. I'd forgotten that my bed was taken up by the boy whose name we didn't know, and was only reminded when I found Mrs Hudson making up a bed for me by the fire. She looked up when I came in and we smiled. We didn't say anything. There wasn't any need.

–

The next days passed calmly and the flood of events slowed to a trickle. Inspector Gregory called to tell us Fogarty had disappeared without trace; a message from Mr Spencer confirmed that the Earl had become quite mellow on receipt of Mrs Hudson's message; Scraggs reported that Mr Fotheringay had taken on as butler a Slav called Volshin; Miss Peters promised to teach me to dance; a number of dusty bottles arrived for Mrs Hudson; Mr Holmes kept weakly and reluctantly to his room; and eventually, one evening, Dr Watson knocked on the kitchen door.

He looked embarrassed.

'I wondered, Mrs Hudson, if I could, er, have the honour of a quick word.'

'Of course, sir. Come in and make yourself comfortable. Flotsam and I have just finished baking.'

He took a seat by the range but continued to look slightly ill at ease. He had a thick pile of papers in one hand, the edges of which he thumbed nervously.

'Mrs Hudson, you may have heard me mention that I have long considered putting down on paper the details of some of the mysteries it has been my good fortune to observe.'

'Indeed, sir. Mr Holmes has alluded to it more than once.'

'I've tried it before, dash it, but I always seem to lose heart. A combination of my diffidence with the pen and Holmes's modesty when discussing his cases has always made the thing dashed tricky.' His unease was evident. 'Anyway, I thought this time I'd do it and be damned, if you'll pardon my language. I've put down all my recollections of recent events and all I can say is I hope I've done you justice!'

Mrs Hudson allowed one eye to flicker upwards for a moment, then came forward, wiping her floury arms on her apron, and seated herself opposite him.

'I see, Dr Watson. An interesting idea. If I may be permitted to see…'

'Of course, Mrs H. Hoped you'd take a look. Any suggestions most welcome.'

She read quietly for a minute or two while Dr Watson fidgeted in front of the fire.

'You mention Flotsam here, I see.'

'Indeed, Mrs Hudson. Flottie played a vital part in proceedings.'

'And you begin your story with an account of how you and Mr Holmes came to quit your previous lodgings in search of our present, roomier accommodation.'

'Absolutely, Mrs H. That decision led directly to meeting you and Flotsam. A most happy event.'

She read on further and for a while there was silence in the firelit kitchen. Having moved fully fifteen or sixteen pages from the top to the bottom of the pile, Mrs Hudson moved the papers to one side and sat in thought for a moment.

'Well, Mrs Hudson?'

'May I speak to you frankly, sir?'

'Of course, Mrs H. I should expect nothing less from you.'

'There's no denying that you tell your story well. But is it your intention that this narrative should be published?'

Dr Watson flushed modestly. 'Oh, I really hadn't thought. Of course, if it was considered good enough for publication…'

'You see, Dr Watson, it's like this. I don't mind so much for myself, but Flottie is a young girl with a future ahead of her. I have high hopes for Flottie. How is she supposed to get on in the world if a story like this propels her into the public gaze?'

Watson looked a little shamefaced.

'My word, Mrs Hudson, I hadn't thought of that. Dashed insensitive of me. Thought you'd be pleased. And without Flottie there'd be a big gap in the tale.'

'Yes, sir, I can see that. Of course there will be times, when visitors are being shown in perhaps, or when errands are run, when it will be difficult to have no-one in Flottie's position. Have you considered a simple substitution? I think perhaps a pageboy would do the trick.'

'A pageboy, Mrs Hudson?'

'You could call him Billy. All pageboys seem to be called Billy nowadays.'

'Well, if you really think…'

'I do, Dr Watson,' she replied very firmly. Dr Watson gave me an apologetic look.

'Well, if it's for the good of Flottie's future, I suppose…'

'And then there's the question of the address, sir.'

'The address, Mrs H?'

'You see, Dr Watson, I believe stories such as this are very popular just now. And Mr Holmes is already set fair to become a very famous man. Do we really want every reader of The Strand Magazine to be able to walk up to our front door any time they feel like it? They'll frighten off Mr Holmes's clients. And Heaven knows, we get little enough peace as it is.'

'But what would you suggest, Mrs Hudson.'

'Well, I can't see why you need to mention the true address at all. There are plenty of addresses that don't actually exist. Something like 221B Baker Street would sound well enough. Those that need us will find us anyway but the passing idlers will be looking in the wrong place.'

Dr Watson nodded sagely. 'Yes, I can certainly see the sense in that. 221B, you think? Hmm, well perhaps… I suppose it has a ring to it. Is there anything else, Mrs H?'

'I can't help thinking that perhaps you overstate my role in proceedings, sir.'

'But you were central to proceedings!'

'Oh, you exaggerate, Doctor. I may have been lucky enough on this occasion to have some of the pieces of the puzzle fall into my hands, but a casual reader of your document would be forgiven for thinking that it was me and not Mr Holmes who is the great detective. But my little scraps of domestic knowledge are hardly likely to interest the public, while his scientific principles will surely prove a far greater inspiration. You must show how he led us through events like a great general.'

'You really see it like that, Mrs Hudson? I confess at the time I thought your actions were rather independent of his. But if that's what you really feel... His role in my narrative is perhaps on the marginal side.'

'And is that going to be good for business, Dr Watson?'

'I say, I hadn't thought of that, Mrs H.'

'What the public really needs are cases that show off his genius. And a man with your strengths as a writer will surely be able to oblige.'

'Hmm, yes. There are a number of cases that might illustrate his talents better than this one. That odd case about blood, perhaps... But this was such a dramatic tale, Mrs Hudson. You see I have called it The Case of the Giant Rat. I feel sure no publisher would be able to resist it.'

'Of course, sir, I haven't come to Scraggs yet. It would surely be unfair to drag his name into this until he is considerably older. And then there's Mr Rumbelow. He has his practice to think about. And then there's Miss Peters's reputation. And Mr Spencer is hoping the Earl will sponsor his new laboratory. I can't believe the Earl will approve of the role that pair played in all this.'

'Hmm... Perhaps you are right, Mrs Hudson. Perhaps this is a tale for which the Earl is not yet ready. You think another case?'

'Indeed, sir. Another case may present rather fewer problems. Of course, I have no objection to appearing at the margins, as it were, sir. And Flotsam – well, Flotsam will just have to make a name for herself in another way, won't you, Flottie?'

But I had drifted away from them, warm and happy enough not to care. Instead I was dreaming into the fire about a future that seemed to burn as bright as the flames and to glow as warm as the fiery embers on Mrs Hudson's hearth.

A Holmes & Hudson Mystery